FAMILY REMAINS

Eric Neher

ISBN-13: 978-1-958557-57-0

To Kelsey and Garrett

CHAPTER ONE

It Won't Make Any Difference

The most dangerous threat to faith is time. For Field Agent Wyatt Wayne, this truth found its way through synthetic optimism during his second year at the Oklahoma Bureau of Investigation. This awakening came by way of a family dispute, which was then concluded by a murder-suicide. The husband learned of the affair his wife was having with their shared drug dealer. He decided to teach her a lesson and then decided to teach himself one, as well.

The silver lining was that he had left the three-year-old twins out of the equation. And it was with this thought that the fall of Agent Wayne's faith began. It was at that moment he realized the world would never change.

The agent allowed himself a moment of recall, reliving the sinking feeling that had overtaken him as he left that tiny one-bedroom apartment. He was thankful he had gotten into his car before the tears came.

It wouldn't make any difference, his father once told him. For as long as Agent Wayne could remember, this had been the old man's favorite answer for everything. Agent Wayne was sure it was just his father's way of justifying his laziness about anything outside of work and television.

But now, he wasn't so sure.

Agent Wayne sat back in his aged leather chair and gazed out the window at the dying trees bordering the OSBI property. It was a reminder of the constant yet repetitive change that being alive presented, and it sometimes terrified him.

But at least he had spared the twins.

Strange that the thought was his automatic response to an impending breakdown.

This world was a violent place, and every minute of every day something died. Agent Wayne had witnessed this revolutionary fact while serving in the Army during the Second Gulf War. As a part of Military Intelligence and having been taught the Iraqi Arabic dialect, his job was to come in after the damage and question the survivors. How often had he walked by covered bodies of men, women, and children?

It won't make any difference.

And it didn't, not in the long run. If anything, it made things much worse.

Was that the truth? Was that the destiny of mankind? Are we on some destructive rinse-and-repeat cycle?

Can we spare the kids?

A buzzer summoned him from his thoughts, and he reached for the intercom near the corner of his desk.

"Agent Wayne," he said.

"Director Thomlinson wants to see you in his office," said a pleasant voice. Carla Ranks was a lower-level agent assigned to headquarters as a badge-wearing secretary. Nice, but a little brittle at times.

"He needs me now?" said Agent Wayne.

"Yep," she said. "He told me to tell you he's got a weird one that should be right up your alley."

"I'm on my way," he said, rising from his chair.

*****

Agent Wayne was well known throughout the agency for his unorthodox methods and high conviction rate, but there had been times when he hadn't even been in the same ballpark.

You're like our own little Agent Mulder, Director Thomlinson had told him once, and Agent Wayne wasn't sure if he had meant it as a compliment. Many other agents treated him as an outsider, referring to him as The Mystic. It was because he tended to let his imagination go and follow it, which was both a blessing and a curse. A hunch was, after all, nothing more than theory without substance, a gamble.

It won't make any difference.

And maybe that was true, but if it was, Agent Wayne was determined to tread the current until there was nothing left to give. What else could he do?

*****

Director Thomlinson was sitting at his desk. He motioned for Agent Wayne to come in and grab a chair.

"We've got a strange one," he said as Agent Wayne took a seat. He then slid a manila folder across his spotless desk.

Agent Wayne opened the front cover and beheld the crime that would soon force him to utilize every ounce of his imagination.

CHAPTER TWO

Jimmy V.

James Varnett, or Jimmy V. as his friends called him, sat in his 2016 Mustang, gazing at the run-down relic. This neglected imposter posing as a house was his last chance, the only thing standing between him and ruin, and the odds didn't look good.

His sales were down, had been for a while, and Charlie Wheaton, Lord of A.A. and enemy to all libations, had no problem letting him know. Charlie was a surgeon. He never used an ax; that would be too messy. It was far better to break a man down into clean sections, preferably with an audience. His precision cuts came from sideways glances or off-the-wall comments, usually regarding the shade of Jimmy's eyes or the cologne that couldn't entirely cover up the stench of Seagram's from the night before. Of course, none of that mattered back when Jimmy V. could sell. But that was then.

To reflect on the rise and fall of his life was, until recently, avoided. Childhood desires to learn why things were the way they were became those of an unwanted stranger. Ridiculous dreams that, as the years went by, were replaced by a ruthless reality: Status was everything. Pride in oneself wasn't inherent but acquired by drive and hustle. And lying, don't forget lying. You must be willing to push off a cliff those who stood at the edge to accomplish your dreams. A set of rules that were both horrific and delusional, creating untrusted friendships and relationships based on not what you were but what you had.

Perhaps it was time for something new. At least Karen, Jimmy's wife of six years, had thought so, having left him for some mysterious savior she claimed treated her right. The thought made Jimmy cringe.

Why stay in Oklahoma City? His mother said after Karen had left him. *Come back to Dallas.*

It was not exactly his first choice for a change, but he would probably have to after today. His construction salesman life was likely over, at least at Charlie Wheaton's Wholesale.

Was that why he stared at this run-down shack in the middle of nowhere? Had The Lord of A.A. set him up for failure? His way of severing an unwanted tie?

I pay for these appointments, Jimmy, he had told him. *I can't keep sending you out on calls when you can't close.*

Of course, Jimmy at first blamed the quality of the prospects, and after that didn't work, went with the classic 'I'm in a slump.'

You're not in a slump. You're in a bottle, The Lord of A.A. said. *And I can't have you out there burning my leads just because you can't put the cap back on.*

You know my wife left me, Charlie, said Jimmy.

I know she did, said the Lord of A.A., and *I also know why.*

That was the most challenging part about talking to Charlie. The usual stories meant to cultivate sorrow and understanding didn't work on the Lord of A.A. He knew too much; he had seen too much.

Once, he pretended to buy into the 'Booze Is The Root Of All Evil' credo. Had even gone to a few meetings where the Supreme Overlord sat as both judge and jury over the circle of liver-spotted disciples. Charlie was a wealthy man, and by then, the late-night excursions and nameless women began to make a severe dent into Jimmy's funds. A change had to be made, even if it was fabricated. It was part of the game when working for Charlie, bringing some animosity. The Lord of A.A. could be benevolent, but only if you showed him that you were genuinely willing to be subjugated. Jimmy had been forced to bow before him and play the part of the sniveling lost soul that Charlie hungered for. And it was then things began to change.

Soon, he rose from a mid-level forgettable to one of the go-to guys. Where once it was hardly noticed whether he was present at the company Christmas parties, it was now mandatory and not just him but his wife. And for a while, they were happy, or at least pretended to be. Jimmy was becoming a winner, and with these accolades came a pressure that had him waking up in the middle of the night in a cold sweat. For once you raise the bar, it could never be lowered. Not without the spying eye of Charlie falling upon you. This is where the animosity came in, knowing you were constantly under surveillance. Each pitch that didn't sell was scrutinized and broken down. Each reason for a late arrival was questioned under a blinding light. It was no wonder Jimmy picked up right where he had left off, drinking until the bar shut down. Diving into whatever woman took him home, using his looks like a weapon on both her and himself.

It was then Karen decided to leave him. He didn't realize what she had done until three days after she was gone. Jimmy told her he was going out of town on business, traveling through northern Kansas to close whatever jobs he could find. She had believed his bullshit for so long that to him, lying to her was second nature. But his truth was a dark secret: It was a relief to be rid of her.

Through all of this, Charlie kept watch.

Come back to the meetings, he demanded, but Jimmy refused.

The Closer was now a free man. He was free of guilt, free of the self-deprecating circle that flocked around the Lord of A.A., and free to fall from Charlie's grace for as far as he wanted, just as long as he was closing. A new age began, a golden age, and as long as Charlie was making money off of his fallen angel, Jimmy's future was safe. But that was then.

*****

Now, his entire future was resting in the run-down house before him. A slick sweat broke out on his brow, and he felt his hands tremble. Once, on one rare occasion when he was home, he had heard Karen scream from the garage. Jimmy had run out, expecting to find an intruder, but instead, he saw a baby opossum cowering in the corner. Its black eyes were wide with terror. Jimmy had taken a shovel from a rack and smashed the infant creature over the head.

Later that night, after Karen fell asleep, he stared up at the ceiling, wondering why he had done that. He certainly could have just as easily scooted the thing back outside. Why did he feel the need to kill it? It disturbed him more than he thought possible. And its eyes, its terror-stricken eyes locking on to him just as he brought the shovel down, still found their way into his dreams. Was this how the creature felt, the way that Jimmy felt now? Trapped in a corner with no way out? Maybe it was Kharma? He certainly would have handled it differently if given another chance, much like in his marriage.

This house was his last chance to pull himself out of the fire he had created. Yes, he created it. He wasn't stupid and had learned a thing or two at those meetings, although he would have never admitted to it until recently.

First, acknowledge you have a problem. Well, for Jimmy, that was obvious. Second, take it one day at a time. That was the important one—not just one day at a time but one moment at a time; seize whatever opportunity was placed before you and be glad you had one.

Jimmy reached down and picked up the appointment slip:

Mrs. Glenda Jones (Widow)
23121 East Cty. Rd.
Blanchard, Ok.
Product: Windows

It wasn't perfect. The house showed no pride of ownership, and the lawn looked as though it was free to do whatever it wanted, but at least it was an appointment. The slip said that she was a widow and, with any luck, a recent widow who had just received what little life insurance her husband could afford. That might be hoping for too much, but for Jimmy, hope was about all he had left.

Jimmy pulled a business card out of his breast pocket and lifted himself out of the 2016 Mustang for the last time.

CHAPTER THREE

Mrs. Jones Has Visitors

Jimmy stood on the porch, gazing through a pane of glass in the front door. It was frosted, and all he could see was a yellowish prismed glow. He straightened his tie and reached out, giving the panel a quick three-rap knock, and waited. He tilted his head and leaned forward but heard only the breeze sifting through the grass.

The sun was just above the horizon, and the air was becoming chilly. It would be another cloudless October night. Maybe the old lady was in the backyard covering her plants or doing whatever these country folk did when the weather changed. Jimmy stepped off the porch. Knee-high grass, brittle and brown, snapped under his feet. He went to where he could see the back of the property marked by a rusted cyclone fence that looked like it might keel over at any moment. The backyard was just as unkempt as the front, and Jimmy hoped that the ticks had all died from the oncoming winter; the last thing he needed was a case of Lyme disease. The only thing in the back was a roofless doghouse and a late-model Winnebago. Jimmy turned around and made his way towards his car, gazing into the house's windows, but they were all covered by thick curtains.

Apparently, he had just driven an hour and a half for an appointment where no one was home. Maybe that had been Charlie's plan the entire time. Send the drowning man out to deeper waters and hope he never comes back. There would be no contract tonight and no more loans against his books. The Mustang would become wanted tomorrow, and his alimony payment would be due the day after. His mother was four hours away and would save him, just as she always did. All he would have to do is admit to his failures. Admit that she had been right all along.

In her mind, Jimmy never should have left home, should have never left the nest for a woman who held nothing but resentment for her baby boy. It never once occurred to his mother that she was why Jimmy had left. It was her smothering affection tethered to the constant micro-management of his life that had pushed him away. Her concern was genuine. He never doubted that. But her reasoning was selfish and based on her fears of abandonment and betrayal. For her, the truth of her failed marriage and its grotesque ending was a family secret that would forever be forbidden to discuss. Even when they went to his father's grave, she would only pretend to miss him because, in her mind, appearances were everything, and the truth was only a mirage.

Maybe that worked for her, but his truth was much more concrete. The car payments and alimony were not fantasy; they would take his car and then take him. Jimmy let out a sigh of resignation. The small townhouse he rented with his wife was on the way. He would stop and grab what little clothes he had and then jump on I-35 south.

For a moment, he considered calling the office and giving them the lead result but decided against it. They would figure it out eventually, and then Charlie would have another example of a life devastated by booze that he could share at the next meeting.

Jimmy made his way to the driver's side of the Mustang and was startled by the sound of the front door being opened. A woman stood at the threshold, her face partially covered by the wide brim of a straw hat. She was wearing a dark blue one-piece pull-over dress that looked to be from some Amish nineteenth-century catalog. The thought of leaving had sunk so deep into his mind that Jimmy had almost forgotten why he was there for a moment. But it soon came back, and he gave the woman his warmest smile.

"Mrs. Jones?" he said.

The woman glared down at him from the porch.

"Aye," she said in a raspy voice. "That's me."

"My name is Jimmy Varnett, and I'm with —"

"I know who you're with," she said. "I'm the one that called you."

"Do you mind if I come in?"

The old lady took a step forward, and Jimmy could make out her chin's long, curved slope, which reminded him of Jay Leno. But he had a feeling that was about as far as the similarities went; this woman wasn't one to joke with.

"Come in," she said. "But wipe your feet."

The woman held the door open as Jimmy stopped at the mat, scraped his shoes, and entered the room. She waited until he had passed and then shut the door, activating the deadbolt lock.

"Is this a high crime area?" he said, hopefully.

The window sample out in the trunk was armed with a double lockset and tempered glass.

"In this day and age, you can never be too safe," she said.

"I agree," said Jimmy, looking around.

The interior was certainly much better than the exterior. At least it had been painted in the last decade. The carpet was an old green throwback shag, and the walls were done in a heavy Spanish texture tinted eggshell. In the center of the room was an oval coffee table, and around it sat a couple of Lazy-Boy chairs. A sofa splashed in Harvest Gold and Avocado Green was pushed against the far wall. For Jimmy, it was like going back to grandma's house.

"I really like this room," he said.

"I think it looks like white trash," said the woman.

Jimmy felt his smile falter and forced it back. The woman just looked at him, her eyes wandering down his body and back up to his face. He had been in situations before where the signing of the dotted line was contingent on something more than just a quality product at a reasonable price. He would sometimes oblige but only if the commission was right, and never with an old lady sporting a ski-jump chin.

"So," he said. "How long have you lived here?"

The woman just looked at him, her mouth now tilted in a cockeyed sneer. Maybe that was her attempt at a smile, but its effects were chilling. Then, he heard a slight creak from down a narrow hallway. He tried to look around the old woman, but all he could see were shadows.

"Do you have company?" he said.

"Are you a married man?" said the woman.

"Yes, very much so, with two kids."

She pointed at his finger and said, "Then where's your ring?"

"Oh, well, I lost it while working on my wife's car."

"And you couldn't find it?"

"I tried, but it fell behind the radiator. I'm taking it to the shop tomorrow."

Another sound of bending planks came from the hallway, closer than before, and it was answered by a similar sound from just outside the front door.

When he was ten years old, before the tragic end of his father, his family had taken a trip down to Corpus Christie. Jimmy had been running along the beach, his bare feet kicking up the sand behind him as he watched the waves crashing. How could there be so much water? The answer was lost on the young Jimmy, who soon discovered that he didn't care as long as he could keep running. His mom and dad looked as big as ants when a feeling of dread gripped him, and Jimmy stopped. Two feet before him sat a gelatinous mass of goo with shiny strings spanning out from under it.

The thing looked like an alien—a quivering, slimy blob rocking with the shallow ocean tide. Jimmy suddenly realized how far away he was from the safety of his mother and father. He was alone, and he was in danger.

That feeling of dread, that indescribable warning that had stopped him that day on the beach, was back.

A voice floated out from the dark tunnel of the hallway, barely above a whisper.

"I like him," it said.

"Who was that?" he said.

The smile was now gone.

The old woman cocked her head towards the shadowy hallway.

"He's a liar," she said.

"He's just scared," said the willowy voice.

Jimmy stepped back towards the door and said, "Look, I don't know what's going on here, but I've obviously caught you at a bad time, so I'm just going to leave."

He turned to do just that when a dark shape stepped out of the shadows, and Jimmy almost screamed. It was a woman much younger than the hag in the hat. She was dressed in the same type of pull-over dress, but unlike the old woman, her face was quite visible, and it was horrifying. Her left eye was lower than the right, and the pencil-thin lips of her mouth looked as though her face had been sliced with a crooked blade. Surrounding all of this was a sickly colored flesh that seemed to sag off a boneless surface. Her nose was bent and flattened on one side. But it was her chin that Jimmy locked onto. Its protruding slope bent out even further than the old woman's, and he could see the yellowish tint of the teeth in her jaw. Jimmy shrieked and turned for the door, reaching for the handle.

"I don't think he likes me," said the girl.

"He doesn't deserve you," said the older woman. "It doesn't matter anyway, just as long as he can serve his purpose."

Jimmy struggled with the lock for a moment and pulled the panel open. A man the size of a mountain filled the doorway, his bulbous eyes reflecting in the low light of the living room. The giant reached out, but Jimmy was quicker, his adrenaline now at full release. The old woman let out a laugh as Jimmy passed by her. The younger girl was just able to move out of his way as he rushed down the dark hallway. The corridor suddenly split and Jimmy went left.

From behind, he could hear the heavy thud of the giant's feet closing in on him.

"Don't hurt him," the girl cried out.

At the end of the hallway, Jimmy could see a divided panel with a pane of glass in its upper half. Jimmy had found the back door. It stood just twenty-five feet away. The giant's footsteps were growing louder. Jimmy shot out like a quarter horse, his arms pumping. He was nearing the end of the hall when a shape, like a shadowy blob, slithered out before him.

It's the alien from the beach! It's found me!

Jimmy came to a stop. His breath was now heaving, burning his lungs like a furnace. The giant's shadow filled the hall, and soon, it would have him. The creature on the floor suddenly rose, and Jimmy realized that this wasn't the beach monster but a man who either had no legs or couldn't use them, and from him came a hiss like some viper out of a nightmare.

"Get away from me," said Jimmy, and then the giant turned the corner.

The crawler moved on its hands and began coming towards him like a spider.

Jimmy looked around with panic in his eyes. He could leap for it. Try to clear the crawler, but what if he couldn't? All the creature had to do was stick up an arm, and Jimmy would tumble. Would he be able to recover before the giant had him? He didn't think so. He glanced over to his right and saw a door. It would probably lead to a bedroom or a bathroom, but either way was fine as long as it had a window. The giant was now only ten feet away and had slowed down, knowing his prey was trapped. Jimmy lunged for the door and turned the handle. The panel opened, and he rushed inside, slamming it behind him. The room was pitch black. He fumbled around until he felt the relief of a turning lock. He slid his hand up and down the wall, finally finding the light switch. It was a bathroom without a window. He had done nothing more than trap himself. Suddenly, he remembered his cell phone. He reached into his pants pocket and pulled it out. He quickly dialed 911 and waited. In his mind's eye, he could see them gathering in the hallway like a herd of undead, could see them backing away to give the giant the room he would need to bust the door down. Could the giant do it? Absolutely, he could. Maybe not on the first try or even the second, but surely the third would send the panel splintering. The phone had yet to make a sound. Jimmy pulled it away from his ear and looked at the screen...**No Service.**

"Shit," he said.

The door was struck as if hit by a truck. Jimmy cried out and backed away until his ass was resting against a porcelain pedestal sink. Another blow rattled the panel, and he saw that the top hinge had been knocked loose.

This was a good door, he thought and almost burst out laughing.

The door withstood another blow. Jimmy looked around for anything that he might use as a weapon. The room was barren, with no broom, mop, or shovel. He stepped over to a cabinet hanging on the wall and opened it. The top shelf held only towels. The second shelf held an assortment of eyeliner and hair products.

There had to be something else that he could use. He looked at the shower curtain hanging over the clawfoot tub and saw the small hooks holding the curtain wrapped around a pole. This was not a cheap aluminum piece bought at Walmart, but it was made of iron and probably dated back to the time of Lincoln. An image of the giant busting through the door and Jimmy bashing him over the head flashed through his mind. Could he do it? Could he crush another man's skull? He wasn't sure. This would be much different than hitting a baby critter. Would it even stop him? The man had to be at least seven feet tall and as wide as the doorway. Jimmy put his phone back into his pocket and reached for the curtain, pulling it off the wall.

His hand froze just as the curtain hit the floor. The ceramic tiles of the shower's wall were splattered in crimson. Trails of red webbed their way around the edge of the tub. Jimmy stepped back, his hands shooting up to his mouth as he began to retch.

This can't be real, he thought, slamming his eyes shut.

A burst of laughter erupted from the other side of the bathroom door.

"Looks like he found Mrs. Jones," said a raspy voice.

Jimmy opened his eyes, hoping that what he had seen would be gone. The woman was still in the tub, bathing in her blood, her throat sliced so deeply that her head struggled to remain attached.

Another collision impacted the door. The panel broke into three pieces and fell to the floor. The butchered body in the tub had extinguished any thoughts of heroics, and all he could do now was cower in the corner, much like the infant creature that he had killed.

The giant entered the bathroom, and Jimmy felt his knees unhinge. His face had many of the same features as the young woman's, but his chin was wider, and his eyes looked like they were falling out of his skull. Jimmy went limp as the vice-like grip of the giant's hand clutched his neck, and then he felt himself effortlessly lifted off the floor.

"Bring him out here," said the raspy voice.

The giant pulled Jimmy out of the bathroom and slammed him against the wall in the hallway. The old woman came up to where her face almost touched Jimmy's, her breath like stale bread and onions.

"Get me the shot, Marianna," she said. He watched as the young woman approached her with a syringe.

The sight of the needle released another round of adrenaline, and Jimmy slammed his hands down against the giant's wrist. He felt Goliath's grip waiver, allowing Jimmy to push off the wall. The large man stepped back, rubbing his wrist with a confused look on his Neolithic face. Jimmy darted between the old woman and the giant, pushing the younger woman down to the floor as he did. The back door was just to his right, and he raced for it. He might not have enough time to climb into his car and start it, but that didn't matter; once he was outside, it would come down to a foot race, and he was pretty damn sure that he could beat them all.

This hope was brought to a painful end when his legs were abruptly slammed together. He was just able to get his arms underneath and stop his face from colliding against the wood floor. He tried to pull himself up, but something had latched onto both of his ankles, constricting them like an anaconda. Jimmy looked down and tried to scream but only managed to whimper. The creature from the beach had caught him at last. Jimmy began flailing at the tumor now attached to his legs. The thing gave out a hiss and bit Jimmy's hands, slicing his little finger as it passed by its face.

The battle was ended by the giant's foot coming to rest on Jimmy's chest. It was like a boulder, and he could feel his ribs struggling not to break. Jimmy lay there looking up at the man, trying to breathe, unable to do anything else.

"This one's a fighter," said the old woman, kneeling beside him.

Jimmy could see the syringe in her hand.

"Just don't hurt him," said the girl.

"I'm not going to hurt him just as long as he behaves."

The thing still had his ankles clamped, and the giant's foot felt like it was beginning to crack his sternum. The girl was peaking around the giant's waist, her misshapen face contorted with concern. An odd calmness washed over Jimmy. If they had wanted him dead, he would already be dead. The giant could have seen to that with little or no problem. They needed him for something. He looked down at the thing clutching his legs and saw its narrow eyes staring at him. The thing had the same protruding chin as the others, only it wasn't as defined. Its head was completely bald, with a long-jagged scar running from above the right eye to the base of its neck. It was completely white. Even in the low light of the hallway, Jimmy could see that this thing was an albino.

He turned his face towards the old woman and saw her tapping the syringe.

"Why are you doing this to me?"

The woman paused momentarily and gave him a look that mirrored his disgust.

"Do you think we want to?" she said.

Jimmy had no idea what she meant by that but knew from experience that good things can happen once you get people talking.

"I haven't done anything to you," he said. "I don't even know that lady in there. If she did something to you, she probably got what she deserved, but I'm just a salesman. Let me go, and I swear I won't say anything."

The old lady laughed contemptuously and continued to tap the syringe.

"My company knows where I am," he said.

"Of course they do, honey," said the woman.

She then reached out and grabbed Jimmy by the left wrist. Jimmy jerked his hand away and felt the boulder on his chest become heavier.

"Don't fight me on this," said the old woman. "If you do, Nith's foot will hit the floor."

The air was stricken from his lungs. The pain from his ribs shot through his body, causing him to go rigid. He felt the woman's hand on his wrist again but was helpless to do anything about it. The pain from the needle entering his arm barely registered, and he soon felt numbness beginning to spread, filtering through his nerves as his eyes became heavy.

"Tie him and take him to the RV," the woman said, sounding miles away. "Then put the woman in a chair and burn the house."

"What about his car?" someone else said.

"Burn it."

CHAPTER FOUR

A Dark Ride

A feeling of being lifted and dropped brought Jimmy out of a nightmare.

He opened his eyes and found that the darkness was still with him. It felt as though he was coming down from a four-day binge, his throat dry and his head pounding. Crawling stings infected his scalp like invisible ants, but when he tried to scratch, he found that his hands could not move. They had been tied behind his back.

It was then that the memory of what happened rushed over him. His heart was pounding in his chest as he struggled to sit up and found that his legs had been tied as well. Jimmy tried to cry out, producing a muffled grunt caused by a dirty sock taped over his mouth. His stomach clenched, and he was sure he would be sick. It would rise and have nowhere to go.

Jimmy lay back, forcing himself to focus on the steady whine coming from below. It was the sound of tires rolling off the pavement. They had kidnapped him, thrown him into the Winnebago that was outback, stuffing him into the luggage compartment. How long had he been out? A few minutes? Hours? There was no way to tell. *Burn it down,* the hag had said, and he was sure that Mrs. Jones and her house were well on their way to becoming a pile of ash and his 2016 Mustang. The repo man was welcomed to it now.

Maybe there was still hope. The fire would be seen. Surely someone would notice the bright orange glare lighting up the sky. How far was that house from the closest town? At least forty miles. How long until the fire department arrived? Probably an hour at least Long enough for the house to be reduced to a smoldering pile of untraceable ash.

But they would see his car. Would they still be able to read the plate? Would they have left the plate? Of course, they wouldn't, not with that old lady calling the shots. What the authorities would find was a crispy corpse in the living room of a burning house with a charcoal car sitting out front. Jimmy's only chance at being saved depended on a fat man who never wanted to see him again. Would Charlie even check on the appointment? He probably would, but only after he was sure Jimmy was gone.

The sound of the spinning wheels had changed. The RV was slowing down. Jimmy tried to shift his body but discovered that he had very little room to move. Something had wedged him into a corner. He lifted his head, searching for any sign of a hatch or door, but all he could see was black.

The brakes squealed, and he lurched forward. The RV had come to a stop. He heard the muffled sound of a door opening and shutting. There was a quick rattling to his left, and a hatch was flung open. Jimmy lay there helplessly shaking as the giant reached in and grabbed him by both ankles, placing him on his feet. To his right stood the old lady, her narrowed eyes shining with the light of a waning moon. The sky was brightening to a dark shade of purple to the east. Had they been driving all night? The air was cold, and Jimmy shook where he stood with his teeth chattering. A strong odor of diesel was in the northern breeze. He could hear the distant sound of large motors or generators growling like invisible beasts, angrily rumbling from somewhere deep within the darkness.

A sudden movement caught his attention, and he looked down just as the albino spider creature jumped out of the R.V. and scuttled its way up to a large house shrouded in darkness. It did have legs, although no bigger than the arms of a toddler. A motion light blasted back the blackness as the thing began climbing the steps to the front porch, causing Jimmy to wince. He struggled to peek through his half-opened eyes, following the thing as it disappeared. For a moment,

Jimmy was sure that it was a blob, after all, sliming its way under some narrow, hidden crack. After his eyes adjusted, he saw it had gone through a small doggy door. But that wasn't all that he noticed. Four large columns rose from the large semi-circle front porch, connecting to a canopy roof. Decorative rocks veneered from both sides of the veranda, covering long-running walls that heightened into a second story, each ending in marbled custom-made corners. The place was a mansion—a two-million-dollar home inhabited by monsters.

"Get him inside," said the old woman.

The giant reached into the extensive waistband of his jeans and pulled out an eight-inch hunting blade. He then bent down and cut the cords binding Jimmy's feet. Jimmy again felt the massive hand wrapping around his neck, and he was half pushed and half carried toward the front door. They reached the first step of the porch, and Jimmy's big toe clipped the edge, sending him stumbling. The giant grabbed him under the shoulder, elevating him, then placed him on the porch like a struggling infant. The pain from his toe sent shockwaves, and Jimmy leaned against the mountain.

The door was an eight-foot-tall oak behemoth with a brass lion knocker. The giant kept one hand clamped securely around Jimmy's neck and reached for the handle with his other. Grinding hinges screeched with a hair-raising sound as the panel swung open. Jimmy expected to find a room covered in blood with body parts scattered on broken tables and ripped-up chairs, but what he saw made him gasp just the same.

The foyer was well-lit, with a tall ceiling supporting an expensive-looking chandelier. To each side of the doorway stood a waist-high bronze statue of a double-headed lion with wings spread in flight. Jimmy was pushed into the main room, where an even bigger chandelier beamed with colorful light. This room's ceiling peaked with a dome thirty-five feet above. To the left was a polished oak staircase curved to a second-floor landing. The stairway wall was decorated with portraits, and Jimmy could see that many of those painted faces bore the same elongated chin and flattened cheeks as the group that now held him hostage. But there was no sign of violence. There was no smell of decay. No blood-stained floors or body parts.

The giant squeezed his neck and jerked him to the right. He led him down a hallway filled with even more portraits. Jimmy looked to the left and the right, watched the heavy stained doors pass by, and noticed the intricate design of the redwood baseboard.

Whatever else these people might be, crazy, kidnappers, murderers, they were also loaded. What the hell did they want from him?

So why did they grab *him*?

The old hag acted as if their plans were right on schedule, right down to the burning of the house. And what was it that the hideous creature with the Picasso eyes said, *I like him?*

What did she mean by that?

The hallway seemed endless, with the portraits now becoming photographs, although they seemed just about as old. One caught his attention as they went by. It was an ancient black-and-white of a family, a royal family judging by the clothes. It was a mustached man sitting in a chair next to what had to be his wife. Around them stood four young women and one boy who looked to be nine or ten. He had seen this photo before, perhaps at school as a kid or at someone's house. Wherever it was, the photo left an impression. The family shared regal expressions, except for one of the girls. There was an air of mischievousness engraved on that face. Her name was so close that he could almost taste it with his grime-covered tongue. Fantasia. Was that it? Jimmy was pretty sure that that was the name of a stripper he had met in Tulsa. No, it wasn't Fantasia, but it was close.

*****

The giant brought him to a stop. They reached the end of the hall and faced another door, but this one was different. The panel was made of iron, and at its center was a wheel, like one of those you might find on a submarine. In the center was a large slit made for a key.

Jimmy began to shiver. He watched the giant bring out a large key and disengage the lock. His knees trembled as the giant turned the wheel. The door swung in, and Jimmy felt a rush of cold air pouring out. A flight of metal-meshed stairs dropped into an ominous yellow glow like the first plane of hell. The giant nudged him forward and followed as Jimmy was forced to descend. Failed sanitizer and bleached waste assaulted his nose. The sock in his mouth was now dripping with spit.

They reached the last step, like they had stepped into a mad scientist's dream. It was a basement, unlike any other one that Jimmy had ever seen. The walls were done in jagged chunks of dark lava rock. They were stacked end over end and climbed to a foam-tiled ceiling with hanging lights covered in wire, much like a psycho-ward. One long metal table sat in the center. Next to it was a steel desk featuring a microscope, a Bunsen burner, a couple of beakers, and a lot of other things that Jimmy had only seen in movies.

There was a sink against the far wall, and next to it stood a cabinet. The giant nudged Jimmy forward, but he refused to move. A paralyzing bolt of fear seized him. On each side of the cavern-like basement was a set of cages like the cells of a dungeon. Jimmy felt the sharp point of the hunter's knife sticking him between his shoulder blades. The giant pressed the blade a little further until Jimmy could feel the warmth of his blood soaking into his shirt.

"Your choice," said the giant, digging the blade deeper.

Jimmy stood with his knees shaking, staring at the opened cell. Was he ready to die right now? What an odd question to be presented with, one so few ever had to face. A rush of anger took hold, along with shame. He was no hero, never had been. Survival for Jimmy consisted of walking away or running when given the chance. But now there was nowhere to run—no open door leading to an escape and not even a bottle to dull that fact.

Jimmy took a shuddering breath and walked into the cage. The giant smiled, revealing ivory-colored teeth jutting out from his underbite, and slowly closed the cell door. The iron panel clanged shut, and the giant secured the lock. He then motioned for Jimmy to come towards him. Jimmy just stood there, his body trembling.

"Come here if you want me to free you," said the giant.

Jimmy walked towards him and turned around, placing his hands through the bars.

If they were going to kill me, they already would have, he told himself, and he really wanted to believe it.

He felt the knife slice through the rope and was overcome by pricking needles shooting through both arms as the blood struggled to return. Jimmy reached up and ripped the sock out of his mouth. The air in the cavern was foul, but it tasted sweet compared to the dirty sock, and Jimmy filled his lungs.

The giant watched him, his enormous eyes sticking out like hailstones.

Jimmy tried to get a read on this man. He looked fierce, but his looks were often misleading, and if there was one thing he had learned from being in sales, it was to never judge a book by its cover. How many deals would he have lost if he had sized a person up by what they wore? The smart ones dressed poorly and kept their money a secret, especially from their family. Maybe this man was a gentle giant, like Lenny in that Steinbeck book. Perhaps all he had to do was show a little kindness.

"You don't want to do this, do you?" said Jimmy.

The giant looked down at him, his bulbous eyes narrowing.

"Do you want me to let you go?" said the giant. "I could, but how far should I let you get? Maybe as far as I let her get."

Here, he nodded towards the cage across the cavern. Jimmy could see the shadowy image of someone covered on a bed just beyond the wall of iron bars and heard the faint sound of something beeping.

"She tried to run," said the giant. "She won't be running anymore."

Jimmy looked up at those narrowed eyes and saw something terrifying—sinister cruelty coupled with a calculating cunning void of any soul. The giant might look like he had been sent to the future from the time of the Neanderthals, but that, much like the old woman, was where the similarities ended. This man, this freak of nature, was not stupid, far from it, actually, but he *was* cold, and he *was* a killer. Jimmy had no doubt about who had sliced Mrs. Jones' throat, and he was pretty sure that this man enjoyed it, had done it before, and was looking forward to doing it again.

"Why don't I do that? Just let you go," continued the giant. "And then when I bring you back...and I will bring you back, we can let the Heiress see you for what you really are."

For the first time in his life, Jimmy was speechless. Fear had encased him, disabling any chance for rational thought. The mild beeping from across the room now rang out like an alarm, a warning of what could happen to him.

"And once she sees you for what you are," said the giant, "she won't want you anymore, and then what? Do you think we'll just let you go?"

The giant let out a rumbling laugh and then turned, making his way up the stairs.

CHAPTER FIVE

The Neighbor

Jimmy cringed as the sound of the slamming metal door echoed from above. He stood motionless, fighting against the waves of terror. Across the cavern, there was another prisoner. One who had tried to run.

She won't be running anymore.

So, he wasn't the only one unlucky enough to be caught by this twisted group. This fucked up family, for what else could they be?

Anastasia...that was her name.

The memory of the girl in the photo broke through his panicked mind, throwing itself out there like a life preserver, giving himself something to grasp onto before utter hysteria could take over. *She was murdered along with her entire family in a basement much like this.* That thought did not help. *She was Russian, her family was The Romanov's, and they were all killed during the Bolshevik Revolution.*

Yes, that was it. At one point, he was sure he felt romantic sorrow for the girl and her family. It was, after all, a tragic story. Much like the one he now found himself in. And not just him.

Jimmy walked over and pushed against the cage door. It remained as solid as a brick wall. He placed his face against the bars, trying to see the woman across the cavern. The lights were low, but Jimmy could just make out the bed. It was like the one you would find in a hospital. He could see that the back half of the bed was slightly tilted, revealing the ghostly shadow of a face. She looked in her mid-thirties, although it was hard to tell. Her dark hair was plastered over half of her face, and he could see a series of tubes running out of her arm. He gazed to her right and saw a stand containing a fluid bag and a machine beside it with a flashing red light synchronized with the beeping. These people who held them captive seemed to be well equipped with medical devices, the kind that forced you to live whether you wanted to or not.

"Hey," he said. "Are you okay?"

The only response came from the flashing machine. A sudden fear that she was dead raced through his mind. And not just dead, but also a part of some mad experiment, like creating Frankenstein's monster. Jimmy quickly kicked the thought out of his mind.

She won't be running anymore, the giant had said.

Did they put her in a coma?

"Hey," he said again, this time a little louder.

A moan danced across the room, and he could see that the sheet that was covering her had shifted.

"Can you hear me?"

Another moan answered him, and he saw her head turn slightly. The end of the sheet began to slip slowly off the side of the bed, divulging one bare and dirty foot.

"Can you hear me?"

The remainder of the sheet hit the floor. Jimmy was about to call out to her again when his throat constricted. A chill seized him, causing his hands to fly up to his mouth, stifling an oncoming scream. The girl was naked. Jimmy could see the lump of her belly rising with each breath she took. Her body was thin but shapely, and he could see the flare of her hips and the cleanly shaved part in between. But it wasn't any of that that had Jimmy now feeling like he was falling into the abyss. A saturated gauze was wrapped over the stump of her right knee. Blood soaked through the makeshift bandage and was leaking onto the bed.

The woman let out another moan, and Jimmy answered with one of his own. The horror of what he was seeing cut him to his core. Not just because of the way they had butchered her but because of what it meant for him. Perhaps he was closer to the truth with his

Frankenstein theory than he had thought. The girl, and by way of association, he was certainly not seen as human by these sick bastards any more than a cage full of lab rats. And that's what they were, judging by the metal table and the hospital bed: lab rats, chosen for some sick experiment, but what?

Jimmy looked feverishly around his cell and saw it held only a rusted cot with an old, stained pillow and a thin motel blanket. In a corner sat a five-gallon bucket. Its intention was very clear. He stumbled his way over to the cot and collapsed.

An echoing grind sounded. The iron door from above was opened. But they could not release him; the woman across the way was proof of that. An image appeared in Jimmy's mind of the freshly wiped hunter's knife gleaming yellow in the psycho light. He could see the murderous smile spreading across the giant's grotesque underbite. Jimmy pulled his knees up to his chest and shivered.

It wasn't the giant who appeared at the cage, but the old woman, and with her was the girl. In the old lady's hand was a tray containing a salmon filet with a side of walnuts. A small glass of milk sat in a cup holder. The old woman stopped at the cell door and placed the tray into the food slot.

"Eat this," she said.

Jimmy just looked at the tray.

"It's not poisoned, you jack-ass," she said. "And we're not leaving until you do."

Suddenly, the girl looked across the room.

"Mother," she said, her hand pointing at the naked woman in the other cell.

The older woman looked over, let out an agitated hiss, and said, "Go cover her up and check the dosage."

Picasso crossed the cavern and opened the cage. Then, she went over to where the sheet lay crumpled on the floor. The girl lifted the sheet and draped it over the woman's body. She walked over to the beeping machine and adjusted one of the dials.

"It should be fine now," the girl said.

The old woman turned her attention back toward Jimmy. Her eyes focused on him like a predatory bird with purpose. For a moment, he was sure that the crazy bitch was about to turn into some flaming eagle, slip through the bars and rip out his throat. The old lady only stood there with the tray held in the cell door slot. The girl stepped out of the other cell, closing the door behind her, and came to stand beside her mother.

The resemblance wasn't uncanny, although it was unmistakable. Where the older woman's shoulders were straight, almost rigid, the younger woman's shoulders seemed to slope like melting snow. They both had dark raven hair parted in the middle but the girls was thinner. Her dry and flaking scalp was clearly visible through the beehive-like bun at the back of her skull.

"Eat this," the old woman said. "You're going to need it."

The unconscious woman across the way was much further along in this game than he was, and look where it had gotten her. He felt sure she had at least started playing by their rules, but it didn't seem to matter. Plus, there were now only the two women and no giant. He might have a chance if he could just get them to open the cell.

"There's something wrong with my stomach," he said. "I feel like I'm going to be sick." He then went over and plopped down on the cot, clutching his midsection.

The old woman let out a small laugh and then turned, going to the cabinet beside the sink and opening the door.

"One has to be qualified for certain procedures," she said absently, pulling out a small electrical circular saw. "I know you probably think that my boy Nith took away that woman's leg, but you would be wrong. He did catch the ungrateful whore and break it. Yes, he split her shin right in half."

The crazy lady then took a step toward the girl's cell and said, "But I knew she would heal, and I knew she might again try to escape."

The woman was now reaching for the cell door.

"Well, that's just something I couldn't allow, especially now that our future rests with her. So, I made an adjustment. One that a few Tylenol couldn't fix."

"Please don't," said Jimmy. He had jumped off the cot and run to his cell door, his hands shaking on the bars.

"I'm not going to kill her," said the old lady, approaching the unconscious woman. "She's too far along for that. But a finger, well, she'll hardly notice."

The girl's hand was suddenly on his, her off-set eyes brimming with tears.

"Just eat the food," she said. "She won't hurt her if you just eat."

Jimmy watched the maniac with the blade begin to spread the woman's fingers out across the mattress.

"Please," whispered the girl.

"Stop," he cried out. "I'll eat. I'll eat the shit. Just leave her alone."

CHAPTER SIX

Karen

Karen awoke with a single tear trickling down her cheek. This was happening more and more as the days passed, which she found both startling and infuriating. She sat up in the queen-sized bed, throwing the silk sheets to the floor. She felt her nails digging into her palms and forced herself to unclench her hands. Was she being punished? It hardly seemed fair, considering the hell that Jimmy had put her through over the last few years. Then, add the skepticism of his twisted mother; it was a wonder that she lasted for as long as she had. And yet, she knew that without his enemy's help, she would still be there, locked inside of her loneliness, watching as another sun began to rise and wondering who Jimmy was with.

Why should she be the one being punished?

Karen had become a product, a rusted trinket Jimmy only brought out for special occasions. Her own desires shelved and forgotten.

The other side of the bed was cold. The clock read 7:45, and she was sure that Charlie had been gone for at least an hour. His early morning A.A. meetings meant as much to him as the very air he breathed. Much more than she would ever mean, and she was fine with that. It coincided with the promise that she made to herself as she stood there watching the last of her things being loaded into the

U-Haul.

I will no longer lie to myself. It was not as easy as it sounded.

Maybe that was why she woke up crying, unable to remember the dreams from the night before. Could her subconscious be trying to protect her from a truth that she refused to face? She did not love Charlie, that was easy enough to admit. How could she? It wasn't because the man was twenty years older, or the fact that his belly hung well below his waistband. Karen had learned very well the risks of having a handsome man. No, it was his driven passion for purity, his single-minded purpose that came from having found *The Answer.*

And *The Answer* left no room for friendly discourse. Jimmy had been right.

Even their lovemaking was nothing more than Charlie's way of becoming closer to *The Answer.* The only position he could perform was missionary, leaving her crushed under his weight and submissive. Thankfully, it never lasted long and ended with his belly gyrating on top of her like a spilled case of Jello as he cried out to God and only to God. Never once did he cry out her name during climax, and she often wondered if he remembered she was there at all. When he came, it wasn't because of her but because he had reached *The Answer.* She was nothing more than a bridge to get him there.

Perhaps the mystery of her morning tears wasn't so mysterious after all.

I will no longer lie to myself.

Karen stood up from the bed and went to the bathroom. The sun beamed through the obscured window above the whirlpool tub, reflecting off the granite sink. Her bare feet felt the chill of the imported off-set tile that decorated the floor. She sat on the toilet, her eyes even with a brass towel holder mounted on the wall. This room, this house, screamed of unscrupulous wealth, releasing her first truth of the morning: *I have to leave here today.* That one message sent a wave of relief, and suddenly, her tears went away.

I will no longer lie to myself.

There is nothing more terrifying than being alone. To be locked in a dungeon of your own making, its walls containing elements of shame and guilt. Lost and afraid...drifting.

That was what Charlie had saved her from. He had offered her a way out, and she had taken it. Karen flushed the toilet and made her way back into the bedroom. Her clothes, what little she had, were still packed in a duffle bag in the corner. She pulled out a pair of jeans and a T-shirt. She threw on her clothes and zipped the bag. All the rest of her things were sitting in a storage shed funded by Charlie. Karen glanced at her cell phone sitting on the bedside cabinet, and for a moment, she considered calling him, but what would she say? Thanks for bailing me out of prison, but it's time I moved on?

She was sure he would be pissed. Better to jump into her Nissan and go and just leave her shit behind. He could sell it if he wanted and call it even. Jimmy had been paying the alimony on time so far (Charlie had seen to that), and it would be enough for her to start somewhere else. And exactly where did she think she was going? Her only family lived in Denver, a ten-hour drive, and she was down to her last two hundred dollars. The alimony payment wouldn't be in for another couple of days. Karen felt her hands tremble as the walls of the plush bedroom started to close in, stifling the air and causing her heart to pound.

I will no longer lie to myself.

She had done it again: she had built her own prison.

The sudden ring of her cell phone caused her to gasp. She sat there watching as the screen lit up. It was Charlie, no doubt, calling to check on her. He did care for her in his strange way, much like a pet owner. Karen considered ignoring the call, but she needed him, at least for a couple of more days. She could suffer through that.

"Hello?"

"Hey, baby girl," said Charlie. "I didn't wake you, did I?"

"No, I was up."

"Good," he said. "Listen, have you heard from Jimmy lately?"

"No," she said. "Why would I?"

"Oh, I didn't mean anything," said Charlie. He then paused, and Karen could sense that something was wrong.

"What is it, Charlie?"

"Karen, the police are here at the office. They think they found Jimmy's car."

"What are you talking about?"

"No one's in trouble," said Charlie. "But they want to know if you could come in for a chat."

"Where's Jimmy?" she said.

"They're not sure," said Charlie. "They said the car's been burned. It was missing its tag."

"Then why do they think it was his?"

"The car was found at his appointment," said Charlie, his voice almost a whisper.

Karen thought about this for a moment. It was obvious that Charlie knew more than he was letting on. Why wouldn't he just tell her?

"What did his customer say?"

"I can't really get into that," said Charlie.

"What do you mean?"

"It's not good," he said, sounding flustered. "I think you should be here."

Something had happened to Jimmy. Maybe it was a jealous husband or a jilted lover. God knows he had blazed a dangerous trail. It occurred to her that they would know she was now living with his boss. She had left him for his boss, and she was sure that they would have a few questions about that. Was this something that Charlie had considered? He probably had, which was why he now sounded coy.

"I'm on my way," she managed to mumble and ended the call.

I will no longer lie to myself…I'm not going anywhere.

CHAPTER SEVEN

The Gripping Test

Even as he drank the milk, he knew something was in it. Jimmy could taste the sour additive but could not do anything about it. The circular saw was still in the old lady's hand, and she was watching him closely. *They're not going to kill me,* he told himself as the last drop ran down his throat. That may be true, but it didn't mean he wouldn't wake up with one less foot. Within minutes, he could feel the drug beginning to work; his sight became blurred, and his eyelids felt like a pair of weights.

"You best get over to that bed," said the old lady.

Jimmy didn't want to, but he knew that if he did, it would be over. But he couldn't help himself, and he soon felt cool air rushing past his face as he fell onto the mattress. Soon, the yellow ceiling lights were no more than a tunnel growing further and further away.

*****

Jimmy's eyes flew open just as the scream escaped his throat. He tried to sit up but found that he couldn't move. A face hovered over him with a wide grin filled with yellow teeth. The giant was pinning him down. Jimmy could still feel the lingering orgasm as his penis continued to be throttled. He looked down toward his waist and felt his stomach turn. It was the blob. His muscled torso was draped over Jimmy's waist, his rubber-gloved hand pumping away. Behind him stood the old lady, and a clear petri dish was in her hand. They were draining him.

"That's enough," said the old woman.

The blob released his grip and slid off the cot. The woman placed a lid on the dish and followed the blob out of the cell. Jimmy felt the pressure of the giant's grip loosen, and for a moment, he considered trying for the open cell door. What did he really have to lose? The giant stood looking down at him as if daring him to try. Jimmy could see it in his calculating eyes. Why the others wanted him alive seemed to matter very little to the giant.

Jimmy lay there, refusing to move, his slacks wrapped around his knees. The giant waited a moment longer, then turned and walked out of the cell, slamming the door shut behind him. He then made his way back to the stairs. Jimmy struggled to pull up his pants, his head swimming from the lingering effects of the cocktail. The effort of trying to stand sent the dungeon spinning. Jimmy fell back onto the thin mattress and watched the old woman and the blob as they placed their sample next to the microscope on the metal table. The woman reached into a drawer, pulled out a glass slide, opened the petri dish, and carefully placed a couple of drops onto it. She then slid it under the lens and stepped back. The blob-man lifted himself and peered through the ocular lens.

"Well?" she said.

"Adjust the focus one notch to the left," said the blob.

The woman reached under his arm and turned the knob.

"That's good," said the blob.

He dropped his scarred albino head a little closer to the lens.

"He will do," he said, monkeying his way off the table.

"What about Marianna?" said old Leno.

"The Heiress finished her cleansing seven days ago," said the blob. "We'll give it a couple of days and then start the process."

He then nodded toward Jimmy and said, "Make sure to keep feeding him the high-protein diet, but judging by this, we should have no problem."

The woman took the slide and the petri dish to the stainless-steel sink and cleaned them. She then took a towel, wiped them dry, and placed them both in a drawer under the table.

"What of the other one?" she said, pointing at the one-legged woman.

"She's coming along," said the blob. "But it doesn't help that Nith still mounts her when he can."

"I know," said the woman. "But he's upset. It helps him."

"Still, we need to keep him off her," said the blob. "At least until the child is born."

"I'll talk to him," said old Leno. "It's unfortunate that we find ourselves in this position."

"It's not the first time, mother," said the blob. "You know that."

"Yes, I do, Phillip," she snapped. "I just don't want to bury more children."

"You mustn't think about that," said the blob. "This new blood will act as the jumpstart we need."

"And how many of these 'jumpstarts' will we need?"

"It's hard to say for sure," said the blob. "I would guess at least three for each of them, if possible."

"The liar should be good for three," said the woman. "But that woman will be lucky to have the one she's carrying. There's no way she'll make it through another."

"I agree," said the blob, rubbing his hand across the scar on his head. "We'll need a replacement."

"We'll wait to make the call," said the old woman, "and see if the liar is compatible. If not, we may need to find two replacements."

The old woman then leaned down and kissed the blob on the top of his sickly pale head.

"If only you could continue the line, Phillip."

"You know I could care less, mother," he said. "I have my own gifts."

"That you do, my prince," she said, and together, without giving Jimmy another look, they made their way up the stairs.

Jimmy lay on the cot, his heart pounding as the iron door shut. The clarity of what he was there for struck him like lightning. A moment of complete nausea overwhelmed him, and he struggled over to the five-gallon bucket. His retching echoed off the lava rock walls, briefly harmonizing with the steady beeps of his neighbor's machine. The woman across the way was as good as dead. They had said so themselves as they stood there analyzing his semen. They would help her for as long as it was necessary, but once that monstrous child that she was being forced to carry was born, they would do away with her and find another.

At least three for each of them, the blob, known as Phillip, said.

The liar should be good for a couple, the hag said.

Jimmy felt another urge to be sick and forced it back. The horror of what was expected of him acted like a net encasing him, and he found it hard to breathe. The drug that he had been given earlier had worn off, leaving his head throbbing.

He found his eyes wandering over to where the poor woman lay unconscious, and for a moment, he felt envious. At least she wouldn't have to deal with the hell much longer. For Jimmy, the nightmare was just beginning.

A shriek escaped from his throat as the lights went dead. The immense darkness swallowed him. From across the room, the faint red glow of the monitor continued to blink, calling out to him, warning him to behave and allowing a brief hellish glimpse at what would happen if he didn't.

CHAPTER EIGHT

Karen and the Agent

The parking lot at Charlie Wheaton's Wholesale was mostly empty. Karen parked her Nissan next to a Crown Victoria with government plates. For a moment, she considered just pulling out, hitting the I-40 west expressway, and going. What could they really do? She hadn't done anything, certainly hadn't burned Jimmy's car. Surely, they would know that. She hadn't even spoken to him since the divorce was finalized. So, what could they do? Most likely nothing, but it would look suspicious, and she was sure that they would eventually find her and bring her back.

That feeling of being punished again crept over her. The guilt of leaving Jimmy for his boss was like a scab that refused to go away. To have her ex-husband's alimony payment provided by the very man who jiggled on top of her left a sour taste in her mouth. Maybe it was because Jimmy still didn't know, and Charlie, the guy with *The Answer,* seemed to be okay with that.

How many women had Jimmy been with while you were married?

It was the voice of reason chiming in again. And it was right. To feel any remorse after what she had been through was nothing more than Karen strapping her own back. A sudden thought broke through her rambling mind.

What if something has happened to Jimmy? What if he was dead?

I will no longer lie to myself: I'm not going anywhere.

Karen got out of her Nisson and leaned against the car's roof. For a moment, she thought she was going to collapse. She forced herself to take a deep breath and hold it. Eventually, the shaking in her legs slowed, and she made her way to the double glass doors.

A young, pretty woman at the front desk smiled as Karen entered the lobby, but it looked pained and badly rehearsed.

She knows about you and Charlie, the punishing voice in her mind said. *The entire office knows.*

"Karen, right?" said the woman.

"Yes."

"Charlie is in the back. I'll let him know you're here."

Karen sat at one of the waiting tables while the woman picked up her phone. She didn't know this woman. Didn't know many of the people that Jimmy worked with, not well enough to remember their names. She might recognize a few faces from one of the rare times that she had gone to a function, but Jimmy had always tried to keep that part of his life a secret, and he may well have paid for it now. She was sure that Charlie wasn't alone and was probably being questioned as she sat there.

When the woman's phone rang, she picked up the receiver, mumbled something into it, and hung up.

"Go on back," she said.

Karen made her way down the light, tan-colored hallway, the soles of her tennis shoes squeaking on the ceramic plank floor. She felt the palms of her hands become moist and quickly wiped them on her jeans. Charlie's office was the last door on the left, and she saw that it was partially open. She stopped, took a deep breath, and gave the door a quick knock.

"Come in."

Charlie was sitting behind his desk, his tie loosened, and his plump face flushed. Sitting across from him was a man who looked a few years older than herself. His dark hair was neatly combed to the side, with a stray curl hanging down onto his tanned forehead. Karen couldn't help but do a double-take at the man's tie. It was glossy black and decorated with a row of jack-o-lanterns. Halloween was only a couple of weeks away. Both men stood up as Karen entered the room.

"Karen Presley," said Charlie. "This is Agent Wyatt Wayne. He's with the Oklahoma Bureau of Investigation."

"I know what you're thinking," said the man, reaching out his hand to shake hers. My name's very old west, but I assure you I have been known to cry at the movies."

Karen smiled at that despite her anxiousness.

The agent turned towards Charlie and said, "I was hoping to have a few moments alone with Ms. Presley. Do you have an empty office we could use?"

"You can use this one," said Charlie. "I need to check on some orders, anyway."

"I appreciate it," said the agent. "We'll only need it for a few minutes."

"Take as long as you want," said Charlie, and Karen could see the relief wash over the large man's face as he lumbered out of the room. Agent Wayne waited until Charlie had cleared the threshold and then reached past Karen, shutting the door. He then motioned for her to sit down and walked around to the other side of the desk.

"Would you like something to drink?" he asked as he sat down. "I'm not sure what they have to offer, but we can send for something."

"I'm fine."

"Ms. Presley, I'm not going to take much of your time," he said, leaning back in Charlie's chair. "Your husband's car-"

"Ex-husband," Karen corrected.

"Right. Sorry. Your ex-husband's car was found at a crime scene. It is part of the crime scene, I should say. When was the last time you spoke to him?"

"We divorced four months ago," Karen said. "That was the last time."

"And you haven't talked to him since?"

"No."

"No text messages or emails?"

"I haven't had any contact with him at all."

Agent Wayne leaned back in the leather chair. His face was a portrait of compassion, but his green eyes held the same quality as a bird of prey: sharp, unwavering, and relentless.

"This may be a stupid question," she said. "But has anyone tried to call his cell, or can't you just trace it?"

"Believe it or not, we actually tried that," he said, giving her a humorous grin, his eyes remaining laser-focused.

She wondered briefly if he held that gaze during sex.

"We found his phone inside his car, melted along with everything else."

"Did you talk to the customer?"

"Unfortunately, that's not possible." Agent Wayne said. "Her house was burned and apparently with her in it."

"Was it an accident?"

"Judging by the shape of the woman's body, I'd have to say no,"

"I don't understand," said Karen. "Do you think Jimmy had something to do with it?"

"Quite frankly, I don't understand either," said Agent Wayne. "At this point, anything's possible. Do you think he could do something like that?"

Karen remembered the time Jimmy had killed the opossum in the garage. She had never told him about how he would sometimes wake her in the middle of the night while he suffered through a nightmare, his body trembling. Of course, that was when he was home. Jimmy was a lot of things; a bullshitter, a conman, a cheater, but he was no killer, of that, she was sure.

"No," she said, finally.

"Actually, I don't think he did it," said Agent Wayne. "Normally, murderers don't burn their own cars at the scene. Can you think of anyone who might want to hurt Jimmy?"

Karen let out a laugh and quickly covered her mouth.

"I didn't realize that was a joke," said Agent Wayne.

"Sorry," she said. "It's just that Jimmy was constantly fooling around, it's why I divorced him, and I'm sure he pissed off a lot of people in the process."

"So, you think that maybe some jealous lover or husband could have done this?"

"I'm just saying that with Jimmy; who knows? Maybe he was seeing the lady who lived in the house."

"Was he into women in their early eighties?"

"Was she rich?" she asked half-jokingly.

"Just the opposite," said Agent Wayne.

"Then no," said Karen. "Unless she had a twenty-year-old body."

"What about you, Karen? Can I call you Karen?"

"That's fine. What about me?"

"How are you holding up? Are you worried about Jimmy?"

"Of course I am," she said. "We were married for six years."

"What did he say when you told him you were leaving him for his boss?"

Here it finally was. The point that all roads lead to. For a moment, she considered denying it, not because she was guilty of anything but because of her inner punishment. Until now, she had told no one about Charlie, not even her mother in Denver, who would have been too drunk to remember anyway.

I will no longer lie to myself. I am using Charlie.

This truth crested on a wave of shame. The woman, who had once been a promising student of journalism, was now using her ass like a whore on 19th Street. Not for money, at least not at first, but for a ticket out. And she had sold it to a man who had the means to provide just that. That it just happened to be Jimmy's boss mattered little. It could have been anyone. That was where she had been in her life...where she was.

She felt a rush of anger flood through her veins. Fucking Jimmy. Karen would have been gone if he had just managed to behave for a couple of more days. But now she was facing an agent of the Oklahoma State Bureau of Investigation as a possible suspect in a murder and being questioned about her lover. What had Charlie told this man? Probably everything, judging by the thankful expression on his fat face when he left the office.

"I never told Jimmy about Charlie," she said. "I doubt Charlie did either."

"According to him, he didn't," said Agent Wayne. "Do you think that someone should have?"

"Look," said Karen, and she could feel the heat in her face rising. "You have no idea what that man put me through. Does he deserve to know about Charlie? Maybe he does. But I'm not staying with Charlie much longer, anyway."

"Ah, found someone else?"

Karen felt her lips begin to tremble as her eyes welled. She sat there with her shoulders shaking, muffling sobs into her palms. Suddenly, she felt a hand on her shoulder, and she tentatively looked up to find Agent Wayne gazing down at her, the sharp look in his eyes gratefully gone. He was offering her a tissue. Karen took it and dabbed her eyes.

"That was mean of me," said the agent. "And I apologize. I know a little about your ex-husband. I know about the DUI's and I also know some things that you probably don't. And believe me, I understand the need for you to get away. I just hope you haven't made it worse for yourself."

"I'm not sure how that's possible," she said. "I know that Jimmy should have been told, but a part of me doesn't even want to admit it to myself."

"Listen, you have no reason to feel guilty about anything," said the agent, reaching into his shirt pocket and pulling out a card. "I want you to call me if you see anything strange."

"How much more strange can it get?" she said, putting the card into the pocket of her jeans.

"This isn't the first case to come our way like this. A young woman went missing six months ago out of Broken Arrow."

"What would that have to do with this?" said Karen.

"Nothing, except that she had just won a lawsuit against Charlie Wheaton's Wholesale for faulty work. It must have been a pretty shoddy job, because the judgment was for a few grand."

"You think it was Charlie?"

Agent Wayne walked over to the door, grabbing the handle.

"I don't know what to think yet," he said, opening the door. "But if you do see or hear something, then please give me a call."

*****

Karen made her way back down the hallway towards the front door. Thankfully, Charlie was nowhere to be seen. She pushed through the panels and felt the cool October air. Could Charlie Wheaton be capable of murder? Would he have killed Jimmy? And why would he kill him? Because of her? It didn't make sense. Not to mention the old lady and her house.

Two more days was all Karen would have needed, and then she could have gone from this nightmare. Her rule had always been to leave her mother out of it, be it Jimmy's cheating or the divorce. If she couldn't handle it herself, then she shouldn't have gotten herself into that situation. That would be the slurred reply of her dear mother. An alcoholic whose fondness for Jimmy had been based on his ability to keep up with her as she popped the top off a bottle of Crown.

But there was something different about this. Something that went well beyond a simple mistake. People were dead and missing and the law thought that Charlie, the man she was sleeping with, might have something to do with it. Agent Wayne hadn't told her not to leave. Maybe she would call her mother, after all. All she could do was say no. Karen reached into her pocket for the keys to the Nissan and froze. There, leaning against the driver's side of her car, was Charlie. His hands folded over his protruding belly.

"Pretty crazy, isn't it?" he said. "Where do you think he is?"

"I really don't know," she said, pulling the keys out of her pocket.

"So, you didn't hear from Jimmy the day he went missing?"

"No," said Karen, walking towards the driver's side door.

Charlie stood there, blocking her way.

"I haven't talked to him since the day we were divorced."

"You'd tell me if you had, wouldn't you, Karen? I mean, that cop was asking me a bunch of questions about you. I think he thinks you might have something to do with it, and I can't help you if you don't tell me the truth."

At that moment, it was clear to Karen that she wouldn't stay at Charlie's house another night. Something about the offhand tone of his interrogation sent up a red flag. His nonchalant effort at going for the backdoor sent a shiver down her spine, and for a moment, she had a terrifying thought that she might not make it to her car. Suddenly, his plump face broke into a smile, and he reached for her, causing her to take half a step back. Charlie seized her by the shoulders and pulled her close.

"I'm just worried about you," he said. "I'm worried about us. I don't want to lose you."

"I understand," she said, wrapping her arms around his wide midsection. "But if you're innocent and I'm innocent, we shouldn't have to worry, right?"

Charlie squeezed her tight momentarily, and Karen felt the air being forced out of her lungs.

"You're right, baby girl," he said, releasing her. "Go back to the house and get some rest. I'm going to try to get out of here early today. Maybe we can go to a movie later, get our minds off this shit."

"That would be nice," said Karen, sidestepping him and pulling the door handle.   She jumped in and started the engine, fighting the urge to lock the doors and floor it.   Instead, she looked up at him and produced her most loving smile.

"Don't hurry on my account," she said. "I'm going to take a nap and try to get rid of this headache."

"Yeah," said Charlie, concern etched across his face. "It's been a stressful day, and it's not even noon yet."

Karen glanced back in the rearview mirror as she pulled out of the parking lot and saw that Charlie was still watching her. The look of concern was gone, replaced with an expression that reminded her of some ancient stone statue; cold and impossible to read. The sensation of being scared lingered as she tried to fight back the panic and maintain the speed limit. If she were asked what it was about that encounter that had frightened her so much, she wouldn't be able to answer. There was nothing tangible. It was more of a sense. A sudden feeling of dread, like when a room drops in temperature or you see something out of the corner of your eye. Throw in the bizarre conversation she had just had with Agent Eagle Eyes, and it was no wonder she was beyond amped.

Karen looked down at her gas gauge. It read half a tank. That would be good for a couple of hundred miles. Add that with the two one-hundred-dollar bills that lay nicely rolled in the side pocket of her bag, and it would be enough. She wouldn't even bother calling her mom. She would just go and hope whatever little money she had left once she got to Denver would last until she could find a job. Until then, she would have to suffer the drunken rages of her mother, but it still beat staying here by a long mile.

CHAPTER NINE

Birds Eye View

The girl's name at the front desk was Monica Hendrix. A pretty blond who didn't seem too surprised when Agent Wayne pulled up a chair next to her. Being hit on was just a way of life for her; it probably happened wherever she went.

"So, you're an agent?" she said as he sat down. "Like James Bond?"

"Not quite like that," he said. "Although I do like martinis, shaken, not stirred."

"Do you think Jimmy's okay?" she said.

"I hope he is," said Agent Wayne. "How well do you know him?"

"Well, I saw him every day up here, but that's about as far as it went. I never had lunch with him or anything."

"I hear he is a bit of a player," said Agent Wayne. "He never asked you out?"

Agent Wayne's eyes drifted over to the large window at the front of the office. He could see Charlie Wheaton leaning on a car in the parking lot, talking to Karen.

"He tried a couple of times," said Monica. "But I always reminded him that he was married."

"What about after the divorce?" said the agent.

He told Karen about the woman who had disappeared from Tulsa, and that had been true, but Charlie Wheaton's Wholesale was one of the largest construction companies in Oklahoma. Its list of customers (both satisfied and unsatisfied) was vast, so the odds were that something bad would eventually happen to someone they had dealings with.

"You know, that's the strange thing," said Monica. "Once he was single, he barely noticed that I was here. I guess he kind of changed."

But someone had murdered Mrs. Jones out in the boonies and had done their best to cover it up. Had there not been a group of high school kids out with Dad's stolen bottle of bourbon, they might have gotten away with it. As it was, the kids called 911 before the fire had a chance to destroy the body completely.

"Divorce can do that to a man," said the agent. "Do you know his ex-wife?"

But not before the car had been totaled. It was just blind luck that his registration in the glove compartment managed to survive. The crime was about as bizarre as they came, and it had no clear motive. The wife leaving Jimmy for the boss was one angle, but it was weak at best.

"I don't know her," said Monica. "She came to a couple of Christmas parties but didn't socialize much. I never talked to her. She was kind of standoffish."

Outside, Charlie reached out and embraced Karen. Karen wrapped her own arms around the man and then quickly let go and got into her car. Agent Wayne remained focused on Charlie as she pulled out of the parking lot. He was still standing there after she was gone, his hands folded over his gut.

"What about now?" said the agent. "Does she ever come up here to see Charlie?"

Charlie reached into his pocket and pulled out a set of keys. Then, he made his way over to a silver Mercedes SL-Class, opened the door, and squeezed in.

"Not really," said Monica. "But everyone here knows that they're together. They think it's a secret, but this place has no secrets."

Agent Wayne watched as the Mercedes pulled out of the lot.

"I wouldn't be too sure about that," he said.

"What do you mean?"

"Nothing," he said, flashing her a smile. "I just like to sound mysterious."

He then reached into the breast pocket of his shirt, pulled out one of his cards, and said, "Do me a favor; if you see or hear anything that you think might help, give me a call."

He stood up and made his way towards the door.

"That's it?" she said, sounding surprised.

"Did I miss something?" he said.

She smiled at him, and her teeth were perfect.

"Well, besides advice on that tie, I guess not."

****

The interrogations turned up nothing. That wasn't entirely true; it uncovered a torrid relationship between a wealthy man and a sad woman. Agent Wayne sat in the Crown Victoria, watching the traffic go by. All these people continued with their lives, oblivious to the dangers surrounding them. After ten years in the Bureau, Wyatt Wayne had seen many things. Buildings blown to pieces, gunshots, stabbings, and children sold for fun. And yet people went on as if nothing bad ever happened. Their lives locked in perpetual motion. Of course, that was nothing more than a fantasy; some of them would find out. Many would struggle once their train went off the track, forced to watch as the life they had known slipped further and further away. Lost in a maze of ill intent and hunted by predators who could sense the panic within, like hounds to blood.

Karen Presley did fit this profile. She had flown off the track a long time ago when she uttered the words *I do.* Perhaps even before then. He hadn't been lying when he told her that he knew a few things about Jimmy that she didn't. Like the two trips he had taken to a doctor. One for genital warts and one for gonorrhea. Not uncommon for a man who regularly cheats on his wife.

If it had just been that, he could probably have told her and gone to lunch with a clear conscience. But it was the one where Jimmy had picked up the nineteen-year-old girl from a rundown eastside apartment and driven her to a clinic for unwanted pregnancies that forced him to remain quiet. Should he have said something? Maybe. Should Karen have told Jimmy about the relationship with his boss? Maybe.

I'll be leaving Charlie, she had said.

Ah, found someone else?

Agent Wayne had regretted asking her that as soon as the words fell out of his mouth. But what she didn't know was that he was just buying time, debating whether he should tell her. Then she broke down, and he had his answer.

Karen Presley did not kill her ex-husband, and that should have been the end of his concern, yet her image continued to linger. Why? True, there was an inherent sadness about her that drew out the humanity in him, but there had to be something more to it than just empathy. She was attractive; he couldn't deny that, but something so primordial had never affected his work in the past.

The image of Charlie Wheaton watching as she pulled out of the parking lot popped into his mind. He would certainly have reason to murder Jimmy, although what he would gain hardly seemed worth the risk. Still, men had killed for less.

Agent Wayne closed his eyes and tried to transcend, placing himself in the rich man's place. The woman he was with was twenty years younger and probably rode him like a carnival ride. It was probably the best sex that he had in years, maybe ever. But would he kill for it? Did he really think that she would go back to Jimmy? And how did the old woman with the slit throat fit in?

It didn't add up. Nothing about this case was adding up. He had come to a dead end. The burned house was seventy-five miles away, and since he *was* at a dead-end, maybe it was time to start over. Perhaps they had missed something, although it was unlikely. But until an answer magically appeared, he had little else to go on. Plus, it would take his mind off Karen Presley. Agent Wyatt Wayne opened his eyes, shifted the car into drive, and left the parking lot.

CHAPTER TEN

A Memory Returns

The dreams circled like sharks. Waiting for him to make a mistake and slip into the waters of unconsciousness. Jimmy found himself fighting against a hangover from the drug that the old woman had given him, its residual effect reaching for him, trying to drag him down into a place that he refused to go.

The monitor continued to pulse from across the dark cavern, producing its own anxiety. The more Jimmy tried to ignore it, the louder the beeping became until his skin was covered in goosebumps as he clutched the pillow over his ears. Sleep would have been a comfort but for the dreams. They went beyond nightmares; it was as if they were animated revelations acted out by the horrors of his past. How long had they been stored away, festering and perhaps rehearsing? Just waiting for the right moment for the curtain to rise.

His father was a bastard. He knew this. The car wreck that had taken his life had been front-page news. It wasn't because his father was a celebrity or politician but because of the nefarious circumstances surrounding it. Laura Scott had been his secretary for ten years. He had hired her when Jimmy was only six, back when his mother and father still liked each other. Those were happy times. That would soon change.

As an attorney, Jimmy's father was well-known and liked. His practice did more than pay the bills; it provided a luxurious lifestyle. Not just because of the money, it also created the envy Jimmy's mother desired. Providing the perfect house, son, and marriage. So perfect that the thought of throwing it away over her husband's affair terrified her. Better to let the bastard dip his dick into The Other Woman; it would be one less thing that she would have to do.

The truth is, after all, a mirage.

This illusion remained until the night the median wall on 23rd destroyed the convenient fantasy. His father's brand-new BMW struck the center barrier doing sixty-five in a thirty-five mile per hour zone, crumpling the front end and tossing the car onto its side. The gas tank ruptured, causing a fire to ignite, which quickly spread. A trucker saw the accident and pulled his semi over, grabbing a fire extinguisher.

"I've seen a lot of things out there on the road," he told a reporter from Channel 4. "but I ain't never seen nothin' like that."

Laura, AKA The Other Woman, had been found with her head crushed into his father's lap, shattering his pelvic bone. Jimmy watched this report while sitting on the couch beside his mother, her hand on his. He felt her grip tighten to the point of hurting, her nails digging into his skin. She drew in a gasp and then stood, wrapping her arms around the bathrobe she was wearing. That night, a disease had been released, infecting them both like a virus, spreading its way into their minds, taking up residency, and never leaving.

For Jimmy's mother, the loss needed to be forgotten, tucked away—just another mirage to be ignored and discarded. But for Jimmy, a kid just starting high school, it was a topic of morbid fascination. It became a conversation starter for the other kids as he quietly walked by, pretending not to notice. Until he eventually joined in on the laugh for survival. And he had learned to use the tragedy, for women, after all, love a good hard-luck case. How ironic that his sole course of solace would eventually lead him down the path that had cost his father his life.

These parallels were not lost on him. His father had fooled around on his mother with just one woman (and maybe he really did love that woman) but he had fooled around just the same. Jimmy had been with many. This was the irony; his life now depended on an act that had been slowly killing him for years, and he was sure that when the time came to perform, he would fail, and that would be the end of Jimmy V.

A sudden light caused him to cover his eyes. From above came the threatening grind of metal. The door opened. A cleansing flood of adrenaline washed away the remainder of the drug. A thump echoed off the lava rock like a slow-moving bouncing ball. Jimmy stared at the mouth of the stairwell, the place where one of the monsters would descend. He didn't have to wait long. His heart sank as the albino crawler came into view, a book strapped to his waist.

CHAPTER ELEVEN

A Failed Attempt

When Karen first arrived at the thirty-five hundred square foot home, it felt like she had entered a fortress built just for her. It was a warm place where the frigid ice would melt, allowing her to heal. Charlie had been good about that, giving her the time and space she needed before mounting her for payment.

It had been a sanctuary...*The Answer.* And yet, even as the wounds were healing, a tumor appeared. This was the beginning of her punishment, self-inflicted and undeserved but there, all the same.

Karen sat in the Nissan near the steps of the stained concrete front porch. The house that had once provided comfort now emanated coldness like an empty tomb. The windows seemed to be watching her, daring her to enter, hoping she would.

Stop scaring yourself, she thought. *Just get the bag and go.*

She opened the car door and was immediately struck by a sudden blast of wind from the north, freezing her momentarily in place. She had gone out that morning in a panic and had forgotten her coat, but she would grab it this time along with everything else if she could find the courage to open the front door. Again, an unsettling feeling spread over her as she ascended the porch. Karen unlocked the door and pushed. It slowly swung inward. There was no reason for her to feel this way; the house was empty, well-lit, and every bit as warm as it had been on the first day she arrived. Karen took a deep breath and made her way through the living room area, passed the game room with the movie projector, and came to the master bedroom.

She went to the corner where her bag lay, stuffed the loose clothing back in, and picked it up. She turned back towards the bedroom door and felt her blood freeze. A low hum was filtering through the walls, becoming louder. Karen clutched the bag in her arms and made her way back through the house stopping at a window in the front room just as Charlie was struggling to remove his large body out of his Mercedes. Instead of pulling up next to her, as he had always done before, he parked behind her.

He knows.

She realized that she was now standing near the front door with her bag in hand. What would he do when he saw her?

You still have time to put it back.

But should she? She wasn't his slave, after all. Why should she not tell him the truth? Or even a partial truth? She could tell him that her mother was sick, but he would only insist on going with her. And if she refused, then what? Would he understand and just let her go?

I must not lie to myself.

The encounter at the parking lot had unnerved her and had filled her with a sense of dread that she couldn't explain. Perhaps it still affected her, causing her to cling to a panic that held about as much substance as smoke in the wind. But he *had* parked behind her.

Charlie was now lumbering his way towards the porch. Karen began to back away from the window, her hands digging into the bag like a life preserver. She could hear his hard sole shoes clicking on the stained steps. Karen was out of time; a choice must be made. But it was already made. Her fragile state of mind decided that even as Charlie was getting out of the car. Karen couldn't afford a confrontation, not now, not when she had just been purged from a six-year-long battle.

She turned and made her way back down the hallway, re-entering the bedroom just as the turning doorknob sounded out like a warning shot. She tossed the bag back in the corner and jumped onto the bed, placing one arm over her eyes. From down the hall, heavy footfalls drew closer.

There was a sudden silence, and in her mind's eye, she could see him standing in the doorway, his eyes darting from her to the bag and then back to her. She sensed him approaching the bed.

Please don't let him want sex, she thought.

The bed sank to her left as he sat down next to her. She moved her arm and gave him a sleepy look.

"Sorry I woke you up," he said.

"I was only dozing," she said, sitting up. "Did something else happen?"

"No, I left right after you."

Karen looked into his eyes, but he was too hard to read.

"I can't believe Jimmy is missing," she said.

"It's tragic," said Charlie, "but not too surprising. His lifestyle did tend to piss people off."

He gestured to her as an example and said, "And who knows how many husbands out there had it in for him."

"But why the old lady?"

"Maybe she saw something," said Charlie, placing his hand on her knee.

Karen forced herself not to pull away.

"Kind of a no-witness thing."

He then squeezed Karen's knee and stood. Karen felt her pulse quicken as he walked over to where her bag sat, zipped in the corner. It had been open before; had he noticed?

"Are you happy here?" he said.

"I'm grateful," she said.

"That's good," said Charlie, gazing towards her. "But are you happy here, with me?"

"Right now, I think I'm still in shock," she said. "I spent six years with him, Charlie. It's hard to just hit the reset button and start over with someone else."

"I get that," said Charlie, looking down at her bag. "But you know I care about you, right?"

"I know," she said. "I care about you, too."

Charlie's eyes remained on the bag.

"Are you planning on leaving me?"

The first chance I get, she thought but said, "I'm not planning on anything right now. Jimmy's *missing,* Charlie. Aren't you a little concerned?"

"Of course I am," he said, snapping his gaze back at her. "But I'm more concerned about you."

"Don't be," she said. "No matter what happens, I'll be fine."

She said this with as much conviction as she could muster, but the truth was brittle at best, and she was sure that Charlie knew it. He looked at her for a moment longer, his eyes locking onto hers. Karen held his gaze, refusing to look away.

Finally, Charlie released her from the vampiric stare, and his face lit up with a smile.

"You still want to catch a movie later?" he said.

Karen returned the smile and said, "You pick it, and I'll go."

Charlie then walked over and leaned down for a hug. She wrapped her arms around him momentarily, and he stood back up, a smile still stretched across his face.

"Good," he said. "I don't know if you know this, but I was married once. Her name was Sarah."

"I didn't know that," said Karen.

"She left me fifteen years ago, right before I started my company. The same year I quit drinking."

"Where is she now?"

"She was murdered," said Charlie.

"I'm sorry," said Karen, a chill seizing her spine.

"Don't be," he said. "It's strange though. She left me because of my drinking, and who could blame her? She was afraid of my 'dark moods,' as she put it, and I guess I sometimes scared her."

Karen watched as Charlie's gaze again drifted over to her bag.

"I came home one night, my head swimming in bourbon, and she was gone. I'm sure that she had help."

He looked back at her and said, "Does this sound familiar?"

Karen ignored the question.

"How was she murdered?"

"She had been... decapitated. They found her body off old Route 66," said Charlie, "most likely killed by whoever she had left me for."

"They never caught him?"

"Nope," said Charlie, placing his gaze back on her. "I want you to think about that while deciding what to do. It's a dangerous world, Karen. There are people out there, soulless people, intent on causing pain."

Then, without another word, he turned and left the room. Karen could feel her pulse pounding away as the sound of the front door being shut was soon followed by the motor of his Mercedes coming to life.

She waited a moment longer, stood up, grabbed her bag, and returned to the living room. He was gone, but for how long? Long enough to make it to the car and find the nearest highway? The house was hauntingly silent as if waiting for her decision. A shiver swept through her.

It's now or never.

Karen opened the front door and crept out onto the porch. A blistering shriek came from above, causing her to almost drop her bag. It was only a blue jay squawking from a nearby tree. Thirty feet stood between her and the Nisson, but it seemed like a mile. Karen stepped off the porch, her legs shaking with every step. She reached the driver's side door, threw her bag in, and followed. She started the Nisson, shifted into reverse, and hesitated. She hadn't locked the front door and considered going back, which produced a nervous laugh. It was amazing how the mind worked while in overdrive.

Karen pulled out of the driveway, pausing to check both sides of the street, sure that Charlie's Mercedes would be parked near a curb, but the road was empty. Karen pointed the car west, away from the direction of Charlie Wheaton's Wholesale, and put her foot down, speeding through a four-way intersection. The neighborhood was gated, with each mansion sitting on two-acre lots, closely cropped and decorated with imported plants and immaculate statues. The epitome of the American Dream, and they could have it; her only wish was to be in Denver by midnight.

But she had to be smart. Her funds were limited, and although she wanted to put many miles behind her fast, the price of fuel would be much higher once she was on the interstate; it was better to fill up now before she got out of the city.

The early afternoon traffic was light, and according to her weather app, she should have a clear road through Kansas. Charlie would call as soon as he arrived back at his house, and then she would have to make another decision: Would she answer it? She decided she would have to; she owed him that much and would tell him the truth. He wouldn't understand, and perhaps he would blame himself, which she would then insist that he did nothing wrong; *except scare the shit out of her.* But she wouldn't mention that. How could she? She couldn't even explain it to herself.

Up ahead, she saw the $2.19 a gallon sign lit up in red neon at a Quickmart on the next intersection. The store was only a half-mile away from the I-35 northbound exit.

Karen pulled up to the furthest pump. She only had cash, which meant she would have to go in and leave the person at the register one of the one-hundred-dollar bills, fill the Nisson, and then go back in for the change. But that would get her over halfway. Relief became all-consuming at the thought of being that far away from Charlie before having to stop. A call would have to be made to the agent, and she decided to call him once she reached Salina. Hopefully, he wouldn't demand that she turn back, and what if he did? What would she do then?

Worry about that if it happens.

The important thing right now was to fill up and get out of Dodge before the man with *The Answer* returned home. Karen dragged the bag onto her lap, unzipped the small pocket on the side, reached in her hand, and felt her heart sink. The pocket was empty. Karen pulled open the seams to the point of ripping, sticking her face so close that it looked as though she might try to climb in. She unzipped the main part of the duffle bag and began tossing out the clothes onto the passenger seat, checking the pockets of every shirt and pair of jeans as she did. She then turned it upside down and shook it furiously.

The money was gone.

Had she lost it? It was there yesterday. She saw it when she had taken out her last twenty, she was sure of it. A shiver coursed through her as she remembered Charlie hovering over the bag. He knew that she had the money and knew where she kept it. She had offered him a hundred when he took care of her storage, and he had refused. But that was before he sensed that she might leave.

Is that what he had done? Grabbed her money so she would have no way out? Why else? He didn't need it, but he sure as hell knew that she did. A blast of rage knocked away the fear: The bastard had stolen her money because he didn't want her to leave him, and now she was trapped. Charlie Wheaton had gone too far, and Karen had no choice but to confront the man and demand that he return the money. For a moment, she considered going to the office and confronting him in person, but that would take too long, and right now, her anger was working like fuel. Karen grabbed her phone off the console and made the call.

CHAPTER TWELVE

The Odd Tracks

Agent Wayne wasn't the first to arrive at Mrs. Jones' house. The local police had called in their own detective. It wasn't until they found the singed paperwork inside of Jimmy's car that the OSBI had been notified, brought in as additional help if needed.

Agent Wayne had stayed in the background at first, allowing the local investigators to continue unhindered, but it soon became apparent that they were getting nowhere. The fire had accomplished what it was no doubt intended for, burning away any chance for prints or follicles.

The police seemed satisfied with the theory that Jimmy had done it, although determining a motive proved somewhat elusive. It was then that Agent Wayne decided to step even further back and run a few checks of his own. That was how he had learned about the missing woman in Tulsa and her affiliation with Charlie Wheaton's Wholesale. From there, it was only a matter of asking the right people the right questions, and soon, the entire affair between Charlie and Karen was revealed. But all of that was circumstantial, and their alibis were solid.

Mrs. Jones' house now looked like a charred skeleton. Agent Wayne sat in the Crown Victoria, allowing his imagination to travel. The old woman had been a widow for twenty years and had the unfortunate luck of having outlived her only son by three years. There had been one grandchild, but she had been struck by a car and killed back in '82, so Mrs. Jones was utterly alone. Her only help came from the church she attended in town. She had been unable to drive, didn't even own a car, and was forced to rely on others for a ride. It was a sad scene, but not completely unheard of in the rural wastelands.

All of this made it hard to believe that a woman in her eighties and living off social security would request an estimate for anything that had to do with the upkeep of her house. There had been a small life insurance policy after her husband had died, but she had run out of that money years ago. And yet the phone records showed that a call had been placed to Charlie Wheaton's Wholesale from this house the night before she had been murdered. Why would she do that? Senility was a possibility, of course, or loneliness, and salesmen are paid to talk. Maybe Jimmy had learned of Charlie and Karen just as Mrs. Jones refused to sign the dotted line. Could that be enough to push him over? Absolutely, it could. But why burn his own car?

Agent Wayne let out a sigh and opened the driver's side door. The smell of smoldering wood and melted chemicals still hung in the air like a toxic leak. The old lady's lawn looked like it hadn't been cut all summer. Agent Wayne could see the broken blades of grass where the first responders had mowed their way up to the house. He was about to make his way to where the front door used to be and stopped. One set of tracks broke away from the cluster, winding their way down the side of the house. Would the first responders drive to the back? Maybe they would, but it didn't seem necessary with a house this size. Agent Wayne followed them. They went past the house about ten feet and turned sharply to the left, veering in and coming to a stop just a few feet away from the back wall. No emergency vehicle would park that close to a roaring fire.

The possible reasons for these tracks probably fell into the thousands. Still, this was an old woman who, as far as he could tell, had no one. And these couldn't be much older than the ones made by the first responders.

A chilly breeze whispered through the tall grass. He paced the distance between the broken blades of grass, then reached inside of his coat pocket and pulled out his cell phone. He flipped to the camera and took a couple of pictures. He then made his way back towards the car, clicking the camera as he went. The town that sent the emergency crew was El Reno, another forty-minute drive.

The tracks were too far apart to be a car, and since he had been at a dead-end anyway, he might as well see if any of them had pulled into the back. And if they hadn't, then what? That would give him something to ponder during the drive back to the office.

****

The El Reno fire station was a recently built flat-roofed matter of local pride. The red brick walls were divided by massive round-top windows with colonial grids that matched two large clear bay doors. It held two pump trucks and one command vehicle.

He entered the station and was met by a portly man who looked to be in his mid-thirties. He was wearing a white T-shirt over loose-fitting sweatpants, which were tucked into a pair of well-worn cowboy boots. The man certainly dressed for comfort.

"Good afternoon. My name is Wyatt Wayne. I'm with the OSBI," he said, showing the man his badge. "Who is the chief here?"

"That would be me," said the man, extending his hand. "Roger Dean."

Agent Wayne shook his hand and said, "I'm investigating the murder of Mrs. Jones out on East County Road."

"Yeah, I was there," said Chief Dean. "Can I get you something to drink, coke or coffee?"

"A coke would be good," said the agent.

"Come with me," said Chief Dean.

Agent Wayne followed him down a hallway. The Chief stopped and opened a door, motioning the agent in.

"Have a seat," said Chief Dean. "I'll be right back."

The room had a long-running table at its center, with cushioned chairs pushed in on both sides. The walls were decorated with pictures of fire engines from the past and photos of the men who used them. A toy basketball hoop had been placed over a trashcan in the corner, and a forty-eight-inch flat-screen television was mounted on a wall.

Chief Dean returned with a couple of soda cans in his hand.

"Sit down wherever you'd like," he said, placing the cans on the table and pulling out a chair for himself.

Agent Wayne sat across from him, taking a coke.

"I appreciate you taking the time," said the agent.

"I have all the time in the world," said Chief Dean. "Unless the alarm goes off."

"Do you get a lot of calls out here?"

"You'd be surprised," said the chief. "Especially when it's dry like it is now. One idiot with a cigarette and you might not come back for days,"

"So, you were out at Mrs. Jones' house?"

"I was the first one there," said the chief. "I went ahead of the trucks. I do that in case people are trying to get out. I pulled her body out of the house."

"Yeah," said Agent Wayne. "I saw the pictures."

"You know, I remember a time when we used to ask questions like, who would do something like that? But nowadays, it's far too common."

"I know what you mean," said Agent Wayne. "I really have only one question."

He then took out his phone and brought up the picture of the tracks trailing off to the side of the house. "Do you recall whether or not any of your men drove to the back?"

Chief Dean looked at the picture for a moment and shook his head.

"I'm sure we didn't," he said. "There was no reason to. The house was only burning in the front, and once we extended the ladders, we had all the range we needed."

Agent Wayne pulled up the picture of the tracks beside the back wall.

"We would never park that close," said Chief Dean. "Unless we wanted to fry our truck."

"That's what I thought," said the agent, placing the phone back in his coat pocket.

"Do you think someone else was there besides the salesman?" said the chief.

"It's beginning to look that way," said the agent.

"I thought it was strange that the guy had torched his own car," said the chief.

"I couldn't agree more," said Agent Wayne, rising from his chair. "I've taken up enough of your time."

The chief stood up, drank the rest of his soda, and tossed the empty can through the net.

"Swish," he said with a grin, then reached out and shook the agent's hand. "I hope you catch whoever did it,"

Agent Wayne brought out a card and said, "I think we will. But if you remember anything else, please call me."

"You can count on it," said the chief.

****

There was a small amount of traffic on eastbound I-40. It would be an hour before Agent Wayne arrived at the office, giving himself plenty of time to think. Chief Dean had confirmed his suspicion and Agent Wayne was now confident that someone else besides the police and fireman had been there.

Someone had killed the old lady and had burned the house. That was a fact. They had also torched Jimmy's car, had even tossed in his wallet and cell phone, and removed the tag. That also was a fact. So, it wasn't a matter of trying to set him up, or they wouldn't have done anything to the car. It was more like they were trying to make him disappear. But why? What could anyone possibly want with a twenty-nine-year-old salesman? An image of Charlie Wheaton watching Karen leave the parking lot flashed in his mind. The guy's alibi was solid. He had been with Karen at a Mexican restaurant that night, and his story had been checked out. But that didn't mean that he didn't have someone else do it.

But why?

CHAPTER THIRTEEN

A Brief History Lesson

The thing's name was Phillip. He was perched on his two hands near the side of the cage. He wore a white pullover Polo shirt draped over a red and green checkered kilt-like skirt. His browless pinkish eyes looked through the bars at Jimmy, who was hunkered in a corner on his cot, his shivering arms locked around his knees. This deformed albino with a scar running across his head had raped him, more like milked him, and Jimmy was sure that if he were allowed a long life, he would relive the event through countless dreams. It was horrifying having to face this mutation, this bringer of nightmares. Jimmy was the victim, and with that came embarrassment and anger. Did Phillip understand that? Of course, he did; the deformed man wasn't stupid. That might be the most terrifying part. The fact that these throwback creatures who looked as though they couldn't manage to open a door were, in fact, very intelligent, smart enough to create elaborate traps and perform amputations.

"How are you feeling?" Phillip said, boosting himself onto his backside, giving Jimmy a clear view of his deformed feet. "I'm sure you have questions?"

"What is wrong with you?" said Jimmy.

Phillip looked at him for a moment curiously, then let out a short laugh.

"That's not what I was expecting," he said. "But a fair question, I guess, and it leads to what you really want to know. Why you?"

"Would you tell me if I asked?"

"There's no point in lying to you," said Phillip, reaching up and rubbing his scar. "What you are seeing is the beginning of the end. I am one of the last in a long line of nobility."

"Are you saying you're a King?"

"Not a King, more like a Duke," said Phillip.

"Sure, you are," snapped Jimmy. "And you jack guys off because it's your divine right."

"In a way, you are correct, although it's not what you think."

Jimmy released his legs and let his feet fall to the floor.

"Listen," he said. "I'm not the greatest at figuring out riddles but I think I have a pretty good idea about why I'm here." He then pointed across the room at the pregnant woman in the other cell and said, "Why we are both here."

Phillip cocked his head towards the woman.

"Yes. Well, that was a tragic event and one I hope to avoid with you."

"Why do you need us at all?" said Jimmy. "Surely there are other ways."

"Ah... now comes the hardest part," said Phillip, pulling the book tethered to his side onto his lap. "Trying to explain a tradition spanning centuries to someone who will never understand, yet I will try. You deserve that, I think. And maybe it will help us both."

Phillip unbuckled the book's strap and slid it through the bars.

Jimmy stared at it lying on the floor but didn't move. The book was large, its cover made of antique leather with loose strings winding through its spine like some ancient work of magic.

"It has pictures," said Phillip.

Jimmy gazed over at the mutated man, then slowly stood and made his way over to the book.

"How's your history?" said Phillip. "But, of course, I already know the answer."

Jimmy picked up the book and returned to the bed, setting it aside.

The steady beep continued from across the room. Jimmy gazed

over to where the shadowed form of the woman lay motionless, her body still working, but he was sure that her mind was gone.

A tragic event, and one that I hope to avoid with you, Phillip had said.

Had he come to barter with him, then? His life for what? Breeding with the girl? Of course, that had to be it. The giant had certainly accomplished his mission with the poor woman. He was overly proficient, according to what Phillip had said to the old woman earlier, dangerously so.

"You never answered my question," said Jimmy. "Why do you need us?"

"If you open the book to page one," began Phillip, sounding like an elementary school teacher speaking to his class, "you'll see a picture of a man."

Here, he paused. Jimmy looked at him for a moment.

"I assure you that the book is not a bomb," said Phillip, grinning. "And you just might learn something."

Jimmy flipped open the cover. The page was a full-length photo of a painting—a portrait of a man whose features resembled those of the old ladies so closely that they might have been twins. His jaw stuck out well beyond the scope of normal, and his cheekbones were nonexistent. He was wearing a throw-over tunic tightly secured by a braided belt. His hair fell in waves around his shoulders, reminding Jimmy of some '70s rock singer.

"That is Lionus the II," said Phillip. "Last King of Spain from the line of the Henley's. Does that name mean anything to you?"

"Not at all," said Jimmy.

"Of course it wouldn't," said Phillip. "Some called him The Bewitched, some The Cursed. But I call him a victim."

"I don't understand," said Jimmy.

"Turn to the next page," said Phillip.

Jimmy did and found that the following two pages contained a chart filled with names. He flipped the book onto its side, holding it up like a centerfold. At the top read Lionus I of Castile (1470-1503), and beside it read Joan of Castile (1470-1556). From there, the names branched off like a flooded river, some containing the title of Holy Roman Emperor, some merely Duke. It was an aggression of royalty that spread throughout Europe, including Hungary, Denmark, and

Austria. It seemed they were everywhere, the family tree growing and expanding quickly as the decades passed.

But then something happened. Jimmy noticed that the tree began to dwindle, thinning out right around the 1600s and stopping with the death of Lionus the II in 1700.

Jimmy placed the book down and gazed at Phillip, who was still sitting with his hands folded on his crooked lap.

"You called this Lionus guy a victim," he said. "Why?"

"Take a look at his parents," said Phillip.

Jimmy picked the book back up and read Darrius IV of Spain and Maria of Austria.

"Okay, and?"

"His father was his mother's uncle," said Phillip.

"They're inbred?" said Jimmy.

"A tradition that goes back to the beginning," said Phillip. "One that has been bestowed upon us by God and carries with it His test."

"This is crazy," said Jimmy. "Is this why you look like you do?"

"That is a part of God's test," said Phillip solemnly. "Along with never-ending loss. Our family has accepted this for generations. Our children are born, and many die before they reach the age of two, and those who do survive but show signs of any mental weakness are disposed of. Our cemetery is full of those chosen to ascend; they wait for us and are surrounded by the faithful."

Jimmy felt numb. This madness went beyond comprehension, a mass delusion of Jim Jones proportion. Did they really think that they were the kin of Jesus? A small drawing on the top right corner of the page caught his eye; it was a double-headed eagle, like the statues near the front door. Scrolled across the bottom of the picture were:

House of Henley

"Are you telling me that you are related to this Lionus guy? How is that possible? According to this, he never had kids."

"He didn't," said Phillip. "His body was too wasted for that, but he did have a sister. Her name was Theresa, and she was unaffected. Because of her and the touch of God, we could continue, venturing out into the new world and continuing on the path given to us by the

Lord. Do you understand what I'm telling you?"

"You're too fucked up to have kids?"

Phillip drew back as if he had been slapped, his pink skin darkening, and Jimmy felt his heart skip.

Be careful, a voice whispered in his head.

"All I mean is that you can't have children," said Jimmy. "That's why you have us here, isn't it? To continue the line?"

Phillip's face went from blood red to the color of a corpse within seconds. For a moment, Jimmy was sure that his life was very close to ending. He had angered this man, the only one who seemed to care about what would happen to him. He would have to remember that if he wanted to avoid the giant's blade.

"But why this?" he said. "Why not just go to a clinic? Why kidnap and risk getting in trouble?"

"What you speak of is an abomination," said Phillip. "It is the production of children by an assembly line, with no choice or interaction; a process and nothing more."

"Isn't that exactly what you're doing now, forcing us to produce children without a choice?"

"But you do have a choice," said Phillip. "That's why I'm here."

Phillip leaned his face closer to the bars and said, "You have been chosen, James. You are not just some random names picked out of a hat."

"What are you talking about?"

"Turn to the last page," said Phillip.

Jimmy looked at him doubtfully. There had to be some setup here, something they had learned after his capture. Certainly, Lord Phillip here was smart enough to know how to check bank records. Maybe they had found out about his divorce. He wouldn't put it past them, and with their money, they could certainly offer him a way out: All he had to do was impregnate the girl. But then what? Were they going to just let him go with a bag of cash? After all that he had seen?

There was no way he would walk out of here with a *Thanks for Playing* card. But it still didn't answer the fundamental question: why choose him to begin with?

You are not just some random name we picked out of a hat.

Jimmy turned to the last page in the book, where a crumpled

yellow newspaper clipping had been taped:

April 15, 2004- Body of Woman Found On Route 66.

Investigators are seeking any information that can help identify the woman's identity. She was found on the side of Route 66, two miles east of El Reno. If you have any information, please call 1-800-670-2600.

Below the column was a follow-up article:

April 21, 2004- Body On Route 66 Identified.
The body has been identified as 32-year-old Sarah Wheaton. She had been last seen three weeks before her body's discovery. According to her husband, Charles Wheaton, she was going to her family's home in Salina, Kansas.

Both of her parents confirm this and are stunned by the news. We will report any further facts as they emerge.

Jimmy felt his heart leap into his throat. He had turned his back on Charlie and not just Charlie but also *The Answer* and was proving to the others who were struggling on the fence that you didn't have to conform to be successful. And he had been right, at least for a while, anyway. That was why Charlie Wheaton hated him—hated him so much that he had set him up, had given him to a family of twisted killers. Had he known that they would kill the old lady? Would he have cared?

A cold, empty spot inside of his gut answered no. But what could possibly be in it for him besides knowing he would never see Jimmy again? Perhaps that was enough.

Jimmy again looked at the article and noticed a Polaroid picture glued to the lower right side of the page: Charlie was sitting at a table with a candle burning at its center, his hands stretched out, and he was clutching a woman's hand. Her young features were almost ghostly in the low light, but Jimmy had no problem distinguishing the painful truth and gasped. It was Karen, her face frozen in laughter. A rumble suddenly erupted in his stomach as the lava rock chasm began to spin, forcing Jimmy to close his eyes.

"Are you ready to hear my offer?" said Phillip.

Jimmy opened his eyes. His vision blurred. He reached up and brushed the newly formed tears away.

"How do you know him?" he managed to ask.

"We go back a long way," said Phillip. "Back to when he was a blithering drunk, much like yourself."

"Does he have my wife?"

"As far as I know, she's still with him."

"Why would she do that?" said Jimmy.

"Do you really have to ask?" said Phillip.

"I didn't even know he was married," Jimmy said, dazed.

"That's how it began," said Phillip. "As I said, he was once an alcoholic and a womanizer. Of course, this was back when I was still in my teens, but even then, we knew that foreigners would soon have to be introduced."

Here, Phillip leaned back on one arm as if talking to an old friend and said, "It's a cycle, you know? And it becomes obvious when the cells need replenishing."

Phillip ran his hand down his body as if giving an example.

"Marianna and Nithard were eleven when our mother was sure that the curse had returned and knew we must plan for the future."

Jimmy listened to the man speak but couldn't keep his eyes from wandering down to the picture of Karen. She had left him for the enemy. Had she known that? Jimmy was sure that she had. He had bitched about Charlie enough over the years. Had he really been that bad to her?

The answer came like a flickering movie: The rain had been pounding on the windshield when he pulled up to where a young woman stood waiting for him. Christine Miller was her name, and she had just turned eighteen. He had driven her three hundred miles for the abortion that night. A shudder passed over him as he remembered conning her into one last romp on the way at a rest stop. The kiss that he had given her when he finally dropped her back at her apartment the next day had burned his lips like poison. And that knowing look in her almond eyes as he drove off, her shivering body standing there like a forlorn statue, like a terrified baby opossum. It was mortifying.

"There are people out there who have lost their souls," continued Phillip. "They stumble through life, surprised they have made it to the next day. Most of them don't deserve to, mind you. But some do and, if given a chance, will do almost anything to improve their lives. Charlie is one of those," said Phillip. "We met him wandering the streets in Broken Arrow. He was passing out flyers, trying to make a living and provide for a wife he couldn't stand. Mother stopped the car beside a curb and asked him what he was peddling. I think it was aluminum siding, and she told him she was interested and offered to give him a ride to the house. Of course, he refused the ride; all his supplies were in the trunk of his old Taurus, so he followed her instead."

"Are you saying that you used Charlie to breed?"

"Heavens no," said Phillip. "Have you seen him? We want to replenish the bloodline, not make it worse. But after a couple of hours of listening to him, my mother had learned a lot about this man. He was greedy, which was good, and besides his wife, he had no one, which was better."

"I don't understand," said Jimmy.

Phillip sat back up and gave Jimmy a smile.

"She made him an offer that would change his life. And I want to make you an offer that will change yours."

"You want me to impregnate your sister," said Jimmy. "And then what, you'll let me leave?"

"I think you know better than that," said Phillip. "But in case you haven't noticed, we're wealthy. We didn't get off the boat empty-handed."

"I still don't understand," said Jimmy. "You're going to give me a pile of money and what? Leave it in this prison with me so I can stare at it?"

"That wouldn't do you much good," he said. "We are offering you a chance at nobility, not to mention a fresh start...a clean slate, if you will."

"I'm listening," said Jimmy.

What choice did he have?

"My sister likes you," said Phillip. "Perhaps she might even love you if given the chance, but she is no whore. For us, marriage is a formality that is never overlooked. And once the vow is taken, it is observed for life."

Jimmy listened to this insanity as his pulse continued to quicken. This proposal was presented with the sum of five hundred years of inbreeding. Cousins marrying Uncles and Nephews marrying Aunts, each generation devolving into unrecognizable freaks, driven by the belief that it was God's will. It would have been funny if Jimmy was not completely at their mercy.

"Which brings me to the offer," said Phillip. "You will marry Marianna and provide for her many children; in return, all of your troubles will disappear."

"You want me to marry your sister?"

"She wants you to marry her," clarified Phillip.

"She doesn't even know me," said Jimmy.

"She knows enough," said Phillip. "Your friend Charlie provided plenty of information, including a charming photo of you."

"Did he mention that I cheated on my wife?"

"Oh yes," said Phillip. "But that doesn't concern us because the penalty for that here is death, and I think you're every bit as smart as you look."

Jimmy looked back down at the articles. A disturbing question suddenly appeared in his mind.

"Did you kill Charlie's wife?"

"Me, personally? No."

"But your family did," said Jimmy. "That was what you did for him, wasn't it?"

"Yes, it was. That, and gave him enough cash to start up his own business. But it came with a catch; if he ever touched a drop of alcohol again, the deal was off."

That explained so much. *The Answer* was nothing more than a contractual threat. For Charlie, to break it would mean losing everything, including, quite possibly, his own life.   "So, his company acted as a front for choosing breeders," said Jimmy.

"Not at first," said Phillip. "We helped his company grow. We actually own fifty-one percent of its stock."

"And what about that woman over there?" said Jimmy. "Was she another one of Charlie's fallen angels?"

"She was a nuisance," said Phillip. "An uppity customer of Charlie's who had caused all kinds of trouble. Fortunately, she came along when she did; Nith was more than ready."

"And no one looked for her?"

"At first, they did," said Phillip. "But she wasn't well-liked. Even her ex-husband made no inquiries about her. She has already been forgotten."

Phillip's words reduced that woman to a product. Had she been given a choice? Perhaps, but she had obviously declined their offer, and the results were horrifying. The woman would be dead soon, was most likely already brain dead, and yet they kept her alive. Her body was nothing more than an incubator, and once the child was born, the machine that carried it would be thrown away. And then what?

They would have to find a replacement for the quota that still had to be met.

"I don't expect an answer from you right now," said Phillip. "It's a lot to take in. Sleep on it and consider carefully what you have to lose. And not just you, but your wife and your dear mother in Dallas."

"Don't you fucking touch them," said Jimmy, jumping from the cot and spilling the book to the floor.

"Me, personally? Never," said Phillip, giving Jimmy a smile that looked like a razor's slit.

He then pivoted around and hand-crawled his way back to the stairs. Jimmy felt the air rushing into his lungs in panicked gasps. He steadied his shaking legs and walked over to the wall of bars, listening to the thumps of Phillip climbing the stairs.

"Don't you hurt them!" he cried out. His only answer was the clanging of the metal door.

CHAPTER FOURTEEN

An Eye in the Sky

Karen rushed out of the house with her bag in hand. Of course, she lied, and it was no surprise for Charlie, who sat two blocks away watching her retreat on his cell phone. The idiot had no idea the entire house had been fitted with the newest Owl 2500 Surveillance System. Everything she did was linked directly to him. He watched as the Nisson backed out of the driveway.

Let her try and run, he thought to himself. *How far could she really get with no money?*

That was the question. How much fuel did she have, and how long until she realized her two hundred dollars were missing? Would she call him then? Most likely, accusing him of taking it and then demanding it back. Charlie would deny it, of course.

For a moment, he considered calling her. Not because of his feelings for her, although she was a good fuck, but because she might actually find a way to leave. Karen was too valuable to lose. That agent's questions were mostly routine, but something in the smartass' eyes gave Charlie the heebee geebees. It was like his words were a diversion as he picked you apart with his gaze, watching your face for any sign of discrepancy. Charlie had not lied. He hadn't needed to, at least for now.

That could all change, and for that reason, Karen was

important. If the agent began to chip his way to the truth, Karen would have to go down. It was a risky venture that could be achieved, especially with the help of the family that had taken him under his wing. His wealth, his prestigious place in the world, hell, his very life, was owed to them. Thanks to them, his marriage had come to an abrupt end. Sarah's murder came as a surprise. Pleasant, yes, but a surprise just the same. They never admitted that they had killed her, but Charlie knew.

Which was why he now felt like an associate of some New York crime syndicate. The family had money, the kind that Bill Gates had, and they were crazy. How they handled that old lady when they grabbed Jimmy was proof. Would they do that to him if he were to fail at a request? Charlie had taken their deal and used their money to build one of the largest companies in Oklahoma; he was a millionaire but also a puppet. For a moment, he fell back into an ongoing fantasy. One which saw him cashing in his chips and climbing on board the first flight out. Where it was going really didn't matter, just as long as it was far from here.

They would find you, a voice within him said, and he believed it.

They would send that giant who towered over Charlie's six-foot-four- frame, and that would be that.

A thought sent a shiver down his spine. Perhaps they were already watching him, much like he was watching Karen. They were that clever. Even the house that the mother had taken him to all those years ago wasn't where they lived. Oh, they had undoubtedly owned it, most likely one of the many properties they had scattered around the state. When Charlie eventually made his way back to that house a little over a year later, it had been sold, and whatever records that might have existed had vanished.

Charlie took in a deep breath and counted to four. A suffocating feeling forced him to lower the Mercedes window. The air had a dirty taste, like diesel mixed with sweat. A sudden urge to vomit struck him. It caused him to drop the cell phone to the floor. Was it guilt he was feeling or fear? Perhaps it was both. An image of Jimmy flashed into his mind. The man was as good as dead. Charlie had seen to that just as he had seen to the lying bitch out of Tulsa. He had no qualms about setting her ass up. She was a cold-hearted whore who had only wanted a quick payday. Jimmy had at least tried, had at least made an effort in The Program. But it was too late for regrets now, and what was done was done.

Charlie pulled the Mercedes onto the road and began to make his way back to the house. The money had to be there before she returned.

If she returned, he thought.

It was then that his phone began to ring.

CHAPTER FIFTEEN

Agent Wayne Makes a Call

The Oklahoma Bureau of Investigation's headquarters was located on the north side of Oklahoma City. It was a four-story relic from the forties surrounded by two acres of closely cropped Bermuda grass. Its location was hidden by a running wall of cedar trees that staggered their way along NE 63rd, its only gap revealing a six-foot-tall electronic gate.

Agent Wayne sat at his desk on the third floor. His office was a 10x12 cubicle painted in Desert Beige, one of a dozen along a fluorescent-lit hallway. This was where the second-level agents were stationed. They were not as posh as the third-level agents on the fourth floor, but they were much better than the poor slobs at the first level who had to share their space.

His boss's comment about being the Mulder of the OSBI hadn't offended him in the least. In fact, he rather liked it. So much, in fact, that a poster of a flying saucer with the words *I Want To Believe* written under it was now mounted on the wall behind his desk.

He loosened the knot on his pumpkin tie and sat back in the chair, watching his laptop come to life. The screen lit up, showing the cast of The Golden Girls with *Stay Golden* captioned across the bottom. He tapped the mouse and typed in Charlie Wheaton's Wholesale. A long column appeared on the screen containing its official website, the year it was established, a Yelp report, and the BBB's rating. He scrolled down to an old photograph of a young woman, unamusingly shocked at having her picture taken. Typed under it was Sarah Wheaton.

Charlie's wife had been murdered. That was no secret. It was still an open case, and her death had happened just before Charlie had started his company. And just where did he get the funds to start that venture? The obvious answer would be life insurance. Agent Wayne pulled up the Sarah Wheaton file and scrolled through the information. According to the file, that theory was tried and discarded due to the small amount that the policy provided. Charlie had received three thousand dollars, hardly enough to start an empire. Agent Wayne read further and discovered that her father, Karl Devon, had been a reasonably well-off real estate developer (he had died just two years after his daughter) and had started a substantial trust fund in her name when she was a kid, but the only way Charlie benefitted from that was if his wife remained alive. So why kill her?

Easy now, he thought to himself. *Let's not jump that gun.*

Agent Wayne reversed out of his search and moved the arrow over to the Criminal Background Check icon. This one-click would link him to the nationwide data files. It covered everything from parking tickets to mass murder. He typed in Charlie Wheaton and waited.

It only took a moment, and a report soon appeared on his screen. The man certainly had gotten around. There was a DUI in Lubbock, Texas, back in 1998 and another one in Tulsa in 2001. A couple of soliciting prostitution charges, as well. All of these had been uncontested, and their fines were paid. Agent Wayne cross-checked the dates of the solicitation charges and found that one of them had happened in Tulsa in 1999 while he was married. Had his wife known? Prostitution for married men wasn't uncommon, but the reaction from the angered wives varied. Women were sitting in prison who had taken the news very badly.

What would Sarah have done? Threatened divorce, of course. But what would Charlie have to lose by that? Her money, for one. But Agent Wayne wasn't sure if she was sharing that. It appeared that Charlie was working awfully hard for a man who was given a silver spoon. Unless he wanted to get away from her. That posed an interesting question. What was their relationship like?

He pecked away at the keyboard and saw that the file had been updated to show Mrs. Wheaton's mother was still alive. A telephone number and address had been placed to the side of her name. Agent Wayne jotted down the number and closed out of the site.

There were two questions that had to be asked of Sarah's mother; the first one wasn't too bad, but the other one was liable to send the old woman into a rage—possibly causing her to call headquarters and demand to speak with his supervisor. That was a scenario Agent Wayne would like to avoid, considering his suspicions. He looked down at the phone number and then glanced over at the phone. No, this wasn't a situation for a call. The telephone was too impersonal. It was a three-and-a-half-hour drive to Salina, a long way for just two questions, yet it beat idling at the dead end.

Agent Wayne picked up the phone and dialed her number. The line trilled away on the other end, and on ring number five was finally answered.

"Hello?"

"Hi, Mrs. Devon?"

"This is her," said the woman coldly. "If you're selling anything, I'm not interested."

"No, ma'am," said the agent. "This is Field Agent Wayne with the Oklahoma Bureau of Investigation—"

"Did you finally get the bastard?" she cut in, her tone becoming energized. "I tried to send you people the information, but you wouldn't take it."

"What are you talking about?"

"The info that the private investigator got for us."

"This is the first I've heard about it," said Agent Wayne. "And just to be clear, when you say him, who exactly are you talking about?"

"Her scumbag husband," she said. "We all know he did it."

A tingling wave worked its way down Agent Wayne's spine.

"Well, actually, that's why I'm calling. I was hoping that I might come up there tomorrow and talk with you. Would that be okay?"

"Honey, I have one good leg and one good eye, so I ain't going nowhere."

"Then I'll be there," said the agent. "How does ten tomorrow morning sound?"

"I'll see you then," she said and hung up.

Agent Wayne placed the receiver into the cradle and sat back in his chair. The private investigator thing wasn't too exciting, although he was sure she would beg to differ. The problem was that most of those bozos found a milk cow like the Devos' and led them along until all of their late bills were caught up.

And, of course, it could be nothing more than her own personal feelings for Charlie fueling her. Agent Wayne stood, grabbed his sports coat off the back of his chair, and exited the office. He would need to be on the road in the morning by no later than six. He considered reporting his plan to the director but decided against it. He already had a reputation for chasing shadows, so what would be the point? The orange haze of the October sun was fading when Agent Wayne started up the Crown. He would turn in early tonight and hope that sleep would find him.

CHAPTER SIXTEEN

Charlie Tries a Trick

Charlie reached over and picked up the cell phone. It was Karen. He considered letting it go to voicemail, but there was too much at risk. She had to stay. His future could depend on it.

"Hey, baby girl," he said.

"Where's my money?" she said, sounding both panicked and enraged.

"What are you talking about?"

"You know damn well what I'm talking about!" she said. "I want my two hundred dollars back!"

"Why would I take your money?" Charlie said, his voice hurt. "I don't need your money."

"No, but I do, and you know it."

Charlie paused for a moment. He could hear the wind in the background and the occasional sound of a passing motor. She was on the road. Charlie eased the Mercedes into his driveway.

"I don't understand what you're saying," he said.

"You don't want me to leave," she said, bursting into sobs. "You're trying to keep me here."

Charlie shut the Mercedes off and walked up to the front door. It was unlocked. The bitch had left his house open to the world, and why wouldn't she? She hadn't planned on ever having to come back, and it wasn't her shit in there at risk.

"Honey," he said, walking into the living room. "Of course, I don't want you to leave. I love you. But if you think that I would rob you to make you stay, you are mistaken."

"I don't believe you," she said.

"Look," said Charlie. "Before you accuse me, maybe you should make sure that it's really gone."

"I turned my bag inside out," Karen said. "The money's gone."

"Did you check the room?" said Charlie. "It's not like you're the neatest person."

The other end was silent, and Charlie could sense the woman's mind spinning. She had waited for him to leave, her anxious thoughts focused on only one thing: getting out.   "Karen," he said as he walked into the bedroom and tossed two one-hundred-dollar bills into the corner where her bag had been sitting. "Why don't you check the room and see if it fell out? I'd do it, but I'm still at the office. If it's not there, I'll give you some money, and you can do what you want. All I ask is that you talk to me first. Is that fair enough?"

The other end was silent. Charlie thought that she might have disconnected the call.

"I'll check," she said, finally.

"And will you promise to talk to me?" he said, a sigh of relief escaping with his words.

"Yes," she said.

"I'll be back at the house at 5:30," he said.

There was another long pause, and Karen said, "I'll see you then."

Charlie made his way out of the house, leaving the door unlocked. Karen would return, find the money, and leave if given the chance. He wouldn't give her that chance. The girl was scared. Maybe it was because of what Agent Wayne had said to her, or maybe it was because of Jimmy or all of the above. Charlie never tried to fool himself about Karen. To him, she was nothing more than a hole to sink himself in. Her feelings towards him, or lack thereof, were a relief. She had never planned on staying with him; he knew that which meant that she wanted nothing from him. That wasn't quite true; she had wanted a way out from the nightmare that was Jimmy, and he had given her that. But now she wanted out of the nightmare that was him.

The why really didn't matter. Only the when. And now wasn't the time for her to leave. Perhaps that time might never come, especially with the OSBI sniffing around his door.

Yes, Karen would have to be stopped. But how? Charlie backed his car out with that question anchored in his mind.

He drove back to the side street and pulled the Mercedes over, the screen on his phone projecting the image of his driveway. An idea struck him, causing the corners of his mouth to curl up in a twisted sneer. He could never make her stay, at least not without threatening her, but there was someone who could. Charlie reached into his shirt pocket and pulled out the card that the wacko agent had given him. If this was done right, the agent would be forced to move his laser-like eyes away from him and over to the woman who was trying to run.

CHAPTER SEVENTEEN
An Odd Call

The sun had fully retreated by the time Agent Wayne pulled into his parking space. The truth was he hated this time of year. It wasn't because of the cold; he always loved the seasons and holidays. It was the fact that the days seemed to die before you even had a chance to get started. He went up the stairwell to the second floor, stopping at a door decorated with a laminated picture of a witch.

As he placed the key into the deadbolt, the conversation with Mrs. Devon was still playing in his mind. The woman had no love for Charlie Wheaton; that was clear, and she would have spent the next hour on the phone explaining why if he had given her a chance. Agent Wayne opened the door to his apartment just as his cell phone rang. He stepped inside, flipped on the light, and took the phone out of his coat pocket.

"Agent Wayne," he said.

"Agent Wayne," said a voice sounding flustered. "It's Charlie Wheaton."

The agent froze with his hand still on the doorknob.

"Why, hello there. What can I do for you, Mr. Wheaton?"

"Listen, I don't know if I should be saying anything or if it even means anything, but Karen just called me freaking out."

"Okay," said Agent Wayne. "Is she in trouble?"

"I don't know," said Charlie. "She was accusing me of stealing her money, which is ridiculous, considering she's living for free at my house."

"Did you?" said the agent.

"Of course, I didn't," snapped Charlie, and it sounded a little too prepared to Agent Wayne. "But that's not why I called you. She was calling me from the road."

"Is that a crime?"

"No, it's not," said Charlie. "It's just that after talking to you today, it got me thinking. The truth is, I really don't know her that well, and with Jimmy missing and that murdered woman...well, let's just say I'm a little nervous."

"So, you think she had something to do with that?"

"I really don't know," said Charlie.

"Did she say where she was going?"

"No, but I know her mother lives in Denver."

"That's a long way to go with no money," said the agent. "Risky, too. Why do you think she left?"

"You're the agent."

Charlie Wheaton was a manipulator, as were so many in that line of work. A loner because solitude was always safe. He was smart enough to realize his shortcomings but ruthless enough to embrace them. His comments stank of a carefully crafted fabrication, and Agent Wayne did not doubt that if he inquired into the rich man's story, it would all check out...he was that good. Still, every lie, no matter how well crafted, had a crack somewhere in its foundation.

"You make a good point," said the agent, sounding embarrassed. "Do you know where she is now?"

"She was heading back to my house to see if her money might have fallen out of her bag," said Charlie.

"Are you there now?"

"No," said Charlie. "I'm at my office."

"I see," said the agent. "Thank you for the call, Mr. Wheaton. It could be important. I would like you to carry on like normal. If something is happening with Karen, I'd prefer if she didn't know about this call."

"I couldn't agree more," said Charlie, and the line went dead. Agent Wayne scrolled through his phone, stopping at a number. The line on the other end was picked up after the second ring.

"Wheaton's Wholesale," said a pleasant voice.

"Charlie Wheaton, please."

"He's not in," said the flowery voice. "May I take a message?"

"No, I'll call back."

The foundation was undoubtedly cracked. Charlie had lied about being at his office, and it was likely just one of many he had told during that conversation. He was sure that Karen's money was missing, and he was pretty sure that Charlie had taken it. Had he known that she was planning to leave? He probably suspected. Did he love her that much, enough to steal her cash and trap her into a relationship that she wanted out of? Was this man even capable of love? Agent Wayne had his doubts.

I'll be leaving him soon, Karen had said.

There was something more to this than just a middle-aged man trying to hold on to his young trophy. Agent Wayne walked over to his leather couch. He sat back, closing his eyes as he loosened his tie. What could Charlie be up to? No threat had been made, at least as far as he knew. Perhaps it wouldn't hurt to give Karen a call. At least then, it would give her the opportunity to share her side of the story.

****

Karen felt another round of tears welling in her eyes. She reached up with one hand, wiped them away, and then brought the Nisson to a stop beside the code box. She pressed in the four-digit code and watched as the wrought-iron gate slowly swung inward. Charlie had taken her money; she was sure of that, just as she was sure that she would never see her money again.

Then why come back?

Because she had nowhere else to go. His plans for imprisoning her were complete; she was trapped. The sudden vibration of her phone startled her. It was probably him calling to make sure she had gone back as she had promised, just like the good harlot that she had become. Karen reached over to silence the cell phone and saw that it was a number she didn't recognize. For some reason, she was sure that it would be about Jimmy. Perhaps he had been found, or maybe it was a call for ransom.

"Yes," she said, her voice trembling on the edge of panic.

"Ms. Presley, this is Agent Wyatt Wayne."

Karen felt her breath leave out of her body in a stuttered sigh.

"Yes, Agent Wayne," said Karen, struggling to keep her voice steady. "How can I help you?"

"Actually, I was calling to see if I could help you," said the agent.

"What do you mean?" said Karen as she slowly pulled through the gateway.

"I just received a call from Mr. Wheaton, and he sounded a bit upset."

"Did he really?" she said. "Did he happen to mention where he hid my money?"

"No, but he did mention that you accused him of stealing it and that you were attempting to leave the state."

"Is that against the law?" she said.

"It is not," said the agent. "But it does look a little fishy."

"Well, don't worry," she said, bursting into tears. "I can't afford to go anywhere."

"Karen. Can I call you Karen?"

The tears poured down her face, winding their way off her cheeks and soaking into her T-shirt. The house was only a block away, but she was forced to pull over until she could regain her vision.

"I don't care," she said.

"Listen to me," said Agent Wayne. "I don't know what's exactly going on, but I have to ask: are you in danger?"

Karen gazed up at the street sign that stood only a few yards from where she sat, shivering in her Nisson. One left turn, and she would be back at the house that she now considered a prison. Was she in danger? Every fiber within her body screamed yes, but she still couldn't say why. Because of the way Charlie had blocked her car in? Because he had taken her money? But had he? He claimed that he hadn't. And what if he was telling the truth? Perhaps it had fallen from her bag. She had been in a rush, panicked because of her trip to the office, and panicked by the very man who now awaited her reply on the other end of the line.

Was she in danger?

"No," she said, finally. "I'm just tired. This whole thing with Jimmy has me a little frazzled."

"I understand," said Agent Wayne. "But I must tell you that Mr. Wheaton seems to think you might have something to do with that. At least he wants me to think that he does. Why do you think that is?"

"I accused him of taking my money. I yelled at him. He probably thinks I'm crazy."

"Do you think he took it?" said Agent Wayne.

"I don't know," said Karen. "I might have dropped it in the house while packing."

"Karen, I want you to do me a favor. Promise me that you will call or text me at least once a day."

"Am I a suspect?"

"As far as I can tell, no," said Agent Wayne. "But my gut tells me something more is going on here. So, can you promise to at least text me once a day?"

Karen eased the car up to the turn. The driveway was empty.

"Karen, are you still there?"

"Yes," she said, stopping the Nisson just a few feet from the front porch. "I promise to text you."

Karen then killed the call and made her way to the front door. The enormous house was even more ominous than it had been an hour earlier. It was like a massive black hole where all one-way visitors were welcome. The bedroom door stood open, and she reached for the light switch as she entered. There, sitting on the carpet in the corner of the room, were two hundred-dollar bills.

I must not lie to myself; those were not there before.

But was she sure? How could she be? Her mind had been flying at breakneck speed, with images of Charlie and Agent Wayne rotating within her thoughts on a terrifying loop. What if she had been wrong? What if she was blaming the one man who truly did care for her? And yet she couldn't quite shake the image of Charlie's cold stare from the rearview mirror as she pulled out of the parking lot.

He thinks you might have something to do with it, Agent Wayne had said.

But Agent Wayne was a cop. He could just be fishing. Or even worse, playing her against him just as she was sure he was playing Charlie against her.

Karen walked over and picked up the bills off the floor, suddenly feeling exhausted. She made her way over to the bed and sat down. The extended waves of panic began to subside, leaving her feeling as though she had just completed a marathon.

There would be no trip to Denver tonight; she wouldn't get past Wichita and certainly couldn't afford a motel. She checked the clock on her phone; it read 5:20. Already, the afternoon was slipping away.

Karen took a deep breath and held it for five seconds, then forced herself to relive the day's events objectively. Charlie had made no threats against her. He had only scared her; if she was honest with herself, she had already been afraid. It was because of that fucking agent and his soul-scorching eyes. By the time she met Charlie out in the parking lot, she was already at nine on a maximum ten dial.

Found someone else? the agent had said like she was nothing more than a whore.   Karen lay back on the bed as those words sent her a blistering pulse of rage. And this was the man who claimed to be worried about her? Bullshit!

The money was not there before.

Maybe, but it made no sense. If Charlie didn't want her to leave, why would he have replaced the money? Why tell her that if she couldn't find it, he would give her more? It had to be the cop. He was playing them both. Charlie didn't kill Jimmy. He had been with her that night, so what was she so worried about?

These thoughts drifted away from her wearied mind, and soon, her clenched hands became relaxed, and her eyelids began to lower. This was how Charlie Wheaton found her twenty minutes later after returning from his curbside perch.

CHAPTER EIGHTEEN

Birth and Death

The grind of the metal door from above acted as an alarm. Jimmy's eyes flew open, and he instinctively pulled the sweat-saturated blanket up to his chin. The blinking light from across the way continued its steady red flash, counting down to the inevitable end. Heavy footfalls began to echo off the lava walls, causing the goose flesh to cover his body. Jimmy lay there motionless, his eyes half closed, his head slightly tilted. A faint yellow light shot through the void, dancing with each weighted thud. It wasn't Phillip coming down for a visit this time, nor was it the old hag and the ugly daughter. A towering silhouette entered the room. The giant had come.

I'm going to die, Jimmy thought to himself.

He felt his heart thumping in his chest and was forced to tightly interlock his hands under the blanket to stop them from shaking.

The giant came to a stop near Jimmy's cell door. He stood there gazing down, his bulbous eyes sparkling within the hazy glow of the flashlight. Suddenly, the beam shot up to Jimmy's face. Jimmy lay there struggling to keep his body still. The giant finally turned and made his way over to the other cell, over to where the naked woman lay partially covered with a sheet. A tinkling sound raced through the silence, and Jimmy tilted his head until he could see the glint of a large key ring. A click was followed by the struggling sound of a worn-down hinge as the giant opened the door to the unconscious woman's cage and went in.

It was then that the words from Phillip spoke out to him like a distorted recorder: *It doesn't help that Nith still mounts her when he can.*

Jimmy felt his breath begin to quicken. He tried to look away from what he knew would happen but couldn't. Instead, he found himself turning over onto his side. The giant let his robe fall to the concrete floor; his naked back was rippled with stacked muscle that went beyond human. The man reached out and tossed the sheet to the floor, then grabbed the comatose woman by the remaining ankle, jerking her close to the edge of the bed, lifting her good leg, and propping it up on his massive shoulder while pushing her bandaged knee out to the side.

A low whine filled Jimmy's ears, and he realized that the sound was coming from his own dry throat. All the caution that he had tried so hard to maintain was being sidestepped, outvoted, and outmaneuvered by the insanity that was now being played out from across the room.

"Stop it!" he screamed, leaping from the cot and rushing to the cage bars.

The giant looked at him with an expression contorted with lust and twisted power. For this was what it was all about. He did this because he could; it was his right. She was nothing more than a toy for him to use, and when she broke, they would find him another.

"You fucking asshole," said Jimmy.

Tears were flowing down his face. His hands were white-knuckled as he pulled against the bars like an enraged primate at a zoo.

"Get the fuck off of her!"

A sound like a lion's purr rolled through the dungeon. The giant gave one last thrust, his body gyrating as one massive hand clung to her leg and the other hand gripped her damaged thigh. Jimmy felt his body go numb as a toxic chill seared through his veins.

Nith reached down and picked up his parachute-sized robe, putting it back on. He then centered his broken toy back on the bed.

"You're a monster," cried Jimmy.

"Did you enjoy the show?" said the giant, reaching down to

grab the sheet and placing it over the woman's body.

He then left the cell, locking the door behind him. The machine's red light continued to flash with an almost strobe-like intensity, and the stuttered beeps now sounded like a solid tone.

"You are insane," said Jimmy.

"Do you think so? You'll–" began the giant but suddenly stopped.

The red light was now flashing at uneven intervals, the sound doubling up and stopping only to give off one quick flash before pausing. The giant stood there momentarily, seemingly unsure of what was happening and what he should do. Jimmy watched the expression on the man's face go from pompous to one of panicked confusion.

"She's dying, you fuck," cried Jimmy, his voice trembling with rage. "You killed her. What do you think your mommy is going to say about that?"

The giant stood there looking down at the woman as the monitor's sound dwindled, his hands clenching and releasing.

"You were supposed to leave her alone, weren't you?" said Jimmy. "What's going to happen if that baby dies?"

Nith whipped his massive head towards Jimmy, his eyes like two moons. Both of the man's hands were now curled into boulder-like fists.

"You're right," he said in a low and menacing voice. "I will be in trouble, so I might as well make it worth it."

He took a step towards Jimmy's cell. The fear that he should have been feeling couldn't overcome the rage still coursing through Jimmy's veins, and he refused to cower. The monster could most likely kill him without much effort, but he didn't care. If he had to die, then so be it, but at least he might manage to gouge out one of those horrific eyes before he did.

"Come on, you piece of shit," he heard himself say, the tears continuing to fall from his flushed face.

The giant reached the cell door, brought up the large ring, placed the key into the slot, and turned it. Jimmy clinched his hands, leaving the thumbs extended out like a pair of dull daggers. This time, there would be no question about whether he could harm this man, for this was no man.

The giant swung the door open with enough force to rattle Jimmy's teeth.

"I'm going to kill you," said the beast, entering the cell. "You know that, don't you?"

Jimmy looked up at the man's eyes, their reflection in the low light acting like twin targets. Yes, he knew that he was about to die. There was nothing he could do about that. All he could do was hope to take one of the giant's eyes out. Two would be better, but he would settle for one.

Jimmy rushed forward, surprising the giant, and swung out with his right hand. Nith turned his face and took the brunt of the thumb across his flattened cheek. Jimmy jumped back, his lungs burning, the tears replaced with sweat. The giant lunged quickly, leaving Jimmy in frozen shock, seizing him by the throat and lifting him off the floor.

This is it, thought Jimmy. *I'm going to die.* From across the chasm, the monitor's pulse had stopped. *And I won't be alone.*

A blinding light exploded, and he thought for a moment that he had died a painless death. He felt himself falling and the air being pushed out of his lungs as he collided with the stone floor.

"Damn you Nith!" screeched a voice. "Get out of there."

Jimmy lay on the cold surface, watching as the giant's feet plodded out of his cell.

"Lock that damn cage," said the old woman.

Nith turned and placed the key. Jimmy struggled to sit up and was glad to see a trail of blood oozing off of the man's face. It probably wouldn't leave a scar, but at least he had scored a point. Just then, Phillip appeared from the metal stairs, his deformed body wrapped in a throw-over nightgown.

"Mother," he said. "There's something wrong with the woman."

The old lady gave the giant a look that could burn wood and snatched the keys from his hand. She went over and opened the cell with Phillip close at her heels. She went straight to the monitor, which was now silent, its light as cold as the room. The old lady grabbed the woman's wrist and held it for a moment, then slammed it down onto the mattress.

"She's dead," she said.

"Get her to the table," said Philip. "Maybe we can still save the baby, but we have to hurry,"

The old lady looked over at where the giant stood. His hands were locked together behind his back, and his overly large chin was lowered onto his barrel chest like a naughty child.

"Get over here, Nith," the old lady barked. "This is your child we're trying to save, so move your ass."

Nith lumbered his way over to the woman, effortlessly lifting his broken toy and carrying her to the stainless-steel table in the middle of the room. The woman's body lay there naked, her swollen belly exposed. Jimmy watched in fascinated horror as the old woman opened the cabinet and removed a small case. She brought it over to where Phillip was now roosting over the woman's stomach. He flipped open the lid, brought out a small half-inch scalpel, and said, "We have to get the child out of there."

The old woman looked up at the giant, her eyes still burning, and said, "When this is over, you'll be digging the grave."

Nith took a step back as if he had been struck. Phillip ran his fingers over one side of the woman's belly, pausing momentarily, then continued to the other side.

"Can you save it?" the old woman said.

"I will try, Mother," said Phillip.

He then began to slice through the dead woman's flesh.

CHAPTER NINETEEN

Biker Ben

Her ass was a work of art. Charlie couldn't help but wonder, as he stood there watching Karen sleep, if maybe that was what she really needed: a good pounding. Would she try to stop him? Perhaps it was what she wanted: proof of his devotion to her. But Charlie wasn't feeling too devoted at that moment. Actually, he was quite on edge, and why shouldn't he be? Karen had tried to leave. There was no denying that. And if he hadn't taken her money, she would have been long gone. Maybe it would have been for the best. At least it would have turned the light towards her as far as the murder of the old lady and Jimmy's disappearance were concerned. But that wouldn't have lasted for long. That agent would know better.

No, it was better to keep Karen close and content until the pieces began to fall into place. The family cared little about the ramifications of their actions, always presuming that they were above whatever the consequences might be. That was unless you were one of the ones left outside in the cold, much like Charlie was now. A shudder raced through his body as Karen snorted and turned over to her side.

No, Karen was much too valuable to let leave, and Charlie's trust in the family went only so far. They were a family—a sick faction whose loyalty was obvious, and any outsiders were disposable.

That line that he now found himself walking was precarious. One wrong step either way would bring him ruin. It was time to take control of the situation. To build his own buffer and begin to make plans of his own. Had the agent called her? Karen's phone sat in her back pocket. He could see it. For a moment, he considered trying to lift it, but it wasn't worth the risk. What did it matter, anyway? Karen was here, and that was what he wanted. Still, there was the risk that she might leave again, which absolutely could not be allowed.

There was a time when the family had Charlie by the balls. Their hideous hooks dug into him, pushing and pulling. His life was led in whatever direction they might see fit. Yet, he wasn't a stupid man, and he hoped that this was a fact that they might have overlooked. He acted like the docile servant they expected, but even while he pretended to be happy doing their bidding, he was consolidating his own crime family. The Program did indeed help many people. However, it also brought Charlie in contact with those who had been forced into The Program as a final solution. These were the people that Charlie searched for. Offering favorable reports to authorities in return for small favors.

Most of them were low-level criminals, addicted to both alcohol and drugs. Some were so desperate that they had no problem busting out a few windows if a potential client needed further motivation. They were happy to do so just as long as Charlie's money was good, and it was always good. What they did with the cash concerned him little. In fact, he hoped they blew it on their habits because nothing beats having repeat customers.

But the real prize came the morning Ben Lanchino walked through the door. Up until then, Charlie's go-to guys consisted of a pencil-thin heroin junkie and a woman who couldn't get past the front door without first slamming back a half pint of rot-gut whiskey. They had both been reliable up to a point, but an addict is still an addict, and the substance always comes first.

This was not the case with Ben. The man arrived via a court order on a Harley Davidson Sportster. His leather jacket was stitched with enough symbols and numbers to create a language. But it was the tattoos that intrigued Charlie the most. The S.S. tattoo decorating his neck and the White Pride splayed across his beefy forearm told Charlie all he needed to know about this man, and he couldn't agree more. Plus, he was huge; not as big as the freaky giant but he was close.

The man had stood before the recovering circle, his face mostly hidden behind a graying beard, and stated his name with a low voice that seemed to carry through the room like distant thunder. His motivation for getting clean had nothing to do with the fact that he had been charged with his fourth D.U.I. That mattered very little to the organization that he belonged to. The reason for his sincerity was the fact that he was becoming sloppy. Charlie became Ben's sponsor, gladly coming to his aid whenever the man slipped, answering his calls at all hours of the day and night. Of course, it wasn't until much later that Charlie learned who Ben Lanchino was. Until then, his knowledge of bikers consisted of Easy Rider and a couple of episodes of Sons Of Anarchy, which he only watched for the sex scenes.

That all changed one night when Ben invited him to the Walter Mitty Club on old Route 66. The place was a strip bar out in the middle of nowhere. Charlie had walked through the door and was immediately assaulted by low-hanging smoke, metal music, and a topless woman whose earnings had gone into her massive breasts.

Ben waved him over to a table where he sat with two other men, each wearing similar leather vests decorated with numerous patches. Charlie sat across from Ben and noticed that the man was drinking a Budweiser but remained quiet. The bombshell asked him what he wanted, and Charlie ordered a Coke.

"See?" said Ben, slapping the man to his right on the shoulder. "What did I tell you? This motherfucker's committed."

The other man gave Ben a slight smile and then took a long pull off his bottle of beer. Ben turned his attention back to Charlie, his eyes flashing with the spinning light coming off the dance stage.

"I'm glad you could make it," he said.

"I wasn't doing anything else," said Charlie, just as the woman placed his drink in front of him. "So, do you come here a lot?"

"I have to," said Ben. "I own it."

Charlie paused with his glass halfway to his mouth.

"You never told me that."

Ben leaned forward, his grin spreading across his bearded face, and said, "There's a lot I haven't told you."

He motioned for the guy to his left to turn, pointing at the large red and white patch on the back of the man's jacket.

"Do you know what this is?"

Charlie leaned in for a closer look. Across the shoulders, in carefully stitched lettering, read Centurions, and under that was a stenciled outline of an ancient warrior riding a chopper with a sword held high above his flaming skull.

"I'm not sure," said Charlie, finally. "But it's pretty scary looking."

"Damn right, it is," said Ben, grabbing his beer. "It's supposed to be."

Ben then stood up and motioned for Charlie to follow. Charlie was led to the back of the bar and down a narrow hallway with numbered doors on each side, which came to a dead end at a metal utility door. The door made a painful grind as Ben pushed it open. They stepped in, and Charlie was shocked to find an immaculate chamber. Ben made his way over to a long table in the center of the room surrounded by ten leather chairs. They looked as though they might be more comfortable residing on the fifteenth floor of some annuity company. Ben rolled one chair out and motioned for Charlie to sit.

Charlie noticed the tabletop had been etched with the same warrior design that decorated the jacket.

Ben sat across from Charlie, handed him his beer bottle, and said, "Take a drink."

Charlie looked at the bottle. For a moment, he wondered if perhaps the old lady was setting him up. Would she go that far? Damn right, she would. But why now?

"Go ahead," said Ben.

Charlie reached out and took the bottle from him. He held it elevated before his mouth, unsure what to do. Ben leaned back in his chair, folding his arms over his substantial chest.

"I really shouldn't," said Charlie.

"Do it," said Ben.

Charlie brought the bottle to his lips, closed his eyes, took a quick swig, and found himself spitting the contents onto the table, not because of the taste but because of the surprise. It was water. Ben exploded into thunderous laughter and stood up. He went to a bar in the corner of the room, grabbed a towel, and tossed it to Charlie.

"I wasn't kidding about wanting to become sober," he said. "I just can't let the others know."

"I understand," said Charlie, wiping the spit off the grooved surface.

Ben made his way over to the head of the table and sat down. It was then that Charlie saw the scythe patch over his right breast. Under it were eight hash marks. Ben saw what he was looking at and leaned back in his chair, his eyes narrowing.

"They mean what you think they mean," said Ben.

"Hey, it's none of my business."

"No, it's fine," said Ben. "I want to be open with you. That's why I invited you here. I consider you a friend, Charlie. You've helped me, and I feel like I owe you."

"You don't owe me anything," said Charlie. "I'm just glad you can remain sober, especially here. That must be hard for you."

"At first, it was," said Ben. "The booze is everywhere, not to mention the pussy, and you know how it is; after a while, it becomes a part of you. A part of what you are. But it also makes you careless, and that's when mistakes happen."

"I know what you mean," said Charlie.

"I know you do," said Ben. "And that's why I like you."

He leaned closer to the table and said, "Let me ask you something: are you a rich man?"

Charlie gazed at him for a moment. This man was dangerous. There could be no doubting that. And he was a criminal. Charlie felt his heart rate kick up a gear as he realized that there would be no way he could escape from this place without at least getting the shit kicked out of him.

"Relax, Ringleader,' said Ben knowingly. "I'm not after your money. I have plenty of my own. Just hear me out. You have a problem. The intoxicated goons that you sometimes use for muscle like to talk. It only took a pint of bourbon and a ride home for Chelsie to tell me all about her midnight rock-throwing adventures."

"Now hold on a—" began Charlie but was silenced by Ben's upheld hand.

"I'm not judging you," said Ben. "If anything, I understand how hard it is. Your business is growing, and you become a target when that happens. Some competitors want nothing more than to see you burn, and then there's the constant juggling with the IRS. Not to mention the crazy customers trying to set you up for a quick lawsuit. Am I right?"

Charlie had never been anything other than a swindler and a builder of false hope, which was why he knew he was being pitched.

"Ben," he said, finally. "What do you want from me?"

"I want to make a deal," said Ben. "Actually, more like a partnership."

"I'm listening."

"Like I said before, your business is growing, and some of that has to do with a few outside-of-the-law maneuvers you have entrusted to a couple of idiots."

Charlie almost spoke up again but decided against it.

"What I am offering you is protection," Ben continued. "And not the junkie burnout kind. Real protection that will free you up to do what you need to do."

"And what is it I need to do?"

"Become the biggest contractor in the state," said Ben. "Isn't that what you want?"

So, this would be a shakedown after all—extortion and probably embezzling. For the first time in years, Charlie wanted a drink. No, not just a drink, a bottle.

"And how much is this going to cost me?"

Ben's eyes seemed to darken like a cloud suddenly hiding the sun.

"I told you. I don't want your money."

"Okay, I'm sorry. But if not money, what?"

"You want to grow, and so do I," said Ben. "Right now, there are outside factions moving in. LA EME and The Angels, to name just two. But there are more."

"So, what can I do?" said Charlie. "I'm not in a biker gang."

"I suggest that if you want to get out of here alive, you never say that again. We're not some nigger tribe from the east side," said Ben, pointing at the stenciled MC on his vest. "We're a motorcycle club."

"Okay," said Charlie. "But I'm not a part of the club."

"I know, and that's what makes it perfect. You are my sponsor at Alcoholics Anonymous and an upstanding citizen, at least on paper."

"You still haven't answered my question."

"All I need from you is an alibi."

"I don't understand," said Charlie.

"Like I said, factions are moving in. Now, I can let them chisel away at my territory or act. I'm not one to just sit by and lose everything I've worked for, so something is going to have to be done. It might get bloody. Most likely, it will. That's where you come in. If you get a knock on your door one Saturday morning concerning my whereabouts the previous Friday night, you will tell them I was with you. Don't worry, I'll call you before it happens, and we'll set up the scene. I'll even provide you someone with a similar distinguished beard and vest to sit with at a place with plenty of witnesses. You can't get hurt."

Charlie sat in silent fascination while Ben told him his plan. How long had he been strategizing this? And just how deep had he gone into Charlie's past? He knew he was rich. That much was clear. But did he know how he had become rich? Did he know about the family? Probably not. Had he pulled up his stock portfolio? Maybe, but even if he did, he would only see fifty-one percent ownership by some company called H.S. Limited. It would mean nothing to Ben.

Still, he was exactly right: Charlie needed some protection and not just from calculating customers and competitors. Those were things he could handle himself. It was that fucking family that caused his sleepless nights.

"Well?" concluded Ben. "What do you say?"

All insurance came at a price. That was a fact of life, and for just a few meetings here and there and a few falsified sworn statements, he could have the protection he so desperately needed. Until then, the family hadn't threatened him, but that didn't mean they wouldn't. They did own half of his corporation and were very capable of murder –had murdered– so what else could he do? The only question was whether to tell Ben about them. Would that change anything? Ben wasn't stupid. Devising this little scheme proved that. Would he pull the offer from the table once he learned the truth? He just might. Better to keep the family a secret for now.

"Let's do it," said Charlie.

Ben stood up and extended his hand. Charlie reached out and shook it. Ben then threw a single key labeled with the number 4 across the table.

"What's this?" said Charlie.

"A gift," said Ben.

Charlie followed him out of the room back into the hallway with the numbered doors, stopping at the one numbered four.

"Enjoy yourself," said Ben. "I'll see you at the next meeting."

He then slapped him on the back and made his way into the main room. Charlie stood there for a moment, his imagination racing. An image of the old woman, her jutting chin and offset eyes, appeared before him like a screenshot. How he hated her. Hated the invisible chain that went with him wherever he went. Ben could be his salvation, and even if this was a setup, it was far too late to turn back now. Charlie placed the key into the lock, turning the handle.

The room was decorated with spaced mirrors, and a low-glow chandelier hung from its ceiling. The floor was covered with light blue carpet, and at the center was a bed. On it, wearing nothing more than a braided necklace, was the girl with double D's.

"I'm glad you could make it," she said. "I'm Gloria."

Charlie paused only long enough to feel his erection beginning to press against his pants and then shut the door.

He had accepted that gift more than once since that night and, in all that time, had only had to hold up his end of the bargain twice. One of those had been a First-Degree Murder charge, which could have given Ben the death penalty. Ben showed his appreciation by kidnapping and delivering the bitch from Broken Arrow a few months back. The man hadn't even asked why. And she, in turn, had been delivered to the family, as promised.

But things were changing. The old lady's murder and the family's insistence that they handle Jimmy themselves left a trail right to him. Was it time to trust Ben with the truth? Charlie wasn't sure if he even had a choice. Karen let out a small moan and turned over onto her back. Charlie left the bedroom, making his way down the dark hall. As quietly as possible, he opened the front door and stepped onto the porch. He pulled his cell phone out of his pocket and scrolled down to Ben's number. It took only two rings before it was answered.

"Hey, Ringleader," said Ben, and Charlie could hear the pounding beat of some rap song playing in the background.

"Are you at the club?"

"What gave it away?" said Ben.

"I need a favor," said Charlie.

"Okay. When?"

"Tonight."

"That's kind of short notice," said Ben.

"It's nothing too bad or too far, but I have to be seen when it goes down."

"Now you've got me curious," said Ben. "What do you need done?"

Charlie told him the plan and was relieved to hear Ben chuckling at the other end of the line.

"You must really like this bitch," he said. "I think Double D's going to be jealous."

Charlie considered telling him the rest but decided against it. He would tell him. He would have to, but not over the phone. That conversation was best handled in person so he could at least try to get a read from the man's face.

"I'll have a couple of boys come by there around midnight. Is the gate code still the same?"

"It is. Thank you, Ben," said Charlie.

"Hey, that's what partners do."

Charlie ended the call and made his way back into the house. He considered taking the couch, but that would seem strange. It was his house, after all, and he was supposed to be in love with her. Charlie went into the bedroom and took off his shoes and belt, setting them on the floor at the side of the bed. He then gently lay down next to her, trying not to rock the mattress or touch her. This entire plan depended on her still being asleep when the time came. Karen rolled over to where her back was facing him. Charlie checked his watch: 7:37, four and a half hours to go.

CHAPTER TWENTY

Closing In

They had left the light on.

The baby had been pulled from the dead woman's body and quickly wrapped in a towel. The old lady had taken the child and rushed towards the stairs with her clan close behind. Jimmy sat on his cot motionless, willing himself not to move until the sound of the slamming door echoed from above.

But they had forgotten to turn off the light. Usually, he would have been grateful, but now the yellow beams lit the uncovered corpse of the brand-new mother, and he found it impossible to turn away.

The steady beeping of the heart monitor was replaced by crimson drops falling from the steel table. Blood had pooled on the concrete floor and was streaming its way towards his cell. Jimmy watched it slither slowly towards him, his mind numb, except for the growing pressure pushing against the front of his skull. Ripples of electricity trickled down his spine, tingling past his knees and stabbing the tips of his toes. He was helpless to stop it, just as he had been helpless to stop the murder of the naked woman who lay just fifteen feet away. Would they leave her long? Most likely, considering they were now trying to save the giant's spawn.

The indignity of what they had done to her had his stomach

clenching. She had been reduced to a defunct factory that would have to be replaced. They would soon bring in another victim, and Jimmy would again be forced to watch the giant do his work. Maybe they would be caught this time. It couldn't be easy to kidnap someone. What about their family? Wouldn't they be concerned? Not if the victim was properly screened.

He had been. And not just screened but set up and captured, and all it took was the murder of an old lady. It was Charlie. The sonofabitch was providing for them like a broker.

For the first time in his life, Jimmy considered the option of suicide. Not because of what was happening to him but because of what he would be forced to witness. The rape and then murder of the woman had been bad enough, but she had already been dead, at least her mind had been. It was kind of a blessing. The next one would be different; she would be very much alive and terrified, just as he had been. And just what would he say to her? Everything will be okay? How could he possibly say that after seeing what he just saw? He couldn't. And then there would be the rape. Would they tie her down and just let Nith have his way, or would they first try to make her an offer? And could he simply sit here and watch? No way. Not again. Better to die.

Jimmy scooted himself back to the corner, pulling both legs up to his chest and hugging his knees. The pressure behind his eyes was beginning to pound with a painful rhythm. Why couldn't they have just turned off the lights? Perhaps they had left them burning as a violent reminder of what would happen if he refused.

"They will kill me," he said out loud, startling himself.

The chamber was a maniacal void, a snapshot of murder frozen in time with its lava rock walls brought out of the Dark Ages and a ceiling spawned from Auschwitz, imprinted with death and insanity. The dungeon had swallowed this woman and was now coming for him. But not all at once; first, it wanted his mind. Was that what the pounding in his skull was? This room beginning its assault, eating away at the last of his very being? Why wouldn't it? It ingested misery. How else could you explain this nightmare?

The dripping from the table seemed louder, as if confirming his theory. Jimmy felt his eyes being drawn back towards the table.

"Don't," he managed to mumble. But still, they drifted.

The woman lay there, her stomach sliced open, her one good leg bent at the knee with her arms draped over the edge. How old was she? Mid-thirties, maybe a little older. What was it Phillip had said? She was an uppity customer of Charlie's? Maybe Charlie wasn't the one doing the killing, but he surely knew about it. And for what? Money, of course, and power. After all, with friends like these backing you, there would be little to fear.

Jimmy noticed that this train of thought had helped with the pain in his head. His brain was finding its path out of madness, grasping deduction and theory as a means to cope. Better to let it continue. Better to turn away from the corpse and search for solutions. But were there any? He was locked in a cell. The place where violation acted as a test for more violations. They would be coming for him soon, demanding a perverted award for allowing him to live. And, unlike the woman draining on the floor, he would have to be conscious.

CHAPTER TWENTY-ONE
Orchestrated Vandalism

The brick exploded through the front window, activating the house alarm. Karen's eyes shot open. She sat up in bed and found Charlie already standing and fully dressed.

"Somebody just broke in," he said. "Stay here."

Karen sat frozen, a blanket clutched to her chin, watching as Charlie made his way over to a wall-mounted cabinet near the doorway. He opened the left side and pulled out a nickel-plated .38. Then started down the dark hall.

"Be careful," she whispered.

She looked at the nightstand for her phone and realized she had never taken it out of her back pocket. The screen read 11:48. After a few moments, the alarm went off.

"It's okay," Charlie said. "You can come out now."

Karen leaped from the bed and made her way out of the room. Charlie had flipped on the living room light and stood over a chipped brick near the middle of the floor. Razor-edged glass decorated the room, glinting off the couch and table.

"Careful," said Charlie. "It's everywhere."

"What happened?" she said.

"I have no idea," said Charlie. "Stay in here while I check

outside."

"Shouldn't we call the police?"

"We will," said Charlie.

He paused at the threshold, turning on the front porch light.

"Holy shit," he said.

The multi-beam illuminated the driveway, clearly showing a busted headlight on the passenger side of his Mercedes. Karen moved next to him and felt her blood turn cold. She could see the irregular lines of a spider-web crack on her Nisson's front windshield. She stepped off the porch and stumbled towards the car. The front tires had been sliced. Slowly, she made her way around, stopping where her gas cap lay just inches away from her feet.

"Why would anyone do this?" she managed to say.

"I don't know," said Charlie. "They hit my car, too."

Karen stood there, her heart pounding in her chest. Someone had destroyed the only thing she truly owned. Not just that, but her only way out. But by now, did she expect anything less? How she wished she would have just been able to fill up her tank earlier. She could have been long gone from this nightmare of a place. Why did she have to drop the money on the floor?

Karen turned to Charlie with tears streaming from her eyes. A violent convulsion rocked her stomach, and she fell to her knees just as vomit erupted from her mouth. Within seconds, Charlie was at her side, grasping for her hair. At first, she tried to brush his hand away, but the spinning world refused to let her. After a long moment, she was able to take a deep breath.

"Come on," said Charlie, placing his hands under her shoulders. "Let's get you back in the house."

She allowed him to help her up, tried to walk, and found herself leaning against his large body for support. They slowly made their way up the porch when a voice shouted out from the shadows, causing her to let out a shout of her own.

"Hey, Charlie! What happened?"

Charlie continued to help Karen into the house.

"Hold on, Greg."

"Who is that?" said Karen as Charlie brushed off the broken glass from the couch.

"It's the neighbor," said Charlie, easing her onto the cushion. "I'm going to talk to him and see if he saw anything. Then I'm going to call the police. Are you going to be alright here for a minute?"

"I'm fine," she said, laying her head back. "I'm just pissed."

"Don't worry about the car," said Charlie, placing the 38 into the waistband of his slacks. "We'll get it fixed."

He turned to go back outside, but not before Karen grabbed him by the hand.

"Thank you, Charlie," she said. "I know I haven't been the nicest person lately."

"Hey, it's been a tough day, baby girl," he said, squeezing her hand. "But it will get better. I promise."

Karen smiled at him and watched as he made his way out of the front door.

*****

The police arrived while Charlie was still talking to Greg. Apparently, the asshole *had* seen something and had called them. A van had been sitting at the curb. Its tag light was out. Greg couldn't get the number. He claimed to have seen three people jump into it after the damage was done, but it was much too dark to see their faces or anything else.

"This is a gated community, Mr. Wheaton, so how did they get in without a code?" said one of the officers.

He was a young man standing next to an older gentleman with stripes on his sleeve. He had just written down Charlie and Greg's full names.

"Maybe they used to work here," said Greg, and Charlie could have hugged the bastard. "The association had a lot of Mexicans working last summer maintaining the grounds."

Charlie did not miss the racist angle, and he figured Ben would have been pleased. He would have to remember to tell him.

"Do you know what company they were with?" said the Sergeant.

"You'd have to get with The Homeowners Association for that," said Greg.

"Do you have their information?" said the younger officer.

"Hold on," said Greg. "I have a card somewhere."

He then turned and made his way back towards his house.

"It's strange that you were the only one vandalized," said the Sergeant, turning to Charlie. "Do you mind if I ask if you have any enemies?"

"Not to my knowledge," said Charlie. "But I own a pretty good-sized construction company, and keeping everyone happy is hard."

"Have you received any threats lately?" said the younger officer.

"Not lately," said Charlie.

"What about with the groundskeepers?" said the Sergeant. "Did you have an altercation with them?"

"Not that I can recall," said Charlie. "I was usually gone when they were here."

"Are both cars yours?" said the Sergeant.

"The Mercedes is mine. The Nisson belongs to my girlfriend."

"Looks like her car took most of the damage," said the young officer. "Does she have any enemies? Maybe an ex or something?"

An image of Jimmy's face flashed in front of Charlie before he could stop it, causing him to shudder.

"Are you okay?" said the Sergeant.

"I'm just cold and a little in shock," said Charlie.

"Do you mind if we have a word with your girlfriend?" said the young officer.

The little bastard was persistent. Charlie had to give him that.

"She's lying down right now. This freaked her out. Can she call you tomorrow?"

The young officer was about to say something when the Sergeant suddenly placed his hand on his shoulder.

"That would be fine," said the Sergeant.

It was then that Greg reappeared with a business card.

"Here you go," he said, handing it to the younger officer. "All their information is on the front."

The officer placed the card in his breast pocket and then faced Charlie.

"We'll give them a call and do what we can," he said. "But there's not a lot to go on here."

I'm counting on that, thought Charlie, but said, "I'm sure you'll do the best you can."

Charlie and Greg watched as the cruiser pulled away.

"I'm sorry I couldn't give them more," said Greg. "It just happened so fast."

"Don't worry about it," said Charlie, returning to the house. "At least no one was hurt."

****

Karen was still on the couch, her face in both hands. She looked up as Charlie opened the front door; sweat glistened on her forehead. Charlie looked down, offering her a smile.

"What did they say?"

Charlie walked over and sat beside her, taking her hand in his.

"They have no idea," he said. "The neighbor saw a van with three guys, but he couldn't give a description."

"Do you think it was a customer?" said Karen, and Charlie noticed she hadn't removed her hand from his.

"It might have been," he said. "It wouldn't be the first time someone's gone off."

"Are they going to try and find who did it?"

"I doubt they'll be able to," said Charlie, removing his hand and standing up.

Karen leaned back and began rubbing her temples.

"How the hell did they get past the gate?"

"They must've had the code," said Charlie, walking over to the shattered window frame.

"I can't leave this open all night."

"Do you have anything to fix it with?" said Karen.

"Not here," said Charlie. "But I do at the shop."

"I'll go with you," said Karen, standing up.

"No," said Charlie. "I can't leave the house here open like this with no one in it."

"You want me to guard the house?" said Karen doubtfully. "Alone?"

"Here," said Charlie, taking out the .38 from his waistband and handing it to her. "Do you know how to use this?"

Karen had gone to the shooting range many times with Jimmy

back in the first couple of years of their marriage. Back when she thought they would be together forever.

"Yes," she said.

"Good. I won't be long."

*****

Charlie sat watching the security gate swing with a smile on his face. The event couldn't have gone any better. But he also knew that he had made a mistake. The question about the code had stumped him. It shouldn't have; he should have seen that coming and planned ahead. Thanks be to the idiot neighbor who might have ruined everything had he not been blind as a bat. Instead, he had provided the perfect solution to Charlie's surprise dilemma. And that Mexican comment was perfect. Not that it really mattered; the police had a lot more than a broken window and a couple of battered cars to worry about.

Charlie eased the Mercedes into a left turn. The clock on the dash read 01:10 am. He reached into his breast pocket and pulled out his phone, scrolled down to Ben's number and initiated the call.

"Hey, Ringleader," said Ben, and there was no pounding music in the background this time.

"Are you at the club?" said Charlie.

"Nah, back at the crib. How'd it go?"

"It was perfect," said Charlie, slowing for a red light. "They fucked her car up. I thought she was going to die when she saw it."

"Well, she ain't going anywhere. I had them drop a half pound of sugar down the gas tank."

"Nice," said Charlie. "And thanks for not fucking up my car too bad."

"Yeah, I told them to make it look convincing but to keep the focus on her Nisson."

"They broke my front window."

"Well," said Ben with a chuckle. "At least you're in the business."

"Very true, my friend. I'm going to have her car towed to your shop tomorrow, of course I'll give her the bad news after it's looked at."

"Sounds good," said Ben. "I already have a head light for you, if you want to bring it in."

"Plan on it," said Charlie, pausing. "Can I meet with you tomorrow at the shop?"

"Is something up?" said Ben.

And yes, there was.

The family was becoming a threat, committing murder that could be traced back to Charlie. Would Ben care? He had been Ben's sponsor for over three years now and had helped him through many backslides not to mention a few legal issues. It was like a brotherhood of their own. Not like the one that Ben shared with his organization. It went deeper than that, containing personal secrets that could never be revealed. Would that be enough for Ben to help him with the inbreds? He wasn't sure.

"It's nothing that I want to talk about over the phone," said Charlie. "What time's good for you?"

"Is it trouble?" said Ben, the friendly tone now forgotten.

"Nothing that involves you," said Charlie.

After a long pause, Ben said, "Meet me at noon."

The line went dead. Charlie stared at the phone for a moment, allowing the tension that had suddenly gripped him to subside. The difference in Ben's tone was like a slap in the face. A reminder that whatever Charlie's illusions were about his relationship with this criminal might be, the truth was very different: Ben, and those with him, were killers. Maybe not of the same caliber as the giant and the old lady, but killers just the same. Perhaps he had just made his second mistake of the day. What would Ben think about his decision to come clean? Would he ask him why he waited for so long to tell him? It would have been the first question Charlie would have asked if the roles had been reversed. And what would Ben say once he found out the OSBI was involved?

Don't tell him shit.

Yes, he could just make something up. Tell him that he was feeling a little fucked up because of the younger woman and that it was messing with his head. But that would still leave the family and the connecting damage that they were causing. If they were caught, and they would be eventually, he could be next. Hell, they would probably blame him, and they would get away with it. Then what would Ben do? Think that Charlie would turn him in for a lesser sentence? Turn state's evidence if he could walk? Charlie's mind was now spinning like a bullet from a rifle. He forced himself to take in a deep breath and held it for five seconds.

No, he would have to tell Ben everything and let the chips fall where they may. Plus, he still had Karen as a failsafe if shit got real, and thanks to Ben, that bitch wasn't going anywhere. He would tell Ben about his plans for her, as well. Charlie pulled into the dark parking lot of his office with a chill scraping down his spine.

CHAPTER TWENTY-TWO

A Motherless Child

The baby had survived the night.

Grenalda Habsburg leaned over the eighteenth-century crib, her eyes focused on the infant's chest, mentally counting each breath. They remained even and strong. The old woman then gazed up at the newborn's face, cautiously looking for any signs of deformity. His chin did seem slightly elongated, but it was nothing compared to Nithards and Marianna's when they had been born. His eyes were evenly placed and as far as she could see. All his limbs were normal. But time would tell.

Damn you, Nith!

Nithard was an idiot. He had placed the family in a dangerous situation. The mother had been a rarity. Her disappearance was soon forgotten and most likely celebrated, but now she was dead. And they would be forced to find another.

Nithard wasn't entirely to blame. She knew this. It wasn't his fault that he was born the way he was. The warning signs had been there for two generations. Grenalda had known this and had even discussed it with her brother as they lay locked in each other's arms. And yet they ignored their own better judgment even after the second stillborn. Their mistake had been love and knowing that God was always watching. To stray from their inherited course could lead to damnation. So, they tried again, and as if to confirm their belief, God granted them a son. Phillip. But like so many other gifts that came from God, there was a catch: The boy was born a mutant, and although he was a genius, he was unable to continue the line. And so, they had to try again.

Two more had been lost before they were finally granted the twins. Nithard and Marianna were born in the last year of her brother's life, but at least he was able to see them before he died. A sudden tear trickled down the old woman's flattened cheek as an image of her one true love flashed before her. Her brother had the chin, it was true, but his eyes had shown with the blue fire of sapphire. What would he say now that a corpse lay in the lab? Now that a liar sat locked up. Perhaps it was better this way. The woman had been a nuisance from the beginning. She would never be able to be trusted. The liar might prove different. He was certainly much better behaved, and Marianna liked him. That was important. Plus, he was a loser whose only family was an ex-wife who was now fucking his old boss and a mother who lived alone. But would he be able to perform? Phillip would see to that.

But there was still Nithard to worry about. What they needed was another woman who, if not grateful for what they were offering, would at least not be as difficult. Any woman should be honored to be with her son, to be with a prince. The man could lift a car, and his lust knew no bounds.

Grenalda reached down and rubbed the tiny point of the infant's chin.

"Shhh...sweetheart," she whispered. "We'll find you another mommy soon."

A scuttling sound grabbed her attention, and she turned to see Phillip in the doorway.

"How is he, mother?" he said.

"He's just fine," said Grenalda. "You did good, Phillip."

"We were lucky," said Phillip, dragging himself further into the room. "But we're going to need formula to feed him."

"Have Lisa bring whatever we need," she said.

"Consider it done. What about the woman's body?"

Grenalda gave the child's cheek one last loving stroke and then turned to where Phillip crouched just a few feet away.

"I sent Nith out to dig a hole. I want you to go with him when he comes back for the body and help him."

"And what would you have me do?" said Phillip.

"Make sure that he keeps his pants on until she's in the ground."

"He scares me, Mother," he said a little louder than he meant to, causing the baby to twitch. "He is putting us in danger."

Grenalda held a gnarled finger to her lips and motioned for him to follow her out of the room. They entered the open hall, and she quietly closed the door.

"I know he worries you," she said. "But what would you have me do? He *is* your brother."

"I understand that, and I know he's important, but we need to get control of him somehow."

Phillip was right, of course. Grenalda knew this, but what choice did they have? And what did Phillip want her to do? Kill him? Could he even be killed? It didn't matter; this line of thinking was blasphemy. The fact that Nithard was here proved that he was one of the chosen, just as Phillip and Marianna were. Best to change the subject.

"Also, when you get back, you should have the liar clean out his pot and make him take a shower. Tomorrow is a big day."

"Yes," said Phillip. "Although, having them consummate before marriage is technically a sin."

"We don't have time for any of that," she snapped. "What's the point of marriage if the man can't get it up?"

"And what about a new girl for Nith?" said Phillip.

"That's something I'll have to consider," said Grenalda, just as the squeak of an activating hinge rang through the house.

"Go," said the old woman. "Help your brother and make sure that the liar is good to go for tomorrow."

She watched as Phillip turned and made his way towards the large stairwell.

Yes, the dead woman would have to be replaced. But with whom? She had been perfect, a friendless whore that the world was glad to be rid of. The liar was like that. His wife had left him for the overweight bastard who mistakenly thought of Grenalda as his partner. Why would such a pretty girl be drawn to such losers? Perhaps it was their smooth, hustling tongues. And, of course, Charlie did have money.

Whatever the reason, it was obvious that she was easily persuaded. There was another possibility that caused Grenalda's lips to curl: Maybe it was because she had no one else to turn to. Maybe she was alone. Was she like the corpse downstairs? An unwanted scab on society? Perhaps. The girl was very pretty and, more importantly, young. But was she fertile? That question could be answered with a simple test. Better yet, having her here might provide the necessary motivation that the liar seemed to lack. Yes, they could all be one big happy family.

But would Charlie agree? Surely the sociopath cared little for the woman; he hardly batted an eye when his wife had been murdered, which was something Grenalda wished she could undo. The bastard didn't deserve such a favor. And yet, because of that, he owed the family big, and he knew it. So, whether he was attached to the young bitch mattered little. She would call the con artist, but first, she must ensure the liar lived past tomorrow.

It was, after all, a big day.

CHAPTER TWENTY-THREE

Coffee and a Tale

Agent Wayne took Exit 92 to Crawford Road off of I-135. Salina, Kansas, was a small hub town with connecting freeways providing multiple escape routes. The four-hour drive gave him plenty of time to consider his upcoming discussion with Mrs. Devos. The woman had lost both her husband and her only child within a span of just two years. The effects of such a loss might have been too much for her to recover completely, and as an investigator, he would have to keep that in mind. Questioning her would have to be done carefully and with a grain of salt. The vehemence in her voice when she spoke of Charlie Wheaton was an emotionally charged condemnation that, as far as he could tell, had no factual basis. Still, they had hired a P.I. According to Mrs. Devos, that person had come up with something that she thought was valuable. But the OSBI had refused to look. That was no surprise, considering the OSBI contained the top investigators in the state. Why should they be interested in what some retired local cop out of Kansas had found?

Agent Wayne had never felt that way. His main concern with private investigators was their motivations. There were far too many pet finders in the world, and their numbers seemed to grow daily. That's not to say that some were not genuinely trying to help, and Agent Wayne could only hope that the Devos' had managed to find one.

Crawford Road was a two-lane broken black top with scattered oaks and cottonwood trees running down each side. Patriotic flags decorated most of the houses bordered by rusted barbed wire fencing. Dented mailboxes stood on leaning, paint-depleted posts, their weathered latches warped and open. This was the heartland. It was a place where a person's choice of worship was often more important than what they did for a living.

Agent Wayne glanced down at the GPS and saw that Mrs. Devos' driveway was coming up on his left. He eased down on the brake and turned the cruiser. The house sat fifty yards off the street. It was a modest two-story colonial with sage-colored lap siding. A pair of evenly spaced windows looked out from the second story, edged with wide white louvered shutters. A narrow gabled roof covered the porch.

The agent brought the car to a stop just a few feet from a stained stairway. A bitter wind hit his face as he climbed out of the car and made his way to the front door. The panel was an eight-foot Knotty Alder with a stain two shades darker than the porch.

He reached out and pressed the copper-plated doorbell, expecting to hear the deep sound of a resonating chime, but was surprised to hear instead the simple *Ding Dong* that matched his apartment.

Overall, the house projected a look of hidden wealth that often came with those who started with next to nothing. And yet the sage paint was chipped, and one of the shutters sagged. To Agent Wayne, it looked like a Roman ruin. A crippled structure whose glory days were now far behind it. That was not too hard to believe, considering two-thirds of what had made this house once shine was now gone. Had Charlie caused this? According to the lady in this house, he had.

The sound of a turning deadbolt brought the agent back to his task. The door swung in, presenting an old woman hunched over and leaning heavily on a cane. Her face was mapped in wrinkles. Her gray eyes were submerged in moisture that he doubted ever went away. The sorrow was apparent as she forced her quivering lips into a smile.

"Mrs. Devos," said the agent. "I'm Field Agent Wyatt Wayne."

"I'm glad you could make it," she said, waving him in.

Agent Wayne stepped through the doorway, removing his coat and hanging it on the rack to his right.

"We've got a storm coming in," said Mrs. Devos. "Are you driving back today?"

"I have to," said the agent. "I won't take much of your time."

"Well, it's not supposed to get bad until around two." said Mrs. Devos.

"That's more than enough time," he said, allowing her to slowly lead him down a canary yellow hallway. The woman wore a blue Allover dress that hung past her swollen knees. Black and orange stabilizing socks stretched up past her calves and were tucked into a pair of feathered Harrison house slippers.

"This is a nice house."

"It used to be," she said over her shoulder. "But nowadays, it's just me, and it's too hard to keep up."

The hallway opened into a spacious living area with matching canary-colored walls. The floor was oak planked, its stained finish worn. At its center was a cottage-style circular coffee table surrounded by a couple of LazyBoy chairs and a Braton Collar Edgeworth sofa, which the agent estimated was worth more than what he made in one month.

"Please, sit down," she said. "Would you care for some coffee?"

"That would be nice," said the agent, easing himself onto the sofa. Mrs. Devos shuffled towards a doorway on the far side of the room.

"Do you need any help?" he said.

"I can manage," she said.

Agent Wayne took the opportunity to gaze at the pictures hanging around the room. Many of them were snapshots of a girl aging from an infant to a young woman that matched the picture in his file at the office. Mrs. Devos reappeared with her cane hanging from its hook over her wrist. She held a tray in her trembling hands, the clinking sound filling the room from the Imperial Porcelain teapot shaking against two matching cups.

"Here, let me help you," said Agent Wayne, leaping to his feet.

"Thank you," she said as he grabbed the tray. "It's horrible when you get too old to serve coffee."

"You seem to be doing fine to me," said Agent Wayne warmly.

Mrs. Devos returned his smile, but it took an effort that

produced sadness within the agent. So many years had gone by since this woman had lost everyone. Her golden years, the years that were supposed to be filled with the laughter of grandchildren and trips to places that she had only dreamed about, had been stripped away by a violent crime. A crime that, as of yet, had gone unsolved. There was no point in trying to show empathy; this pain could only be understood by experience, and to pretend otherwise would just be an insult.

"So," said the woman, pouring them each a cup and handing him one. "What new evidence has the OSBI found against my daughter's husband?"

Agent Wayne took the cup from her and sat back on the couch. He slowly took a sip, buying all the time that he could. She had presented him with a dangerous question. In her mind, there was no need for a jury; Charlie Wheaton was guilty. This was something that he could not confirm or even pretend to acknowledge. By doing so, he would give the old woman a false hope that could easily explode in his face later. But on the other hand, he couldn't flat out deny her suspicion either because then he would risk upsetting the woman, which would get him nowhere. Agent Wayne returned the coffee cup to the table with a satisfied sigh.

"That is delicious," he said.

The old woman sat there with her hands interlocked on her lap, patiently waiting for his response. Agent Wayne reached up and loosened his tie, thankful he had decided to forgo the one with the dancing black cat. Finally, he decided that the best approach would be the truth.

"Mrs. Devos, I'm not really sure I have anything new to add to your case," he said.

"You drove up here from Oklahoma City just to tell me that?"

"Not exactly," said the agent. "I'm investigating a murder that happened a few days back."

"And you think Charlie did it?"

"Actually, I don't know what to think. But I assume you knew him fairly well."

"Better than I wanted to," said Mrs. Devos.

"I know you're convinced that he's responsible for your daughter's death," said the agent. "But what I don't know is why?"

Mrs. Devos lifted her cane and pointed it over the agent's shoulder.

"On the mantelpiece, there's a manila folder. Do you mind getting that for me?"

Agent Wayne stood up and made his way over to the rock opening of the fireplace with the marble shelf and returned with the folder. Mrs. Devos took it from him and unclasped the top, spilling out its contents onto the table. She then pushed them back into one pile and placed them on her lap.

"These are from the private investigator I told you about. This is six months' worth of work."

"Do you mind if I ask who this guy was?"

"It wasn't a guy," said Mrs. Devos. "Her name is Katherine Jenkins, and she's a retired detective out of Kansas City. Her husband was a close friend of my husband's; they played football together at Kansas State. Katherine recommended that we stop the investigation."

"Couldn't she find anything?"

"She found plenty of things that confirmed he was a parasite. But nothing that could tie him to Sarah's murder."

Mrs. Devos then removed a picture from the pile sitting on her lap and handed it to the agent. It was a photograph taken with a quality zoom lens. It showed Charlie standing at a door with the number 12 attached to its panel. Beside him was a brunette wearing six-inch heels and a skirt that just barely covered the cheeks of her ass.

"Not your daughter, I assume," said the agent before he could stop himself.

"No, it's not," said Mrs. Devos.

"I'm sorry," said Agent Wayne. "Sometimes my mouth rebels."

"Don't worry about it," said Mrs. Devos. "We all have our fucking moments."

Agent Wayne burst out in laughter, which she soon joined. At least she still had some semblance of a sense of humor. Of course, he was already aware of Charlie's sexual habits, and now he knew that Mrs. Devos was as well. Good, that might make things easier.

"Did Sarah know about the prostitutes?"

"Of course, she did," said Mrs. Devos. "But she refused to believe it. Charlie would be gone for weeks, claiming to be working, but they were always broke. I can't tell you how many times we had to pay their rent and cover their light bill."

"Why did she stay with him?"

"Because he said he loved her. My daughter was a shy child and was never one of those girls who hung out after school."

"But she looks so friendly," said Agent Wayne, pointing at the nearest picture hanging on the wall.

It showed a girl no older than fourteen sitting on a swing, her metallic braces reflecting in a setting sun.

"She was, but she was also afraid to open herself up. I could never understand why and I gave up on trying."

"How did they meet?"

"Sarah had gone off to college at The University of Tulsa. She was going to become an accountant. She had worked part-time at some construction company where Charlie was working. The nightmare started from there."

"Did she finish college?"

"She wanted to, but that asshole talked her out of it. Told her there was no reason to waste the best part of her life when he could take care of her."

"When were they married?"

Mrs. Devos rummaged around for a moment on her lap, pulling out a yellowed piece of paper, and then gave it to Agent Wayne. The agent took it from her and saw it was a marriage announcement from Tulsa World. It was dated June 16th, 1998.

"Were you there?"

"Nope," said Mrs. Devos, pushing back a stray gray hair out of her eyes. "We didn't even find out until a week later."

The agent looked back down at the clipping.

"It says here that her witness was someone named Alicia Turner. Do you know who that is?"

"It was a friend from school," said Mrs. Devos. "I never met the girl."

"What about his witness? Mike Crandell?"

"No clue," she said. "And that's how it was; we went from seeing our daughter almost every weekend to her basically disappearing into some secret life. We only saw them on the holidays, and we only received phone calls from Sarah when they needed money."

"I must ask you: Were you aware of his arrest in ninety-nine?"

She again picked through the stack on her lap and pulled out a picture.

"This one?" she said, handing it to Agent Wayne.

It was a photo of Charlie with his hands cuffed behind his back, being placed in a police car. Agent Wayne looked at the date inked in at the bottom corner of the photograph: 5-21-1999.

"That would be the one," he said, placing the picture on the coffee table. "Did Sarah know?"

A pained expression crept over Mrs. Devos' face as she leaned forward, placing the stack of information onto the table. She reached over, picked up her cup of coffee, took a quick sip, and leaned back into the chair.

"The only reason we hired our friend was because we were concerned. We didn't know anything about this man, and there our daughter was, leaving her dorm room for a shitty apartment on the west side of Tulsa."

A tear rolled down the old lady's deeply creviced face.

"We weren't trying to ruin her marriage. That's not why we hired Katherine. We just wanted to find out who this man was. And that was the hardest part: finding out and knowing that if we did tell Sarah, she might never talk to us again. So, we decided to remain quiet. As far as whether she knew that Charlie had been arrested, I really don't know."

Agent Wayne decided to give her a moment to regain her composure.

"Do you mind if I look through these?"

"Please," she said, grabbing a tissue from a box sitting next to her chair.

The agent lifted the pile and began to flip through the pages slowly. Many were financial logs of the cash that they had given the couple. There were also a couple of different addresses that included a map. Agent Wayne assumed that these were where Charlie and Sarah had lived at one time or another and where Mr. and Mrs. Devos would sometimes mail their rent.

The photographs were mostly of a younger Charlie going about his day. Some showed him walking into an office or arriving at some client's house. All were dated, and their time noted. There were a couple more, capturing him making his way into a rundown bar alone and leaving with some woman hanging on his arm. Then, the agent came across a smaller envelope meant for letters and saw that it was unsealed. He reached in and pulled out another group of photographs. It was a stack of eight aged polaroids that lacked the clear resolution of the ones before.

"What are these?" he said.

Mrs. Devos gave her eyes a final wipe and said, "Those were taken by my husband after our daughter was murdered. He never could believe that Charlie had nothing to do with it."

The photos were much like the others: Charlie going in and out of a bar. Stopping at a gas station. There was one where he was walking into a building with a poster taped to a wall that read Alcoholics Anonymous. Another picture showed him leaning against the door of a gutted room, talking to an older woman who had an extremely severe underbite. He flipped to the next picture and saw that in this one, Charlie was walking out of a Dollar Store, and standing behind him was a heavy-jawed lady, her eyes glaring at the back of his head. Agent Wayne brought out the previous picture and held it to the other. There could be no mistaking that chin.

"Do you know who this is?" he said, handing them to Mrs. Devos.

"I have no idea," she said, her eyes narrowed. "But she needs a dentist."

"Do you know where either of these were taken?"

Mrs. Devos held up the one with Charlie talking to the woman.

"I think my husband said that this one was at Charlie's office right after he bought it," she said, giving him back the picture.

Yes. Agent Wayne could see it.

"And this one," she began. "I'm not sure."

"How long after your daughter's death was the one at his office taken?"

"Probably six or seven months," said Mrs. Devos. "I know it was one of the last ones Kevin took because it wasn't much later that he became sick."

"I'm sorry to hear that," said Agent Wayne.

Mrs. Devos sat staring at the agent momentarily, her hands interlocked on her lap.

"What are you thinking?" she said, finally.

"According to your daughter's file, Charlie stood to lose a lot of money if something ever happened to her,"

"That's true," said Mrs. Devos. "My husband had set up a trust fund, but she couldn't touch it until she turned twenty-five."

"Yes, I remember reading that," said Agent Wayne, and that had only left her one year to go. "And her life insurance policy only paid out three thousand to Charlie."

"I wouldn't know," said Mrs. Devos. "I had nothing to do with that. But what is your point?"

"The one thing that confuses me is how a guy who had to rely on his wife's family just to get by came into enough money to buy an office in Oklahoma City and start up a business?"

"He is a hustler, Agent Wayne. Maybe he swindled someone just like he swindled my daughter."

"Maybe," said the agent.

A low roll of thunder entered the room. The light from the window behind Mrs. Devos was fading, reminding him that the storm was still very much alive.

Agent Wayne stood up, held out his hand, and said, "Mrs. Devos, I've taken way too much of your time."

"Don't be silly," she said, taking his hand. "I appreciate the fact that you care. You know, that's the worst part? It's like I'm still stuck in that moment, and the world has moved on."

"I assure you, ma'am, I do care." Agent Wayne said, holding up the two pictures. "Do you mind if I keep these?"

"Take whatever you want," she said, trying to stand up.

"Don't bother," said Agent Wayne. "I can show myself out."

Mrs. Devos slumped back into the chair.

"Thank you," she said. "Will you let me know if you find something?"

"You will be my first call."

*****

A slow drizzle had begun when Agent Wayne merged onto the I-135 southbound traffic out of Salina. The meeting had gone pretty much as he assumed it would. The old woman had just wanted someone to listen to her. Had wanted someone to look at those horrific pictures of her philandering ex-son-in-law. To her, it was all the proof that was needed. Unfortunately, all it proved was that Charlie was a low-life who had used his wife and her family as a means to an end. Strange that he would even consider killing his Sarah. She was, after all, the one paying for his hookers.

There was no telling whether Sarah had even known about it. But surely she had suspected. There were only so many times that a strange perfume on a shirt could be ignored. Only so many nights that a woman could spend alone without hearing from her husband.

He would be gone for days, Mrs. Devos had said, and still, Sarah had stayed with him.

Agent Wayne let the fractured center white lines work as a pendulum, allowing his mind to relax and become more receptive to his sometimes-careless imagination.

Assuming Charlie did murder Sarah, he thought to himself. *Where would that leave him?*

First and foremost, without money. At least without the kind of cash that paid for his extracurricular activities.

So, if he didn't kill her for money, then why kill her at all? Another woman? Possibly, except Sarah's father had been on him after the murder like a tick on a dog, and he had found nothing to support that theory. There had been no other woman who appeared consistently except for the older woman with the protruding chin, and even Charlie could do better than that. Agent Wayne reached down and grabbed the photos from the seat. There was no doubt that they knew each other, and the look in the woman's eyes as he left the Dollar Store certainly wasn't one of adoration. Perhaps Mrs. Devos was right. Maybe this was how Charlie had come into his wealth. Had he hustled this person out of her savings? It was worth looking into, not that it would necessarily help as far as Sarah's death was concerned. Still, one never knew. Agent Wayne let the picture of Charlie's office drop and held the other closer for a better look.

There were flyers stuck to the store's windows, but the shot had been taken too far away to see them clearly. Maybe, with any luck, he might get the photograph blown up and at least find out the general location. And with even more luck, maybe someone at that store would know who she was. It was a long shot, but the agent was getting used to that.

Then, his mind took a sharp left, and he found himself thinking about Karen. Perhaps it was because of the similarities between her and Sarah Wheaton. Both were lonely women conned into a poisoned relationship by a man whose only drive in life was greed and power. For a moment, he considered giving her a call but decided against it. He had made his concern for her known and had left the ball in her court. To press it any further would be teetering on harassment. If she needed him, she had his number. Better to leave it like that and focus on finding out who this woman slaying Charlie with her eyes was and hope that she might be able to help in some small way. You just never knew.

CHAPTER TWENTY-FOUR

Charlie Takes a Ride

Charlie Wheaton sat in the parking lot of Legion Mechanic Shop, hardly noticing the rolling darkness to the north. What he did notice was the six Harley-Davidsons parked near the curb in front of the garage. He had followed the tow truck hauling Karen's Nisson from his house and watched as it was deposited just outside of a bay door. She had wanted to join him, but he had refused, claiming that he had to go to the office to meet a contractor and then drive down to Lawton to negotiate with an irate customer. At first, she acted as if she didn't care and still wanted to tag along, but after promising to let her know about the car once he found something out, she agreed to stay. Then she did something unexpected; she reached up and kissed him on the side of his mouth. It wasn't passionate, but it might have led to something more if he had had more time.

The building front sported a harbinger depicting the same warrior rider on a motorcycle that decorated the back of the MC's vests. Charlie gazed at it. The chill that had seized him while he was pulling into the lot refused to go away, forbidding him to get out of the Mercedes. He wasn't one to believe in premonitions but was also never one to discard a bad feeling. And that's what this was: A bad feeling.

Perhaps it was because of his recently shattered delusion that had been leading him along for so long. This notion that helping Ben with his sobriety had placed Charlie in a superior, almost God-like, position had been a mistake. Again, Charlie considered not telling the biker, but the family's threat would still be there, and it was only a matter of time until that agent found something. A sigh escaped from the slit-like frown that now decorated his pudgy face.

Maybe he could tell Ben most of the story but omit the part about OSBI. After all, they weren't looking for the woman out of Broken Arrow. They were looking for Jimmy. The Centurions had nothing to do with that.

Fuck it, it's worth a shot, thought Charlie.

He was just about to get out of the car when the front door to the shop suddenly opened, and he felt his heart sink. Ben walked out, but he wasn't alone. Following him was a tall, thin man with a clean-shaven head. He was wearing a matching vest that had almost as many patches as Ben's. The man's face had the look of a nocturnal predator. It was pale with sharp eyes and a beak-like nose that sat above a thin mustache that slithered down each side of his narrow chin. Together, they made their way over to Charlie's car. Ben gave Charlie a wide smile and a wave, causing Charlie to flinch. Charlie opened the driver's side door and began to get out, but Ben suddenly threw up his hand.

"Hold up, there, Ringleader," said Ben, approaching the passenger side. "Let's take a ride."

Charlie felt his stomach clench and collapsed back into the seat. Ben opened the passenger door and flopped onto the seat just as the guy with him climbed into the back. They each shut their door and activated the seat belts. Charlie sat there for a moment with his leg still hanging out.

"What about my headlight?" he said, his voice sounding weak.

"We'll get to it when we get back," said Ben.

"Where are we going?" he said.

"Let's head out to the club," said Ben. "We can talk on the way."

"Okay," said Charlie. "But I can't be too long. I have a client coming in at two."

This, of course, was a lie. But it was also a test.

"We're just going to grab a couple of cases of beer for the shop," said Ben. "It'll give you time to tell me what you need to say."

Charlie reached up and adjusted the rearview mirror, sneaking a glance at the man in the back. The man sat gazing out of the window, seemingly unconcerned about anything. That didn't make Charlie feel any better. If anything, it made it worse. Why would Ben feel the need to bring this guy?

"This is Lester Floyd," said Ben, as if reading Charlie's mind. "He's kind of my right-hand man."

"How's it going?" said Charlie, pivoting around and extending out his hand,

Lester grunted and reached out, giving Charlie's hand a quick shake.

"He helps me with the more difficult decisions," said Ben.

"I wasn't aware that any decisions needed to be made," said Charlie.

Ben looked at him darkly and said, "I guess we'll see, won't we?"

Charlie pulled the Mercedes away from the shop and out onto the road. The drive to the club would take thirty minutes if the traffic was light and he could only hope that it was. The northern sky matched the color of Charlie's sinking emotion, an ominous gray that promised to bring nothing good.

They drove along in silence for a while. Charlie's eyes darted from mirror to mirror as he switched lanes, pausing here and there for a better look at the man in the backseat. On his vest were the same scythe marks Ben had, and it looked like Lester might have had more. Another difference was the man's title patch; where Ben read President, Lester had SGT. At Arms. Had he been in the military? Until this point, Charlie had little to do with The Centurions, except for the occasional party at the club, but he rarely spoke to them even then. The titles and their meaning were lost on him. It was probably time to do some research, that is if he survived today. He tightened his grip on the steering wheel at that thought. Did he really think that Ben would kill him? If so, why hadn't he been worried before he had called him? Because of that family, that's why. They had him by the balls and as scary as The Centurions were, they were like a child's gang compared to that old lady and her deformed kin.

"So, tell us," said Ben.

"I thought *we* were going to talk," said Charlie.

It was then that the silent man sitting in the back seat undid his seatbelt with the speed of a cat and moved to within inches of the back of Charlie's head.

"Don't make him ask you again, fat man," he said, his voice pitched like a baritone.

Charlie felt the threat of his bowels being released and was forced to clench his cheeks. Sweat had formed on his forehead, dribbling its way down his nose.

"Is it hot in here?" said Lester, sitting back in his seat.

"You need to relax, Ringleader," said Ben, placing his hand on Charlie's shoulder. "You called me, remember? I'm assuming you need my help."

Charlie took a deep, shuddering breath and began spilling out the story, starting with the first day that the old lady had stopped him on the side of the road in Broken Arrow all those years ago and continuing to the death of his wife and the business arrangement that had been made.

"So, they own fifty-one percent of your operation?" said Ben.

"Yes," said Charlie. "But they have nothing to do with the actual day-to-day."

"I see," said Ben. "Go on."

Charlie snuck a quick look at the rearview mirror just as an astonished look swept over Lester's hawk-like face. To his right, Ben's eyes remained fixed on the outside terrain, his expression impossible to read. It was only when Charlie was talking about Jimmy and the murder of the old lady that he stirred, shifting his booted feet slightly.

"That's why I called you Ben," Charlie concluded. "These crazy fuckers have got me involved in something that's way over my head."

"Is that it?" said Ben, and Charlie wished it was.

He had left out the part about the woman they had kidnapped and how she had been taken for the family. He had told Ben that he had wanted to scare her. Force her to drop a lawsuit. Ben had asked no questions and helped without knowing the truth. The woman that they had taken was now most likely dead, and the worst part was that The Centurions were unknowingly implicated in kidnap as well as possibly murder.

Is that it? Ben had asked him. Yes. It would have to be.

"That's it," said Charlie.

Ben stared at him for a moment, his eyes narrowed.

"So, this 'family' killed your wife?" he said.

"Yes," said Charlie. "They cut her fucking head off."

"And you didn't know anything about it?"

"They didn't tell me shit until after she was dead."

"Why would they do that?" said Ben.

"They said that it was a gift and a warning."

"Meaning?" said Ben.

"They knew I didn't care much for Sarah, and they also wanted to let me know what they were capable of if I tried to fuck them over."

"What else do you know about them?" said Ben.

"I know that they're fucked up looking, and they're very rich," said Charlie. "They act like royalty. One of them is seven feet tall and can lift a tank."

"Do you know where they live?"

"I've never been to their house, but they've had me meet them a few times in Lost City. Usually at a gas station or a Dollar Store."

"Where the fuck is Lost City?" said Ben.

"It's a small town forty miles east of Tulsa. If you blink, you'll miss it."

"And now they've taken one of your salesmen. Do you have any idea why?"

"I don't know why they wanted him," said Charlie. "I certainly didn't think they were going to kill anyone."

To Charlie's relief, the club appeared on the left. He flipped the blinker and eased the Mercedes into the empty lot. He pulled into a space close to the door and parked the car.

"Is there anything else you want to tell me?" said Ben, opening the passenger door.

"That's pretty much it," he said. "I just think that my life could be in danger."

Ben got out of the car and then leaned back in. His face, again, plastered with that wide grin.

"Why don't you come in and grab a coke while we load the beer."

"I'm good here," said Charlie. "I need to call the office."

It was then that he felt something hard pressed against the back of his skull. He looked up at the rearview mirror and saw a short barrel .38 being held by Lester Floyd. Charlie never heard the man move.

"Come on, Ringleader," said Ben. "I just have a couple of more questions."

Charlie felt his stomach roll, and the seat of his pants got very warm. The smell wafted through the cab, causing Lester to cover his mouth.

"He shit himself," he said.

"Get out of the car," said Ben, standing up. "I'm sure we have something in here for you to change into, although it might have tassels."

Charlie's mind went numb. They were going to kill him. He had put them in the middle of a murder investigation, and somehow they had found out. A low moan escaped his throat as he struggled out of the car on shaky knees, oblivious to the stream now running down his right leg.

"Make his ass shower first," said Lester, hopping out of the back with the gun still held on Charlie.

"Not until we talk," said Ben.

"Okay," said Charlie, leaning against the hood of the Mercedes, trying to catch his breath. "There's more."

"I kind of figured there was," said Ben. "But save it until we get you inside. I want you to see something."

Ben turned and made his way to the front door of the club. Charlie felt a sharp pain in his lower back from Lester stabbing him with the .38.

"Let's go," said Lester with a laugh. "I can't believe you shit yourself, cuddles."

Charlie felt as though his legs were trying to revolt as he stumbled his way forward. He looked up at the sky. Would this be the last thing he would ever see from outside? Another low whimper escaped his throat as the blacked-out glass door shut behind him. A subtle click of a turning lock caused him to trip.

"Keep going," said Lester.

Charlie stepped down the back hallway towards the room with

the carved table. Once inside, he saw a metal chair sitting in the center of a sheet of plastic placed near the corner. The chair was covered in dark stains, and on each armrest hung a set of handcuffs. It faced a television with a DVD player sitting on top. Ben was standing next to a short, stocky man wearing a vest. Stenciled across its ID patch was V. P.

"Take a seat," the V. P. said.

"Better put a towel down first," said Lester. "He shit himself."

"It wouldn't be the first time someone shit in that chair," said the V.P. moving up beside the trembling man and forcing him down onto the stained cushion.

Once Charlie was in the chair, Ben walked over and placed a hand on his shoulder, giving it a painful squeeze.

"I like you, Charlie," he said. "And I want to help you, but you haven't been totally honest with me."

"I'm going to tell you everything, Ben."

"I know you are. But I want you to watch something for me before you do."

Ben then reached over and pressed the play button on the DVD.

CHAPTER TWENTY-FIVE

Preparation

"Let's get you cleaned up," Phillip said after Jimmy had scrubbed away the blood on the floor. Nith stood at the base of the stairs, his eyes tracking Jimmy's every move.

Jimmy followed Phillip to the back of the dungeon, where a 3x4 cubicle shower sat behind a translucent curtain. A small wooden stool was placed at its side, and on it were a toothbrush, a small tube of toothpaste, a bar of motel soap, and a towel.

"Tomorrow is an important day," Phillip said from just outside the curtain as the sulfur water ran over Jimmy's trembling body. "You will have to perform."

"What if I can't do it?" Jimmy said more to himself than anyone else.

"Then you will die," said Phillip, tossing him the towel. "I don't want that to happen to you, James. I think that fundamentally, you are a good person and will see the benefits of becoming a member of our family."

Jimmy gazed over at the sentinel-like giant and shivered.

"I can help you if you let me," continued Phillip. "I have tasty concoctions that will guarantee success."

"Did the baby live?" Jimmy suddenly asked.

"He is alive and doing fine: Praise God."

Jimmy made his way back to his cell. The baby was alive, swaddled in a pit of snakes, unaware of what his future had in store for him. But at least he had survived.

Jimmy paused mid-step and said, "What about the marriage?"

"Mother will not allow it until you have proven yourself worthy."

"In other words, she wants to know I can get it up."

"Precisely," said Phillip.

The cage, which was now his home, had been cleaned with new sheets placed on the cot. The lava rock protruded with menace, its sharp texture providing the only escape. It was his choice, and it was the only thing they couldn't take away. Jimmy stepped in and heard the grinding hinges from behind that represented his captivity, flinching as the metal door impacted the wall of bars. A smile slithered slowly across his face at the thought of them coming down tomorrow and finding another corpse. Would they be angry? Of course, they would. Not because it was Jimmy but because their search would have to continue. That would put them at risk. How easy could it be to find someone who had spread nothing but animosity and anguish for most of their life? A person who would be barely missed. And yet, they would find that someone eventually. Jimmy had no doubt about that. A thought suddenly thrust through, dissolving the remnants of his mental fog. The innocent child would become a murderer, a killer raised with the mentality of the giant, molded into a sociopath.

Jimmy turned and sat down on the cot and said, "Can you help me?"

"I guarantee that my mother will accept you after tomorrow."

"I'll do it," said Jimmy.

Phillip clapped his hands as if he had just closed the deal of his life.

"I'm so glad to hear you say that," he said, turning towards the giant. "Nith, grab his clothes."

The giant lumbered to the pile, picked them up off the floor, and made his way back to the stairs.

Phillip turned to Jimmy, saying, "I'll have those washed and back to you by tomorrow morning."

Jimmy watched as the deformed man began to pivot, but he paused.

"I'll arrange to have Marianna bring you your dinner tonight. Why not try talking to her? It might make tomorrow a little more enjoyable for you both."

"I'll consider it," said Jimmy.

Phillip turned and crab-walked his way up the stairs with Nith close behind.

CHAPTER TWENTY-SIX

A Movie and a Gun

A dark-haired man was sitting on the very chair that Charlie now found himself shaking in. Both of his hands were cuffed to the armrests. The video was riddled with horizontal lines, and the audio was lousy. But it was good enough to see the absolute terror in his eyes. The camera panned back, showing the table with the carved warrior top and the small bar near the back wall. It was like looking into a horrific mirror.

"You think you can steal from us, and we wouldn't care?" said a voice, sounding very much like the man with V.P. stenciled on his vest. "Why? Because you're doing one of our girls?"

"I didn't steal shit," the man on the video screamed, and it was then Charlie noticed that the man's left eye was swollen shut.

"You deal drugs in our place without asking or even offering a kickback. That's the same as stealing."

The man rocked in his chair, trying to break his hands free. Another man came into the shot. He was thin, and his eyes burned with a rage that could stop a healthy heart. Lester Floyd raised a fist and brought it down on the man's upturned face, splitting his cheek. Blood poured down the man's dirty T-shirt, dripping onto a plastic sheet.

A scream rattled the television speaker, causing Charlie to

wince. He had seen enough and started to turn his head away, closing his eyes. A sudden thumb against the side of his head caused him to gasp in pain. Charlie opened his eyes to find Lester staring down at him.

"Keep watching, cuddles," he hissed. "It's just about to get good."

Charlie felt his stomach tighten and was sure he would be sick. Lester made a quick motion like he would hit him again, and Charlie turned his eyes to the screen. The screaming continued as the video Lester spent another fifteen seconds pummeling the helpless man.

"That's enough," said a deep voice that could only have belonged to Ben. "I don't give a shit about the drugs, Kyle. And I don't give a shit about Larisa, but what I do want to know is why you're really here."

The man's face was unrecognizable. Both eyes were swollen shut, and his top lip had ballooned past his disfigured nose.

"Please," he managed to jumble out. "I'm not with anyone."

"Rip off his shirt," said Ben.

Lester grabbed the man's collar and pulled, tearing the blood-soaked cotton down the middle. Across his sweat-covered chest was a tattoo of a skull wearing a sombrero.

"Well, I'll be a motherfucker," said Lester, a smile camped from ear to ear. "He's a Renegade."

"I'm not," Kyle spit out. "I got this in Reno."

"He's fucking lying," said Lester.

"Listen to me, carefully," said Ben, and Charlie could almost see that face-splitting grin. "Are you listening, Kyle?"

"Yes," said Kyle with tears flowing down his broken face.

"Good," said Ben. "Cause I'm only going to ask you this once, and if you lie, you'll be carried out of here. Do you understand?"

Kyle nodded his head, causing sweat and blood to fly.

'Why are Renegades in Oklahoma?"

"I don't even know what Renegades are," said Kyle.

Out of nowhere appeared Ben, and in his hand was a 45. He came to a stop just behind Kyle, placed the barrel at the top of his head, and pulled the trigger. The blast sent a burst of horizontal lines racing across the screen. When they subsided, the screen showed Kyle slumped over, his jaw shattered.

Charlie leaned over to his right and vomited onto the plastic sheet.

The image of Kyle grew closer until his death-gripped gaze filled the screen, and then the television went dark. Ben walked in front of Charlie with a .45 held firmly in his hand. Charlie lifted his arm and wiped his mouth, his eyes like saucers, focusing on the pistol.

"In case you're wondering, this is the same gun," said Ben. "Kyle, as it turns out, was a Renegade out of New Mexico. They sent him up here as a scout. You see, they were considering moving against us. We sent his head back in a box, and you know what? We never heard from them again."

Charlie sat there with his heart thrumming, sweat pouring from his brow. He tried to speak but could only manage a dry click in his throat.

"Now, Ringleader, I feel like I owe you. The state would have fried me if it weren't for you. So, I will ask you again: Is that it?"

A force, like a bulldozer, burst through Charlie's head, initiating a cacophony of sobs mixed with snot-filled snorts.

"Jesus Christ," said Lester, backing away. "This guy's a real hero."

"Last chance," said Ben, placing the .45 on Charlie's head.

It was as if Charlie had left his body and was watching this strange man; a man that he didn't know, blubbering his way through a complete confession; revealing every dirty secret, every damning piece of evidence. A soiled and smelly coward bent on pathetic survival.

Ben stood there for a moment with the gun still pointed at Charlie's head. He then lowered the weapon and made his way over to the back of the bar, pulling out a bottle of Jack Danials and a couple of glasses. Lester hovered just a few feet away from where Charlie now sat with his chin on his chest, gasping for air. Ben unscrewed the top off the bottle and filled the two glasses.

"Come over here, Charlie," he said.

Charlie tried to stand, but his knees could not hold him, and he collapsed back into the chair.

"Help him up," said Ben.

Lester Floyd stepped behind Charlie, hooking his hands under Charlie's sweat-infested armpits, and lifted the man to his feet, waiting until he was stable before letting him go. Charlie stumbled his way past the smiling man with the V.P. patch over to the bar, the seat of his pants now plastered to his ass. He came to a stop just a couple of feet away from Ben.

"Move down a little," said Ben, waving a hand in front of his nose.

"Sorry," stuttered Charlie, stepping away from the man, having to use the bar's surface as a crutch.

"Take this," said Ben, sliding the shot of whiskey towards him.

Charlie gazed at the translucent glass, at the brown liquid swirling within. He wanted to take it and throw it down the hatch. But the family's threat lingered like lightning blasting through a wind-driven dust storm. His crippled mind was desperately trying to rebuild itself, clutching for broken pieces of logic. Could this still be them? Could they be trying to break him? If so, the mission was very much accomplished.

"I–I don't drink," he managed to mutter.

Ben slammed his beefy hand down on the bar, causing Charlie to jump.

"Enough bullshit, Ringleader," said Ben. "We both know that you're just as dirty as we are, so there's no point in trying to hide it. Especially from me."

"I'm not a criminal," said Charlie.

"Really? Your wife was murdered, her head cut off, and you know who did it. Did you turn them in? Fuck no, you didn't. And even better, you took money from her killer and became a front."

Ben then leaned towards Charlie, his friendly grin exuding an evil that tightened Charlie's skin, and said, "I've done some bad shit in my time, Ringleader, but I've never done anything that comes close to that."

"What are you going to do to me?"

Ben leaned back and said, "I wouldn't give a shit about your marital problems or even those freaks you've hooked up with if only you would have left us out of it. But you got us involved when you had us grab that bitch from Broken Arrow."

"I didn't know what they were going to do," said Charlie.

"Of course, you didn't," said Ben, with mock understanding. "And now here we are, chest-deep in your cluster fuck."

"I've told you everything I know," said Charlie.

"I believe you, Ringleader, and that's the problem: You really don't know shit. That bitch could be chained up somewhere, getting dicked every night, or dead. Don't you think that's a problem?"

Charlie stood there staring down at the whiskey, afraid to answer.

"What if she finds a way to escape and talks? Or if they find her body in some shallow grave? What if they trace her back to you? Have you thought of that?"

Of course, Charlie had and had taken it even further. What if Jimmy managed to escape?

"And now they have your salesman," said Ben in that eerie prescient way. "And you don't even know where they are."

Ben was right. Charlie had dragged them into this and would now have to pay for his mistake. But at least his brains were still in his head and not decorating the plastic sheet, like the guy on the video. So obviously, Ben wasn't going to kill him, not today, anyway. But Charlie wasn't an idiot. He knew Ben's mercy would come with a price, and he only hoped he could afford it. He drew a deep breath and held it momentarily, willing his scattered composure to return, then turned to face Ben, hoping his face was masked with a courage that he didn't feel.

"What do you want me to do?" said Charlie.

Ben reached for his shot glass and then pointed at Charlie's.

"Right now, I want you to share a drink with me."

Charlie's hand whipped out with a mind of its own, grasping the whiskey. Ben held up his glass and said, "Here's to no more bullshit."

He then clinked Charlie's glass, and they downed the whiskey together. For Charlie, it was like tasting freedom. It was as if the shackles of servitude had been snapped from his ankles. Ben placed his glass on the bar and returned the bottle from where he got it. Charlie held his empty shooter, debating on whether he should ask for another.

"Now, here's what you're going to do," said Ben. "You're going to find out where this family is."

"They won't tell me," said Charlie. "And if I ask, they'll know something is up."

"Yeah," said Ben. "That's not my fucking problem. You're their partner. What was it you said? Fifty-one percent, wasn't it?"

"That's what he said," Lester chimed in from the other side of the room.

"So, have yourself a business meeting," said Ben. "Tell them anything, I don't care. I'm going to give you three days. If you fuck me over on this, we'll be making another video, understand?"

There was no other way out of this but to comply. Charlie nodded like a chastised child, the empty glass still in his hand. The thought of calling the old woman still managed to fill him with a dread that overrode the events that had just ruined his one-hundred-and twenty-five-dollar Givenchy's. The woman didn't respond to his requests, never had. And every time they met, it was because she wanted to meet. But this was information best kept to himself. Ben had learned enough, and it had almost cost Charlie his life.

"I'll find out," he said.

"Good," said Ben. "I've got faith in you, Ringleader."

Charlie felt a sliver of courage return and held up his empty glass.

"Do you mind if I have another?" he said.

"Are you fucking kidding me?" Ben snapped, slapping the shot glass out of his hand.   "You don't drink. Now get him out of here."

*****

Charlie drove back towards the city with the windows lowered, and still, the stench hung in the cab like a busted septic line. He quickly gazed down at his Ralph Lauren that he had placed on the seat and hoped that the shit had dried enough to where it wouldn't seep through the shirt and onto the leather of the Mercedes. He reached over and picked up his cell phone from the floorboard. There were seven missed calls, four from Karen and three from the office. He returned one to the office, telling Melanie he wouldn't be in for the rest of the day. He then considered going home, but how could he explain this to Karen? Going home wasn't a good idea, anyway. He needed to be alone, needed time to recover from the trauma that his friend Ben had caused, and he needed time to plan.

Plan for what?

That was the million-dollar question. How was he supposed to find out where The Hills Have Eyes clan lived, anyway? They had only met a handful of times over the years, and it had always been at a different location. The old woman was as intelligent as she was ugly. Even her corporate label was sheltered, funneled into some offshore haven unbeholden to the United States.

Forget it, for now, he thought to himself.

This day was a bust. His nerves were firing like a Gatling, so there was no point in making it worse. He reached down and picked up his cell phone, scrolling through his numbers, stopping at the Cherokee Casino. The line was answered on the second ring.

"Hello, my name is Charlie Wheaton, and I'd like to book a room."

"Yes, sir," said the friendly woman on the other end. "Have you stayed with us before?"

"Many times," said Charlie.

He then gave her his information.

"Oh, Mr. Wheaton," began the happy voice. "I see here you're a VIP. Do you have any special requests for your room?"

"As a matter of fact, I do. Could you please make sure I have a pair of pants, size 46 at the waist and 36 long, sent up? One of my bags was lost at the airport."

"I'm sorry to hear that, and, of course, I'll have them waiting in your room. Any particular brand that you would like me to send for?"

"Whatever you have close by will be fine," said Charlie. "Also, would you send up a bottle of Jim Beam?"

"Sure thing. Do you want a pint or a fifth?"

"Most definitely a fifth," said Charlie.

"Got it," said the woman. "Will there be anything else?"

"Just my room number, preferably on the first floor."

No reason to drag his stinking ass any further through the hotel than he had to.

Charlie ended the call with less than three miles to go. He would have to get a hold of Karen and let her know he wouldn't be home. Of course, she would ask why. But lying to her shouldn't be a problem. She was used to it. And it wasn't like she had a way to leave. The subtle taste of the shot he had taken still lingered in his mouth. The wheel on his sobriety wagon was most certainly coming off, threatening to drop him into the sweet, soft grass of oblivion, and he couldn't wait. Maybe after a few drinks, he would bring out the special phone numbers that guaranteed company for the night. And why not? He would probably be dead in three days, anyway.

CHAPTER TWENTY-SEVEN

Go Wolves!

Agent Joyce Green sat at her computer surrounded by the latest technological catch-alls. Her office was done in a glacier white paint that sharply contrasted the dull gray carpeting. Against one wall stood a row of tan-colored metal filing cabinets, and hanging above them was a large marker board dividing the days of the month. Agent Wayne gave a quick knock on her open door.

"Agent Wayne," she said, swiveling around in her chair. "Come in and tell me some stories from the outside world."

Her pretty round face was bizarrely balanced by the wide-rimmed glasses resting on her nose, her long raven hair tied in a bohemian bun. She was wearing a loose-fit two-piece suit that seemed to swallow her body. Agent Wayne had long suspected that Agent Green was never one to relish attention, at least not that kind of attention. Maybe that's why they got along well.

"Would you take a look at these for me, please?" said Agent Wayne, placing the pictures on her desk.

"They look pretty old," she said.

"At least twenty-five years," said Agent Wayne.

"Looks like they came from an early nineties One Step Polaroid model," said Agent Green, holding up the one taken at the Dollar Store. "That woman has quite the chin."

"Yeah, that's who I'm looking for."

Agent Green pushed her glasses back up the bridge of her nose and said, "I might clear the photo a little and enhance her features."

"I'm more concerned about finding the location of this store."

"I see," said Agent Green. "Let me run this through the Epson, and we'll see what we can do."

Agent Green rolled her chair over to a large scanner at the end of her desk, opened the top, and placed the photograph face down on the glass surface. She then rolled back over and clicked a mouse, causing the monitor to come to life. Within seconds the picture appeared on the screen.

"And now for the magic."

Agent Green's fingers scrambled over her keyboard with blinding speed, and soon, the faded edges began to solidify into linear cohesion. After completing that, she enclosed the photo within a generated box and expanded the frame. Agent Wayne leaned in over her shoulder.

"Can you zoom in on the storefront?" he said. "Maybe closer to those flyers?"

Agent Green moved the cursor over to where three pieces of paper had been taped to the window and enlarged the section. The lettering was still too blurry to read.

"Hold on," she said, clicking away at the keyboard, focusing on the flyers, blowing them up until they filled the entire screen.

One was an advertisement for Clorox Bleach, and another was a picture of a smiling kid holding a half-gallon of milk.

But it was the third one that drew both agents' attention. It was larger than the other two and contained an image of a dog standing on a lone hill with a full moon hovering above it. Written across the poster board in bold purple letters were:

Homecoming Parade
September 15th
Go Wolves!

"That should narrow it down some," said Agent Green. "How many schools are in Oklahoma with Wolves as a mascot?"

"Let's find out," said Agent Wayne, grabbing an extra chair and sitting down.

"Give me a minute," said Agent Green, closing out of the printer screen and going online.

"Looks like there's three," she said, grabbing a pen and a pad of paper. "There's Edmond, Pawnee, and some place called Lost City."

"And I'm sure all of them have a Dollar Store," said Agent Wayne.

"Yep, but hold on," said Agent Green, her fingers moving like a virtuoso. "It looks like the one in Pawnee didn't open until '03."

"Well, at least that eliminates a third of the possibilities," said Agent Wayne. "Can you pull up that picture again and back out a little?

Agent Green popped the photograph up on the monitor, slowly backing off the image.

"Hold on," said Agent Wayne, pointing at the screen. "What is that?"

Agent Green produced another box near the spot he was pointing at, enlarging the section.

"Look there," he said.

"What am I looking at?" said Agent Green.

"That reflection on the window on the lower right side," said Agent Wayne. "Can you zoom in on that?"

Agent Green enhanced the section, and there, barely noticeable, was the faint image of a rear bumper, and on it was a license plate.

"Do you see it?" said Agent Wayne. "It must be parked on the far side of the lot."

"Give me a second," said Agent Green, and within moments, the plate filled the monitor, its numbers as clear as a newly printed magazine: 324AHY.

"Okay," said Agent Green. "What about it?"

"Let's run that plate," said Agent Wayne.

"Ah," said Agent Green. "Aren't you clever?"

She brought up the statewide register and typed in the plate number. The name Gladys Jones appeared within seconds, including the address: 12547 E. River Oaks Rd. Lost City, Ok. 74441.

"We have a winner," said Agent Wayne. "Where the hell is Lost

City?"

"With a name like that, it shouldn't be too hard to find," said Agent Green, again typing away on her overworked keyboard.

"Here it is," she said, leaning back so Agent Wayne could get a clear view. "It's about three hours from here, up by Tahlequah."

"Nice area," said Agent Wayne.

"It is," said Agent Green. "With plenty of places to get lost."

"Hence the name. Can you pull an image of Gladys Jones up for me?" said Agent Wayne. "Maybe I'll get lucky."

A few seconds later, an image of a pretty blond woman appeared on the monitor.

"I don't think it's her," said Agent Green. "Unless she had a lot of work done."

"Yeah," said Agent Wayne. "I never was lucky. That's why I stay out of casinos. I guess I know where I'm going tomorrow."

"Good luck with finding her," said Agent Green. "By the way, you owe me lunch."

Agent Wayne stood up and said, "Consider it done. I'll even let you choose between McDonald's or Burger King."

"Be still my beating heart," said Agent Green, rolling her eyes. "Let me know if you need anything else."

*****

Agent Wayne sat in the parking lot in the idling cruiser. He would have to make the drive to his apartment during rush hour. It mattered little; his day was done and all that was left to do was rest up for his early morning trip to Lost City. He gazed down at the photograph sitting next to him on the seat.

"What did you do to her, Charlie?" the agent said out loud.

The trip to Lost City would be the only blind cast he would make to find out. If it revealed nothing, he would have to confront Charlie Wheaton with the picture and hope he could maneuver through the web of lies the man would no doubt spin. Agent Wayne pulled out onto the Northwest Expressway and was immediately greeted by a mile-long line of red brake lights tapping precariously along at five miles an hour. He reached for the radio, switched on NPR, and mentally prepared himself for the long ride home.

CHAPTER TWENTY-EIGHT

Conversations

Marianna stood near the cell door, holding a tray containing a filet of smoked salmon, mashed potatoes, and a can of diet coke. Tucked under her arm were Jimmy's folded clothes. He sat on his cot, the towel still wrapped around his waist. The girl gazed at him, her off-centered eyes filled with what he could only assume was shy passion. Her throw-over dress had changed from blue to pink, her long, thin hair now free and hanging loosely over tilted shoulders.

"I have your clothes," she said, finally. "They're clean."

Jimmy just sat there looking up at her. She moved forward, placing the food tray in the slot, then slid the clothes through the bars. Jimmy stood, causing her to step back. He came over and grabbed his clothes off the floor. Her eyes followed him as he moved, making him feel like a zoo exhibit.

"Could you please turn around?" he said.

"Of course," she said.

He waited until her back was to him and then dropped the towel. He took his time, allowing his mind to work. This girl had picked him based on a referral from Charlie. Why? Did she think that he would make a fine addition to her family? Was it because of his looks? There had been a time when he considered himself quite the ladies' man, but even he had to admit that the years hadn't been as kind as they could have been. He wasn't quite thirty, and already his hair was crawling back, and the lines around his eyes had taken up permanent residence.

"Okay," he said, fastening the final button on his shirt.

Marianna turned around, her misshapen mouth curling into a smile.

"That's much better," she said. "You look handsome."

"Thank you," he said.

"You should eat," she said, nodding at the plate.

"Yes, boss," he said and walked towards the tray.

"You don't like us, do you?" she said.

"What's not to like?" said Jimmy, returning with the tray to the cot. "I mean, since I've been here, I've been raped and witnessed a murder."

"That woman was never supposed to die," said Marianna. "She shouldn't have tried to escape."

"And why would she do that?" said Jimmy, cutting into the salmon with a plastic fork.

"We're not monsters," she said. "We didn't want to keep her locked up for the rest of her life. We even let her out in the yard, but she was relentless. Every time Nith tried to love her, she would fight him."

"Imagine that," said Jimmy.

"We never wanted to have to do this," she snapped. "We had no choice."

"If there's one thing I've learned since being locked up here, it's that there's always a choice," said Jimmy, setting the tray to the side. "What you are doing is a crime."

"Spoken like a true plebe," said Marianne. "But for us—"

"Save the royalty speech," said Jimmy, cutting her off. "Your brother Phil told me all about it."

"Did he also tell you that my mother will kill you if you don't fuck me tomorrow?" she said, the shyness morphing into a savagery that chilled Jimmy's blood.

"I am aware," he said, trying to keep his voice level.

"I am going to assume that you want to live," said Marianna, her voice softening. "So let me give you some advice. When I come here tomorrow evening, you must do whatever it takes. Handle yourself if you need to, but you are going inside of me. Because if you don't, there will be nothing that Phillip or I can do to save you. My mother will release Nithard."

She stepped forward, placing her hands on the bars, her face drawn into a pained expression. "Do you understand what I am saying?"

"I think I get it," he said.

Marianna stepped back, her arms falling to her side.

"I could make you happy if you only let me," she said. "What do you really have to go back to?"

Jimmy sat there looking at the girl. Her features were like an artist's rendition of a Picasso nightmare. Her chin jutted out, showcasing her ivory-colored incisors. Did she realize just how unnatural she looked? Probably not. Her mother had instilled a lifetime of compliments that had little to do with reality, sheltering her from a world beneath them. Only now, they needed that world and the lower class it supplied.

"I have my life," he said, finally.

"And what a life it is," Marianna quipped, smiling. "You have an ex-wife who left you for a fat man whose only concern is himself. And even if we did free you, where would you go? How would you get there? You have nothing."

"Wow," said Jimmy. "You really know how to get to a man's heart."

"It's the truth," she said. "I'm offering you a better life. Can't you see that?"

"Okay," said Jimmy, scooting to the cot's edge. "But why me?"

Marianna looked down at him, her smile fading.

"When that fat man first told us about you and gave us your picture, my mother scoffed. She said that you would be no better than having Charlie. She thought you were nothing more than a booze-riddled womanizer who lived to lie. But I saw something else, I saw a man struggling to survive. A man surrounded by enemies disguised as friends, who went on day after day, unaware of the trap he was already in. You were oblivious, struggling to keep the very man who was ruining your life happy while he smiled and slowly ran a blade across your throat."

Jimmy found himself hypnotized.

"It was all so sad to me, but I couldn't blame Charlie, not really. You see, it's the world that created monsters like him. They have little choice but to do what they do." Here, she paused, letting out a sigh. "Can you understand what I'm trying to say? You are not innocent, just as they are not, but you were outnumbered, so I guess I felt sorry for you."

The wave of emotion that hit Jimmy was a surprise. He struggled to keep his lower lip from quivering, trying in vain to stop the well of tears from blurring his vision. Marianna had summed up the last part of his life with remarkable precision. Had reduced him to ashes, all within a few sentences. How long had he walked blindly as Charlie slept with his wife? How many distant and worthless appointments had he been sent to just so the asshole could get with Karen? And his loving wife had played an active part in his downfall. But Marianna's mother was right. Jimmy hadn't been innocent.

"So here we are," she concluded. "You are caged but free, and I am in love but unloved."

Jimmy reached over to the roll of toilet tissue beside the bucket, tore off a handful, and wiped his eyes. He found himself hoping that this girl would stay. She was an unexpected comfort, a small spark of light in this dark place, not just this place, but in a life that had been spiraling out of control for quite some time. But they were killers and rapists, he couldn't forget that, and he *had* been kidnapped. And what of the one that was not born to the outside? The child who had been pulled from the corpse of his murdered mother. He wasn't a part of the outside world, and yet his life was certainly doomed; doomed to be raised into this violence, doomed to partake in horrific crimes. Doomed to keep the Henley line going.

"How is the baby?" he said.

Marianna's face seemed to light up.

"He's doing well," she said. "He is a beautiful boy. I've never seen Nith so happy."

"And what about you?" he said. "What happens when he gets older?"

"What do you mean?"

"Will you be expected to have children with him?"

"It is expected," she said, coldly.

"And you're okay with that?"

"It is the way of God," she said, lowering her eyes. "We cannot go against His word."

"But what if we're married? I've been known to be jealous."

A sudden laugh escaped from Marianna.

"We will have plenty of time to worry about that. Besides, you should probably be more concerned with tomorrow."

That thought had been shelved away, at least momentarily, and now it surged forward, filling him with dread. Yes, tomorrow came down to life or death. This girl standing before him showed little nervousness, and Jimmy couldn't help but wonder why. She was expected to have sex with a stranger, someone that she had picked from a photo, like a mail-order bride. His life might be on the line, but their family's future would rest with her. Did this not trouble her? It had to.

"I know that if I fail, I'll die," he said. "But what happens to you?"

"We'll have to find another," she said.

"Just like that?"

"We have no choice," said Marianna.

"Did you and Nith ever–," said Jimmy.

"Of course," she said, her face pallid. "And it wasn't pleasant."

"What happened?"

For a moment, Jimmy didn't think she was going to answer and was about to change the subject, but then she said, "It took three painful attempts for my body to finally be able to accept him, and after I could, he was on me every night. Two months went by, but we couldn't conceive."

So, perhaps there was a little bit of jealousy fueling the giant's hatred towards him. It would explain the large man's desire to see him dead. A thought struck Jimmy, and he was surprised that he hadn't considered it before: What if she could not have children? If this were true, he would only have a couple of months to live.

"At first, my mother was sure that her past decision to be with my father had destroyed the family, but Phillip assured her he would find a way. He's very smart, my brother."

"So, I've noticed," said Jimmy.

"He ran some tests, and we discovered it wasn't because we couldn't conceive. It was because our bodies were rejecting each other. The DNA sequence was too close and was aborting the process before it could take. Do you understand?"

"I think I do," said Jimmy. "It sounds to me like nature had seen enough."

Marianna's eyes narrowed into dark slits, percolating that savagery from before. She clenched and unclenched her hands, and for a moment, Jimmy was sure that a visit from Nithard was soon to come. Suddenly, she let out a short laugh.

"I have to remember that you are funny," she said. "I like that."

"I'm sorry," said Jimmy. "I tend to become sarcastic when I'm scared."

"Don't be scared," said Marianna. "But you should learn to control that, especially around my mother."

"I'll try to remember that."

A voice rang down from the stairwell, "Marianna! You need to come up here!"

The voice held a cracked edge that could only belong to the evil queen.

"I'm coming, mother," Marianna said. She then looked back at Jimmy, and he noticed for the first time that her eyes were crystal blue.

"Are you done with your tray?" she said.

"Yes," he said, standing and walking to the cell door.

Marianna's hand shot through the bars like a coiled viper, coming to rest on his crotch. Jimmy resisted the urge to brush it away and calmly placed the tray in the slot. She began to rub his penis, gently gripping it through his slacks. A rush of nauseous heat surged through his body, and he felt himself beginning to become hard. Marianna continued to stroke him for a couple of seconds longer and then pulled her hand away.

"That was my personal test," she said, her glittering eyes now locked on his. "I don't think there will be a problem tomorrow, do you?"

Jimmy could only reply with a quick shake of his head, the air burning in his lungs.

"Marianna," the voice sounded from above.

"I'm coming," the girl shouted back, grabbing the tray and then turning towards the stairs. She left the dungeon without looking back, without saying another word. Jimmy stood there leaning against the bars, his heart pounding, his breath bellowing. How had she managed to do that? Jimmy had made a living for years by turning the negatives into positives. He had convinced those who balked at his proposal to reconsider and accept what he was offering on their own terms. All these tricks that Jimmy utilized, he had learned from the best. But he had never seen anything like this. Marianna had slithered through his barriers, brandishing compassion like a weapon, creating a comfortable net he could safely fall upon. And in the end, had managed to twist his own negative into a positive. All he had to do was look at the pulsing bulge in his pants to know that it was true.

Jimmy slowly turned away and walked back to the cot, his hand unconsciously covering the front of his pants.

A confused feeling swarmed over him as he sat down. On the one hand, he should be grateful that he now knew he could get it up for Marianna. But what did that say about him? Was he so fucked in the head that even a Neanderthal piece of ass could get him off? The girl was ugly, but she was also genuine and very smart. The way she had read Jimmy was like some kind of soothsayer. And it was that which had sparked his desire. He lay back on the cot, clutching the thin blanket, his mind whipping around like a tattered flag. Tomorrow they will come. Will they have them do it here? Will they send her in and then watch through the bars as if they were watching a couple of near-extinct animals?

Jimmy covered his eyes with the crook of his arm and shuddered.

CHAPTER TWENTY-NINE

Alone

Karen sat on the couch with her cell phone clutched in her hands. Charlie had finally gotten back to her, although it came in the form of a text message:

Going to have to stay the night in Lawton, it read. *Wife says her husband won't be back until then and he demands to see me or he won't pay.*

This was nothing new for Karen. How many nights had she spent alone while Jimmy claimed to be working? Or claimed to be detained by the weather or the promise of some big-ticket deal? It was familiar territory. So familiar that it triggered the dark emotions that she had fought so hard to suppress. It all felt so surreal. The entire day had been spent watching as the front glass was removed from the window frame and replaced. Only to be followed by a cleaning crew who carefully combed through the living room, removing all signs of the violent act from the night before. And through all this she had tried to keep Charlie informed, but he wouldn't answer her call.

Perhaps the mechanics had taken up more time than he had expected, forcing him to leave abruptly for Lawton, a three-hour drive filled with plenty of dead spots. Still, why would he not at least call to see how it was going? And what about her car? It occurred to her that she didn't even know what shop Charlie had taken it to. This realization caused her heart to race and her breath to quicken. The house suddenly felt small, enclosing her like a pit she had carelessly fallen into.

Karen stood up and walked over to the front door, slamming it open. Cold air rushed over her, allowing her a momentary reprieve from the panic that had seized her. But the fresh air and openness couldn't hold back the anxiety for long. There was no true freedom here. It was only a cruel portrait, like looking out the window of a jail cell.

Karen walked to the edge of the porch and sat down. An oncoming storm was momentarily lighting up the pitch-colored sky.

An image of Agent Wayne appeared in her mind, and she became frightened, not because of his warning but because he was just further proof that she could trust no one. He was playing her against Charlie, looking for cracks in an already corroded foundation. And yet, his voice had sounded genuinely concerned. Did she really believe that? Did she think that the man with the eagle eyes gave two shits about her? Did Charlie? Did Jimmy? Did anyone? Her worst enemy had always been trust. That, and an inherent lack of options.

I must not lie to myself; that money was not there before.

The inner voice had returned, speaking timidly as if checking to see if it was safe to come outside.

"I know it wasn't," she said, tears now blurring the distant skyline flashes. "But what am I supposed to do?"

The voice didn't seem to have an answer. No surprise there. The light from the open front door threw her shadow out into the void, illustrating the feeling of hopelessness that enveloped her. She gazed down at the phone still clutched in her hand. She had promised to check in with the agent. Would he call her if she didn't? And if he did, would she answer? Karen lowered her head, taking in a deep shuddering breath. Of course, she would answer. She would have to. She was, after all, involved in a murder investigation. The clock on the phone read 10:36. She scrolled through the numbers, stopping at Agent Wayne's. She paused only for a moment before typing:

Letting you know that I'm fine.

She then sent the message, waiting as the lie traveled through the towers and satellites until finally coming to rest at its intended destination: the screen of her enemy/friend. Karen then slowly rose on shaky legs and returned to the empty house, unaware that what little freedom she had was about to end.

CHAPTER THIRTY

Lost City

Agent Wayne left his apartment just as the sun broke over the eastern horizon. The storm had come and gone the night before, but fortunately, the temperature had remained above freezing. The day had started out promising; Karen had texted him the previous evening, which he found surprising and reassuring. He sent her one in return and again offered his assistance if she needed it, but his phone remained silent.

He passed through Tahlequah and caught State Highway 51 west. The scenery was a Rockefeller work filled with rundown houses. A place where intangible dreams seemed to flicker within the signs posted on the side of the highway in the form of bait shop advertisements and casino specials. And yet, this land held within it a unique charm if one only cared to look. It was a paradise of waterways and untethered wildlife that struggled to remain untouched.

These romantic notions looped through Agent Wayne's mind when the GPS informed him of the upcoming right turn. The agent eased off the gas just as an eroding pavement line became visible around a sharp bend. He eased into the turn, conscious of his soon to be tested front end suspension. After a mile, the road improved, and the agent could accelerate to the posted fifty-five. The sky had become an inviting blue, a cloudless tapestry that suggested a warmth that wouldn't be felt for another five months.

A sudden drop in the speed limit from fifty-five to thirty-five signaled the beginning of Lost City. The highway soon became the town's main street, with rundown brick-veneered buildings crumbling on each side. Boarded-up windows decorated many storefronts, their emptiness exuding a feeling of retreat and financial peril. This was one of many dying small towns nationwide. Their survival usually depended on cheap housing and buyers who weren't afraid to commute to the nearest big city. A dilapidated wooden structure on his left contained two aged police cars and a hand-painted sign that read Police Station. This would have to be his next stop if the store revealed nothing. He never liked to involve the local authorities in routine searches in small towns where everyone knew everyone, especially when the person in question had committed no crime.

Up ahead on his right, a large, yellow-lit board read Dollar Store. The agent pulled into the pitted pavement of the parking lot. The lot was mostly empty, with only a few pick-up trucks and a classically restored 1970's model Thunderbird.

A girl with blonde hair streaked with dark pink stood working behind the counter. She didn't raise her face from her cell phone as the double doors slid open. Agent Wayne paused momentarily, but she continued to type away on her screen. The agent made his way down the center aisle. After all, this was a day of long shots, and you never knew if you might get lucky. But all he saw was an extremely overweight woman in an electric wheel chair throwing a bag of chips into her basket and a young man with long black hair standing on a stool stocking toilet paper. He walked up to the kid, pulling out his ID.

"How are you?" he said, flashing his badge.

"Whoa," said the kid, dropping a bundle to the floor. "You scared the shit out of me."

"Sorry about that," said the agent, reaching down, picking up the paper, and then handing it back to the flushed kid.

"Are you okay?" said Agent Wayne, placing his wallet back into the inside pocket of his coat.

"Yeah," said the kid. "Did I do something?"

The agent smiled and said, "I don't know, did you?"

The kid shook his head.

"What's your name?"

"Dillon Smith," stammered the kid.

"Calm down, Dillon. I just want you to look at something for me."

He then pulled out the picture of the old woman glaring at the back of Charlie's head.

"Do you recognize this woman?"

Dillon looked at the photo for a moment.

"What's wrong with her?"

"Nothing that I know of," said the agent. "Have you ever seen her in here before?"

"Can I help you, sir?" said a voice from behind.

The agent turned and saw that it was the girl that had been behind the counter.

"Maybe you can," said the agent, approaching her. "I'm trying to find this woman. I know this is an old picture, but I was hoping that she might live around here."

The girl gazed down at the photo, and her face cringed as if she had been stung. The reaction was brief and quickly disappeared.

She then pointed at the kid and said, "Go man the register."

Dillon gave her a quick nod and then hurried off.

"You must be the boss," said the agent.

"I manage the store," she said. "Are you a cop?"

Agent Wayne again took out his ID.

"Why are you looking for her?" she asked after giving the badge a once over.

"I'm sorry," said Agent Wayne. "What is your name?"

"Lisa," said the girl. "Lisa Smith."

"Okay, Lisa. This woman isn't in any trouble. I just wanted to ask her a couple of questions. Do you know who she is?"

Lisa looked at him for a moment.

"I've never seen her before," she said, finally.

"Are you sure?"

"It's not like I could forget that face. This town only has about eight hundred people, give or take, and this is the only store in town."

The girl was lying. The agent didn't need to rely on any

extensive training to see that. The question was why?

"Listen, Ms. Smith," he said. "This woman could be in danger, and it's important that I speak to her."

Lisa broke out in laughter, then quickly fell silent.

"I told you I don't know her."

"Why did you laugh?" the agent said.

"I just can't imagine threatening someone with a face like that."

It was an awful thing to say and complete bullshit. But to continue with her would be pointless. The opportunity for the truth had passed. Agent Wayne reached into the inside pocket of his jacket and brought out one of his cards.

"If you decide to remember, would you call me?"

The girl ignored his jab and looked at the card with reservation.

"It won't bite," he said.

She snapped it out of his hand like it was contagious and quickly buried it in the back pocket of her jeans.

"Is there anything else?" said Lisa.

"Nope, I appreciate your help."

The agent pulled out of the Dollar Store parking lot with his gut tied in a knot. The girl's response to his question was contextually wrong. It was what you would expect from somebody harboring a fugitive. The lady in the photograph was a victim, so why would that girl's face flicker with fear when she saw the picture? No doubt she knew the woman or at least knew of her.

*****

Agent Wayne stopped next to one of the police cars and put his cruiser into park. He pulled out his phone, found the number he wanted, and placed the call.

"Agent Green."

"Hey, Agent Wayne here."

"How's life up in the mountains?"

"Strange, actually."

"Strange, like Deliverance strange? Or is it more like Twilight Zone strange?"

"I'm going to have to go with Twilight Zone for now," said Agent Wayne. "But that could change."

"Well, if it does, do me a favor and keep it to yourself. I'd like to keep my high regard for you."

"I assure you that I will," said Agent Wayne. "I need a favor."

"You know me," said Agent Green. "I live to serve. What do you have for me?"

"There's a girl; her name is Lisa Smith. She's probably in her mid to late twenties. Can you do background for me and see if anything comes up?"

"And is she in Lost City?"

"Yes," said Agent Wayne. "She runs the Dollar Store."

"Okay, give me a few minutes, and I'll get back to you."

"I'm about to step into the cop shop, so I better call you back."

"As you wish, my Lord," said Agent Green, and the line went dead.

*****

The station was a single-room facility decked in cracked wainscoting that edged along a heavily plastered wall. A single ceiling fan lazily spun on a warped bronze post, casting waves of yellow light. In the center of the room were two desks facing each other, each containing an outdated laptop with one dust-covered printer sitting off to the side. On one desk was a stack of board games, while on the other was a deck of playing cards and a small case containing poker chips.

Two uniformed men stood talking to each other at a wall-mounted bar near the corner of the room. One poured coffee into the other's cup just as Agent Wayne opened the door. The officer placed the pot back on the maker and made his way over to the desk that held the cards. He was a short, stocky man with copper hair fixed in a crew cut. His clean-shaven face held the reddish glow of either hypertension or a love of bourbon. He gave the agent a rehearsed smile as he fell into the chair.

"How can we help you?" he said in a voice two octaves higher than you would expect.

Agent Wayne brought out his ID. The officer gazed down, and as he did, Agent Wayne noticed the two bars pinned on the man's collar.

"I'm looking for someone, captain," said the agent. "I was hoping you might be able to help me."

"I'm Jake Carter," the captain said, then pointed to the other officer still standing, sipping on his cup. That's Officer Reynolds."

Agent Wayne gave him a wave, which was returned with a raised index finger.

"So," continued the captain, "who could possibly bring the OSBI out to our little town?"

"I'm looking for this woman," said the agent, handing the picture over.

"I can't imagine why."

"It's part of a murder investigation I'm working on," said the agent.

"You think she killed someone?"

"No," said the agent. "But she might have some information that could help."

"So, you think she lives here?"

"I just know the picture was taken at the store in town,' said Agent Wayne. "I started there."

"Really," said Captain Carter. "Who did you talk to?"

"Lisa Smith."

Captain Carter leaned forward in his chair and looked at the picture.

"Was she able to help you?" he said.

"Not really, although she seemed a little put out by my question."

"Lisa has always been tightly wound," said Officer Reynolds. "But that's what happens when you're put in charge of a Dollar Store."

"She did seem a little young," said Agent Wayne.

"But she's loyal," said Captain Carter. "And that can take you a long way in this world."

"I guess it can," said the agent. "What about the woman in the photo? Do you recognize her?"

"I'm sorry," he said. "I've never seen her before. She was probably passing through. A lot of people do."

"Probably," said the agent, *and I can see why.*

"Let me make a copy of this, and I'll ask around."

He stood and walked over to the dust-covered machine near the back wall. After the duplicate was spit out on the tray, he handed the agent the original.

Agent Wayne took the picture, pulled out a card, and placed it on Captain Carter's desk.

"I appreciate your time," he said.

"I'm sorry we couldn't be of any help," the captain said.

"It was a long shot," said the agent, turning to leave.

"One more question," he said, pausing. "How long have you been an officer here?"

Captain Carter ran his hand through his closely cropped hair.

"Damn, what's it been now? Twenty-three years this November. Why do you ask?"

"It just seems like an interesting place to live," said Agent Wayne. "I bet it has a low crime rate."

"You'd be surprised," said Captain Carter.

"I bet I would," said the agent.

He then opened the door and made his way to the Crown Victoria.

*****

Agent Green answered after the second ring. By then, Agent Wayne was making his way out of Lost City, and the knot in his stomach had now doubled in size.

"I have Lisa Smith's info," said Agent Green. "Did you have any luck with the locals?"

"Nothing that I can use," said Agent Wayne. "What did you find?"

"Well, our young woman is certainly no angel. She had her indoctrination into the system by way of becoming a ward of the state, thanks to her father's slippery hands. She then proceeded to explore methamphetamine and graduated by stealing his Thunderbird."

"Is she from Lost City originally?" said Agent Wayne.

"Yes, and you might find this surprising," said Agent Green. "Her criminal record has been erased."

"Wait, what?"

"Yeah, and she served two years in Bassett Girls Reformatory," said Agent Green. "She was released in 2014."

"How did you find this out?"

"I keep a historical record of past reports just in case."

"That's good thinking, although not exactly ethical," said Agent Wayne.

"It comes in handy," said Agent Green, "Wyatt, what's going on?"

"I'm not sure," he said. "I feel like I've driven into a dense fog up here," and then another thought struck him. "What year was that Thunderbird?"

He could hear Agent Green shuffling through some papers.

"'78," she said. "Why do you ask?'"

"A restored Thunderbird was sitting in the parking lot," said Agent Wayne.

"What are the odds?" said Agent Green.

"One thing that bothers me is how a girl with that kind of record could get a job running a Dollar Store?"

"Maybe she was hired after her record had been erased," said Agent Green. "It happened four years ago."

"Maybe," said Agent Wayne. "But this is a small town. There's no way it could be kept a secret. Do you feel like getting back into the outside world for a while?"

"You mean, like a real agent?" said Agent Green. "Do you think the powers that be will let me?"

"I think by the time you're done with them, they'll beg you to leave."

"What's your plan?" said Agent Green.

The plan wasn't exactly a stroke of genius, more like casting a line out into murky water. It was obvious that Lost City was a closed society priding themselves on the fact that they could keep a secret. It would do no good for him to go back. That much was clear; they had locked the door on him. But every house had a rear entrance, and with Agent Green's help, perhaps they might find it.

By the time he arrived at Motel 6 in Tahlequah and had booked two single rooms, Agent Green had received the go-ahead from 'the powers that be' and was leaving OSBI headquarters to pack a bag, sustainable for a week.

Across the street was a Wal-Mart. Since he had never relied on any real sense of style, agent Wayne decided to visit the store for a few articles of clothing and a toothbrush. He glanced down at his watch and saw that it was now getting close to mid-afternoon. That would put Agent Green's arrival right around six.

A grumble spoke out from his gut, and he realized that he hadn't eaten anything since that morning before he left his apartment. But he would wait for her to arrive and then offer to buy dinner. She, of course, would probably chide him for asking her out on a date, which, had they not been working out of the same office, could easily have been a possibility. Agent Joyce Green was as stunning as she was smart, and her mind was like a chess master's. The fact she had been downloading criminal files before they could be erased showed how she stayed two moves ahead. Perhaps with her here, they could devise a way to crack the hidden safe that was Lost City and find that back door.

CHAPTER THIRTY-ONE

Preparations

Marianna stood looking at her reflection in a full-body mirror. She was wearing a

ruffled robe, Valentes, which accented her breasts. She pushed them up a little more until her pale skin threatened to burst out of the embroidered lining. The dress was tightly clasped around the waist, causing her hips to flare. Grenalda stood behind the girl, fixing the young woman's hair.

"You are too good for this man," she said. "He doesn't deserve you."

"Mother, we don't have a choice, do we?"

Of course, she was right. Grenalda cursed herself for being so stupid. Why had she refused to do what was necessary back when she had the chance? They had told themselves it was because of God and their devotion. But eventually, she and her brother settled on love as the excuse. Now, as she looked at their daughter preparing to degrade herself for the sake of the family, she wondered if even that was true.

Damn, this curse! Why couldn't they be left alone? Why were they being forced to dilute their blood with outsiders, with inferiors? What kind of test was this? She must be careful; such thoughts bordered on blasphemy. Grenalda looked over her daughter's shoulder and forced a smile.

"You look beautiful," she said.

"I feel silly," said Marianne. "I hope he doesn't laugh."

"I'm sure he won't," said Grenalda. *Not if he wants to live.*

The liar was given Phillip's concoction with breakfast, which included a mild hallucinogenic mixed with Sildenafil. Right now, he was probably looking at his erect penis and wondering why it was talking to him.

There was a knock on the door.

"Mother," said Phillip. "We have a problem."

Grenalda gave Marianne a loving squeeze on her shoulder and said, 'I'm coming."

Phillip crouched in the hallway with a phone in his hand.

"It's Carter," he said.

Grenalda's eyes narrowed for a moment. The cop hardly ever called, and if he did, it was usually because he needed an advance on his already exorbitant salary.

Grenalda took the phone from Phillip.

"What is it?"

"There was a guy from the Oklahoma Bureau of Investigation here today," Carter said. "He was looking for you."

"For me?"

"Well, not by name."

Grenalda felt a flood of ice release in her veins.

"What did he say?"

"That he was investigating a murder and that you might have some information."

A pain in her hand suddenly raced up her arm, and she realized that she was now strangling the phone. She forced herself to take a deep breath and relaxed her grip.

"He had an old picture of you outside the Dollar Store. I made a copy."

"Is there anything else?"

"He talked to Lisa," said Carter. "But he claims she didn't tell him anything."

"Do you think that she would?"

"Why would she?" said Carter. "After all you've done for her. I think her loyalty is with you."

And what of yours? Grenalda thought to herself but said, "I tend to agree with you. I want to see that picture."

"I'll text it over."

The line went dead, and Grenalda looked down at Phillip, his usually pallid skin now flushed.

"This isn't good," he said. "Why would they be looking for you?"

"I have my suspicions," she said.

The phone signaled the incoming message then. Grenalda gazed down at the screen, and her suspicion was proven correct.

"Charlie," she hissed and then handed Phillip the phone.

Phillip looked at the picture, turning it from the left to the right.

"It's no secret how they figured out where the store was. I'm pretty sure those flyers say it all. But who took the picture?"

"I guarantee you it had to do with that fat man's wife," said Genalda. "Probably her family."

"Do you think the OSBI has figured it out?"

"That's the problem," said Grenalda. "Are they looking into Charlie's wife or the old bitch from where we got the liar?"

"We need to find out," said Phillip. "Maybe we can have Carter look into it."

"Yes," said Grenalda. "Give him a call. It's time for the liar to prove himself."

"You're still going through with this?" said Phillip. "After what we just learned?"

"Nothing has changed," said Grenalda. "If anything, our situation has become more urgent. Besides, Marianne has prepared herself, and the drugs you gave him should be at their peak."

*****

Marianna led the way down the hall. Grenalda followed close behind with a .32 tucked in the side pocket of her throw-over dress. Her mind clicked back and forth between Carter's call and the task at hand. Getting involved with Charlie had been a mistake. His aptitude for fucking things up was habitual. A moment of self-pity gripped Grenalda. She was never supposed to lead this family. That honor had been bestowed upon her brother, who handled the job with almost perfect precision, expanding their vast investments and venturing into new territories. He was a chronic miser who kept only the family in mind. Of course, he would have to die. Why would God have it any other way?

"Mother," said Marianna, snapping Grenalda back from her misery. "I'd like to go down there alone."

"Absolutely not," snapped Grenalda. "What if he hurts you?"

"He won't," said Marianna.

"How can you be sure? This man could use you to try to get out."

"And just how far do you think he would get?"

"I don't like this, Marianna. It would be better if I were there to watch over you."

"No, it wouldn't," said Marianna, her eyes dropping. "Not for me."

"I understand how you feel, but I can't let you go into a cage with this man alone."

"You can stand at the base of the stairs," said Marianna. "I just don't want anyone watching."

Marianna was not like her brother Nith. She didn't relish perversion or become aroused by others' suffering. She was a good person. That wasn't always a good thing. It sometimes left Grenalda feeling a little envious and guilty because she realized that she wanted to watch—wanted to see this subhuman enter her daughter in a cage. How did that picture into the path of the chosen laid before them? Grenalda decided to fall to her knees later and ask for an answer.

"I'll wait for you at the base of the stairs," she said. "But I will be listening, and if I hear anything other than passion, I will kill him."

They reached the end of the hall, and Grenalda spun the wheel, unlatching the metal door. She pulled it open and motioned her daughter through. The next few minutes would say much about the future of the family. Would say much about the future of the liar waiting down below. But no matter how this went, there was still the OSBI to deal with. Them and that bastard Charlie. What had he told them? Surely, they knew that the liar's ex-wife was shacked up with him. They had probably questioned her, as well. What had she told them? She could say little about the family unless Charlie had told her.

Would he? Grenalda didn't think that he would. What would be the point? Still, he was an idiot, and she did not doubt that he would sell them all out if it meant his freedom. Perhaps that was what he wanted the girl for: a playing piece in case things went south. The benefits of having the liar's ex-wife continued to add up. Only now, it seemed that the best thing to do was to keep her hidden and unharmed. Would she be able to keep Nithard off her until the heat was off? She would have to. One way or the other.

They had reached the bottom of the stairs, and Grenalda forced herself to stop. Around the lava corner was the liar. The man her daughter had picked from a picture to breed with. She reached into her pocket and felt the reassuring cold of the .38.

"Go on," she said, handing her the key to the cell. "I'll be right here if you need me."

Marianna continued, turning the corner, and was soon out of sight. Grenalda eased herself onto a stair, her thoughts returning to the fat man. Once this was over, she would have to place a call. If she were right about Charlie, there would be no way that he would give up his insurance. But that mattered little. One way or another, that pretty girl would be coming home with her.

CHAPTER THIRTY-TWO

Time to Shine

They were coming.

Jimmy took in a deep breath and unconsciously reached for his penis. It felt like iron, detached from the fear now flooding over him.

An image of the giant glaring down at him as he entered his sister caused Jimmy's stomach to clench. For a moment, he was sure that he felt himself begin to soften.

Don't think of him, he said to himself as he gripped his penis, tugging at it.

Close your eyes, think of Karen, and get it over with quickly.

That was the key. Never once did they say Marianne had to enjoy it.

Marianna appeared dressed as if she had arrived from the French Revolution. Her hair was done up in a beehive, and the tops of her breasts glistened from a low-cut dress. Jimmy struggled to grasp through the thick fog, leaning closer, unsure if what he was seeing was real. Within moments, the dominant chin filtered through the drug-induced shroud, and he could see her crystal blue eyes, like a pair of watch towers beaconing through the night.

"Marianna," he said, but it wasn't a question. It was more like a statement of relief.

There was an undeniable excitement that had seized him upon realizing that she was there, that she was real. Strange that he seemed to long for his captor's company, her conversation. But what of her touch? It was then he noticed that she had come alone. There was no evil queen or hulking giant to dissuade him with a look. He watched in silence, his hand still unconsciously clutching his erection, as she slid the key into the lock and opened the cell door.

She came in, shutting the cage behind her, then walked and sat beside him. A fragrance of vanilla mixed with crushed roses filled Jimmy's nose, sending a shiver down his spine. The smell was a welcome change from the chemical-laden room fused with his shit pail. Marianne reached out, placing her hand on his knee.

"Are you ready?" she said, eyes locking onto his.

"I have to be," he said.

Marianna traced her hand up his thigh, brushing away his hand.

"It feels like you are," she said.

She then stood up and took him by the hand, forcing him to follow. Her offset eyes continued to look into his as she slowly undid the button of his slacks, neither moving as they fell to the floor. Jimmy's penis sprung out like a man who had finally broken the surface of a deep lake. Marianna again took him in her hand and began to stroke. A sudden heat erupted, and Jimmy felt his pulse beginning to quicken. Marianna pushed him gently back onto the cot, his head barely missing the jagged rock that made up the back wall. She then lifted her leg over him, straddling just inches above his erection, and raised her dress.

Jimmy lay there in conflict. The horror of his reality was being pushed to the side by an overwhelming lust. How could this be? This went beyond anything that her brother Phillip had given him. The drugs might cause physical effects, but what of this desire that had overwhelmed his mind? Marianne slowly dropped to where he could feel her pressing against him, her warmth lingering above him like a much-needed blanket.

"It's our first time," she murmured. "So, I don't–"

Without realizing what he was doing, Jimmy reached up, grabbed her by the hips, and thrust. Marianne let out a moan, her eyes widening with surprise. She struck out with both hands, gripping

Jimmy's shirt, her eyes now shut, her body matching his movement.

His plan for making it quick was forgotten. Time had lost all relevance. All that mattered was pleasing this woman; the question of why was discarded. Without any signal, Jimmy turned Marianna onto her back, seizing her legs and placing them on his shoulders.

Marianna began to shiver underneath him, rocking up her hips. She let out a cry of pleasure, which only caused Jimmy to thrust harder. A rush of heat burst through him, and he fell onto her, grabbing her from underneath, his orgasm seizing his body, leaving him spent.

They lay there with arms still wrapped around each other, Marianna's legs resting on his thighs. Finally, Jimmy rolled off her, his back resting against the lava rock. Marianna gazed up at the ceiling, her breath coming in deep pants, her face flushed. Jimmy felt his breath ripping like fire in his lungs.

After a moment, Marianna sat up, adjusting her dress. Jimmy felt an odd desire to reach out to her, to keep her from leaving. Instead, he said, "I hope I passed the test."

"Oh, you did," she said, rising from the cot. She then leaned down and kissed him on the cheek. "I'll see you tomorrow."

"Do you have to leave?" he said.

"I have to check on the baby," she said, giving him a slanted smile. "But I'll be back."

She then let herself out of the cell, locking it behind her.

Yes, she would have to return at least until his job was done. But, of course, if he had done that job right, they would soon be married, at least in the eyes of the cruel queen, and then what? Perhaps they would grant him guarded trips into the yard, or his own television set mounted across the chasm. It didn't matter. He had performed and, by doing so, would survive. The aftermath of sex coinciding with the coming down from whatever he had been given was like a weight. He soon felt his eyelids beginning to fall. He had just enough energy to pull up his pants before a dreamless slumber took him.

*****

Grenalda had sat listening to her daughter's and the liar's sounds in silence. It was disturbing to think they were enjoying what should have been no more than a business transaction. She waited silently as the moans and groans filled the dungeon like one of Nith's movies that he liked to watch when he thought no one was around. Grenalda couldn't help but feel a little disappointed. She had been sure that the idiot in the cell would fail and had been looking forward to watching the man die. But she had been wrong. Just like she had been wrong about so many other things. Charlie was a good example. The fat man had brought the law down upon them, either knowingly or unknowingly. She would bet that it was the latter; such was the level of his stupidity. And now she would have to figure out how to clean up his mess. One thing was for sure: her involvement with Charlie Wheaton was coming to an end.

A crescendo caused her to rise. It echoed off the lava rock and then died. She sank back down, fighting the urge to creep around the corner. Marianna had agreed to this horror with only one stipulation: to go into it alone. She would honor her daughter's request; it was the least Grenalda could do. The sound of a turning lock soon followed a grind of turning metal. Seconds later Marianna appeared, her hair disheveled, her face the color of an outdated apple.

"Well?" said Grenalda.

"He more than served his purpose," said Marianna.

"Do you think he'll be able to do it again?"

"I think he wants to,"

"Good," said Grenalda, waiting as Marianna began to ascend the stairs. "That's one less thing we have to worry about."

But there was still Charlie. It was time to make a call.

CHAPTER THIRTY-THREE

Charlie Gets a Call

The man in the mirror seemed to have aged ten years overnight. The flushed round face had hollowed into a pallid hue. The eyes were splattered and bloodshot, poorly disguising the fear that had been drowned out the night before. Charlie had left Gloria snoring in bed and raced into the bathroom, barely making it to the toilet before his stomach ejected the leftover whiskey and shrimp tail they had shared from the night before. Strange that he had called her. As far as paying for sex was concerned, there were plenty of better-looking and younger women out there who would have loved a chance at his thousand dollars. And they would have had all their teeth. But this went beyond getting off. He needed a shoulder to cry on, and although it still cost him, the woman always seemed to listen. Not that he told her the truth. Charlie knew better than that. Gloria did work for the very man that was going to kill him, after all. And yet, she managed to comfort him, and it was the thought that counted.

"Are you all right?"

Charlie gazed at the doorway and saw her standing there, looking like she had aged a little. The late morning light from the bathroom window cast shadows across her face, revealing the early forties wrinkles that she tried so hard to hide.

"I drank too much," he said.

"You're a beast," she said.

Charlie gave her a weak smile and said, "Listen, I've got to get to work."

"Hey, I know when I'm not wanted."

"It's not that," said Charlie. "And believe me, if I could stay with you forever, I would."

This produced a grin that seemed to wash away fifteen years, except for the lack of incisors.

"Why, Charlie, that's about the nicest thing anyone has ever said to me."

"If that's true, I'm sorry about your luck."

This caused her to break out in a laugh. Charlie smiled and realized that this was why he had called her: She made him feel good. Gummy Bear had a way of making him forget the troubles of the world. He watched as she got dressed. She put on her last high heel and then walked over to where he was now leaning in the bathroom doorway.

"I don't know what's going on," she said, throwing her arms around his substantial mid-section. "But I heard rumors at the club."

Here, her eyes changed into fearful sincerity. "Don't fuck with Ben, Charlie. He's crazy, and he's a killer."

"Yes," said Charlie, patting her on the ass. "I'm aware of that."

Gloria seemed to want to say something else but instead reached up, kissing him lightly on the mouth, and then turned away. She grabbed her purse off the table and made her way to the hotel door, opening it, and then paused.

"Be careful, Charlie," she said, and then she was gone.

*****

Charlie lay back on the bed. Obviously, Ben was a killer. The video had made that quite clear. But setting up the family seemed even more dangerous. How could he find out where they lived? He couldn't ask the old hag; that would be signing his own death warrant. Maybe he could try to set up a meeting and then follow them. Of course, they would know he was behind them; it's not like he was an expert spy.

A knock on the door caused him to stifle a yelp.

"Room Service."

"I don't need any," he said, his mind shifting into panic.

Could Gloria have been a mole? What if she told Ben that he had called her?

"Sorry to bother you," the voice answered.

For a moment, he sat there, expecting the door to burst open. He could see the leather jackets piling into the room; guns thrust forward, looking for their target. But it didn't happen. That wasn't Ben's style. He would want Charlie's death to be a lesson for the next guy, complemented with popcorn. He briefly wondered how many videos Ben had in his collection of death. Did he already have a slot picked out for Charlie in his library? Charlie gazed up at the digital clock on the television: 11:28 AM.

Noon was closing in, and he still hadn't turned on his cell phone. It sat three feet away on the nightstand like an electronic Pandora's Box. Once he turned it on, once that box was opened, he would be fair game to whatever secret virus the damned thing held, and then there would be no turning back. He closed his eyes and let the recurring fantasy of packing a bag and catching a flight out of this nightmare play out in his mind.   Only this time, he had company.

Gloria had met him at the airport, her new ivory implants beaming from fluorescent lights hanging from the high ceiling of a portal. But just as her arms were about to meet his, her head exploded, throwing chunks of bone and brain all over his face. He wiped his eyes clean and saw Ben holding the .45 that he seemed to love so much. Only his face had changed. It was no longer human but that of a hyena, and he began to laugh.

Charlie's eyes shot open. His body was drenched in a cold sweat that held the rotten aroma of stale bourbon. The clock read 12:46 PM. He had passed out for over an hour.

By now, he was sure that the office was nearing a chaotic walkout. Karen was probably having a panic attack, and Ben was still waiting. And still, Charlie refused to open the box. Instead, he picked up the motel phone and waited for the front desk to answer. Ten minutes later, he opened the door to receive another fifth of Jim Beam. Pandora's Box would have to be opened, but that didn't mean he would have to do it alone. Jim had always been a friend.

After his third drink, he turned on the cell and was immediately assaulted by a string of alerts. Three missed calls and two text messages from Karen. Four missed calls and two voice messages from the office. But nothing from Ben. There was another number that he didn't at first recognize, and it was only after he placed the phone back on the nightstand that it came to him. He grabbed the phone, found the messages, took a deep breath, and pressed play.

The voice held the unmistakable rasp of the old woman: *Call me,* was all she said.

Charlie had to fight back the urge to once again race into the bathroom. He forced himself to take long, deep breaths and waited for the fire in his stomach to assuage.

Why the fuck would she be calling him? The fear of being set up briefly entered his mind, but that was ridiculous. At this point, it was clear that Ben had his own agenda.

The glass still contained a three-finger shot, and he quickly killed it. He then filled the glass and took another drink. He found the number and initiated the call.

"Charlie," the voice on the other end hissed.

"Mrs. Henley. I'm sorry I missed your call. I was with a client."

"I could care less," she said, and Charlie took another drink. "We have an issue. The OSBI has been looking for me. Specifically an Agent Wyatt Wayne."

Like gasoline catching, heat bubbled Charlie's skin, and he had to place the drink on the nightstand with a trembling hand.

"What do you know about this?"

"This agent is looking for Jimmy. He thinks Jimmy killed that woman."

Silence followed. Charlie could hear a baby crying faintly through the phone.

"What did you tell him?" said Grenalda, finally. "I want the truth, Charlie."

"I told him I didn't know anything," said Charlie, gazing back at the drink. "He seemed to believe me."

"He has a picture of me with you taken years ago," said Grenalda. "How do you suppose he got that?"

Charlie risked a spill and took another drink. The bitch could be lying, but he doubted it. That fucking agent was clever. He remembered after his wife died, thinking that he was being followed. He could never prove it and eventually brushed it off as paranoia. But now it seems as though his fear had been justified.

"It had to be Sarah's family," he said. "They were spying on me."

"And they gave him the picture?"

"They had to," he said. "Who else could it be?"

"What about his wife? Is she still with you?"

"Yes," he said. "She's at my house as we speak."

"I want her," the woman wheezed.

Charlie's chin dropped as if unhinged. She was going for his alibi, his get-out-of-jail-free card. The sinister cunt knew it, too. She was making a play for the very same reason.

"Do you think that's a good idea?" he said. "I mean, that agent has talked to her. Hell, he probably still is."

"But you don't know that for a fact, do you?"

"Well, no. But I'm pretty sure that he is."

"And that's why I want her, Charlie. Because you don't know. This Agent is moving in, and you can't even tell which way the wind is blowing because you're an idiot."

Charlie shot the rest of his drink down and stifled a cough. Never had this woman talked to him like this before. He knew she looked down on him as an inferior, but she looked down on everyone like that. But never had she exploded on him with such rage. They had burned that woman and her house just so they could get what they wanted. What would they do to him? Then there was Ben waiting in the shadows with his trusty .45.

Suddenly, it was there. Like a mountain on the horizon. The epiphany struck him with hammer force, and he almost laughed. It would be like the old 'killing two birds with one stone' adage. And if he set it up just right, he might be able to take that flight out of here with Gloria scandal-free. Because, in the end, that's all he wanted: To get out. He could see that now. The business could be sold, and he already had enough money to live comfortably, especially in some third-world country. Would Gloria come? Why wouldn't she? Her money maker was deteriorating with each day that went by.

The old bitch with the extended jaw wanted Karen, and she

would have her. He would give her the ticking bomb and then watch
as the walls came tumbling down.

"When do you want her?"

CHAPTER THIRTY-FOUR
Agent Green Makes Contact

Agent Joyce Green looked anything but professional as she pulled into Lost City in the '92 Ford Bronco her father had left her. Her pleated slacks had been replaced with tight-fitting Wrangler's, tucked into a pair of Justin Ropers one size too big. An extra-large T-shirt with Tulsa County Fair emblazoned across the front hung loosely off her shoulders. Her dark hair was now in a horse tail, with the length threaded through the back of her fake diamond studded baseball cap. She had started her morning visiting the Goodwill store in Tahlequah, picking up the ensemble while Agent Wayne struggled not to laugh.

"If you had just done your job right," she said, shooting him a grin as she was trying on the hat. "I wouldn't have to look like a tossed-out rodeo queen."

"Ouch," said Agent Wayne. "Somehow, I don't think those glasses are going to compliment your attire.,"

"That's why I always carry contacts," she said, taking off her Zelool frames.

He had doubts about the plan but, in the end, had agreed. It was, after all, her plan and one that she put together based on the information that she had gathered about Lisa Smith. The girl had been broken at an early age, betrayed by her father, who, instead of consoling her after her mother's death, chose to use that opportunity to molest his only daughter. The son of a bitch was sick, and apparently, he was dead, as well. He had been found in a ravine on the outskirts of town with his head separated from his body. Lisa, who was incarcerated then, had nothing to do with it. His murder had never been solved.

"Much like Charlie's wife," Agent Wayne had said.

"Do you think there's a connection?" said Agent Green.

"It feels like there is," said Agent Wayne.

"The truth is out here," said Agent Green. She then whistled the theme to the X-Files.

For those unfortunate souls who had suffered the abuse like Lisa Smith, there was always an issue of trust. And not just trust, but a searing anger that derailed any attempt at trying to heal. Their lives had become a track filled with hurdles, each one becoming a little higher than the next until they were finally forced to stop and accept the person they had become. And before you knew it, a wall was built, encircling and suffocating. But no one wanted to be alone; it went against human nature. What was needed was a person who carried similar pain-filled baggage. A shoulder both offered and needed. At least that was what Agent Green was banking on as she pulled into the Dollar Store with tears (thanks to two years of high school drama) now flowing freely down her face. The double doors opened as she approached. Her hand was wiping her eyes as she went to where Lisa sat, gazing at her with concern.

"Can I help you find something?" she said.

"What aisle is your tissue on?" said Agent Green.

"Aisle four," said Lisa, standing up and coming around the counter. "Hold up, and I'll show you."

Agent Green followed her through the store, stifling a sob here and there. Lisa led her to where a row of Kleenex stood stacked between rolls of paper towels and Charmin toilet paper. She grabbed one of the boxes off the shelf and quickly opened it, handing Agent Green a couple of sheets.

"I'm sorry," said Agent Green. "How much do I owe you?"

"We'll ring it up in a minute," said Lisa.

Just then, the double doors slid open, causing Agent Green to flinch. An old man entered the store, grabbed a cart, and then proceeded to amble his way over to the beer cooler.

"Are you okay?" said Lisa.

"I'm sorry," said Agent Green. "I'm just having a rough time right now."

"Is someone following you?"

Agent Green looked at her for a moment, her lips quivering.

"It's okay," said Lisa. "You can tell me."

"It's my husband," said Agent Green. "I was pregnant, which was the only reason that he was keeping his hands off of me, and now I'm not."

"You had an abortion?"

"God, no," said Agent Green. "I lost it, and when he finds out, he'll kill me."

"When did this happen?"

"Four days ago. I waited until today, after he went to work, and packed my bags and left."

Lisa looked out the large front window and saw the old Ford Bronco in the lot.

"Where did you come from?"

"Oklahoma City," said Agent Green. "I don't know why I went this way. I don't know anyone. I just needed to get away."

"What about your mom and dad?"

"Don't get me started," said Agent Green, rolling her eyes. "My mom died when I was thirteen, and my dad is an alcoholic who likes to get a little too friendly."

Lisa's eyes widened.

"Do you have anywhere to stay?"

"I was hoping to find a motel, but the only one I saw said there was no vacancy."

"Don't worry," said Lisa. "I know the owner."

She then pulled her cell phone out of her back pocket. She walked a few feet away from the agent and spoke in a low voice. A minute later, Lisa came back with a smile on her face.

"You're all set,' she said. "Just go to the front office and talk to Larry. He'll have a key waiting."

"Oh my God," said Agent Green. "Thank you so much. I don't have much money."

"Don't worry about it," said Lisa. "The first nights on me."

"You don't have to do that," said Agent Green.

"It's okay," said Lisa. "I know what it's like to have a shitbag for a dad. By the way, my name's Lisa."

Agent Green shook her hand and said, "I'm Joyce Hicks, and the least I can do is buy you a drink."

"That would be great, except we don't have any bars in this town."

"That sucks," she then looked over at the cooler stacked with beer. "How about I get us a twelve-pack? Unless you have to get home."

"Nope, I don't answer to anyone," said Lisa. "But I don't close until nine."

"That's fine," said Agent Green. "It's not like I'll be sleeping."

"Okay then," said Lisa. "You're in room two. I'll come by after I get out of here."

Agent Green left the store with a plastic bag containing a twelve-pack of Coors Light, an open box of Kleenex, and a smile. The ice had been broken, and she could tell that the girl wanted to talk...needed to talk. She would continue with her sad tale, watching Lisa's face, and then, when the time was right, she would let the girl chime in. It would no doubt be shaky initially, but she was sure that she would know Lisa's life story within an hour.

*****

Agent Green opened the lobby door and saw an old man hovering over a glass counter. He reminded her of the butler from The Rocky Horror Picture Show.

"Are you Lisa's friend?" he said, and even his voice held that eerie hissing quality.

"I guess I am," she said.

"Here's the key," he said, holding out the chain. "You're in room two, just down the way."

"Do I need to sign anything?"

"Nope," said the creepy old man, and Agent Green had to stop herself from shuddering as his eyes took a tour of her body. "Lisa's got it covered."

She took the key out of his hand and said, "I think I'm going to like this town."

"Sure, you will," he muttered.

Agent Green turned and made her way out of the lobby, thankful that her long t-shirt covered her ass.

The room smelled of moldy socks blended with Febreze and Lysol. The bed was made and looked like it hadn't been used in months. A layer of dust covered the top blanket, and Agent Green could only hope that whatever might have resided within its fibers was now dead. She walked over, turned on the heating unit mounted on the wall, pulled out her phone, and texted: "I'm in and have a room at the Lost City Motel, compliments of our girl.

She then sent the message to Agent Wayne and quickly deleted it. The clock read 3:37, leaving her five and a half hours to kill before Lisa closed shop.

She fished around in her purse and found an energy bar. It would have to do for now.   There were no restaurants in Lost City, so she would either have to go back to the Dollar Store or head over to the gas station for food. She would worry about that later; right now, she wanted to drive around the community and learn a little more about its layout.

*****

Thirty miles to the east, Agent Wayne was shuffling through a pile of papers on the bed of his motel room. He adjusted them into a timeline, starting with the news clippings concerning the death of Charlie's wife. He then placed the two pictures featuring the chin-heavy woman next to those. He had removed a sticky pad of yellow paper and filled in the gaps. One was the date of Lisa Smith's arrest and release, which he placed after the photo of Charlie and the old woman taken at his newly purchased office. Another sticky note contained the date of Sarah Wheaton's father's death. He placed it between the photos and Lisa Smith. Just for the hell of it, he pulled up the missing customer's name from Broken Arrow on his laptop and wrote down her information, placing it at the tail end of the line. Then, of course, there was Jimmy and the murdered woman.

All of them revolved around Charlie Wheaton. At least so it appeared. And yet, there were holes within the structure. As far as he could tell, Lisa Smith had nothing to do with Wheaton. She was only a kid when those pictures had been taken. But her reaction when he showed her the photograph was textbook. Lisa was hiding something.

An alert came from his phone. Agent Wayne looked down at the screen and smiled; the hick had made contact. Perhaps her plan would work. Maybe she could find that back door and at least learn the name of the mysterious woman. Agent Wayne removed the sticky note containing Lisa Smith and looked at the fractured line-up.

He stood up and made his way to a mini fridge, grabbed a soda, and then paused. The fat man was the common denominator, but he wasn't the only one. Take Lisa and Wheaton's missing customer out of the equation. What did you have? A thought burst through like light flooding a cave. The woman in the picture was undoubtedly livid with Charlie, and he had assumed, much like Mrs. Devos, that she was a victim of one of his scams. But what if it was because of something else?

He plopped back down on the bed and logged into Oklahoma's business records. Charlie had a partner called HS Corporation. Agent Wayne typed in the name and waited. He felt his heart quickening its pace while the buffering circle spun. Finally, a page full of information covered his screen. HS had been started over seventy years ago by a man named Charles Henley III, but it was never opened to the public. Instead, it seemed to have been whisked away into a shroud of secrecy. The name or names of its owner were undisclosed, although it listed the many assets it held. At least a dozen small oil companies HS had stock in or owned outright. These were spread across Oklahoma and Texas. There was stock in McDonalds that dated back to the fifties, which made them wealthier than everyone combined in the state. They had even bought into Microsoft in the early nineties. But their location was hidden. Their address was a list of PO boxes: Oklahoma City, Tulsa, Dallas, and Corpus Christi.

The only way to find out more about them would be to get a court order, and without a reason, it would never happen.

Just another long shot gone to shit, he thought to himself and was just about to close out of the search but paused.

The long list of acquisitions was overwhelming; it was no

wonder that he had almost missed it. Near the middle of the second column, in small, almost irrelevant print were the words Dollar Store (Lost City, Ok.)

Why would a company worth billions of dollars trouble with some hillbilly store in the middle of nowhere? Another thought struck him, and he typed in businesses located in Lost City. There were only a few, one of those being the Lost City Motel. He brought the HS Corporation's assets back up. Sure enough, it was listed. And not only that but Diamond's Filling Station and Cora's Floral Design.

But she's loyal, Captain Carter had said. And that can take you a long way in this world.

Indeed, it could, especially if you were paid to keep your mouth shut.

HS Corporation seemed to own the town, and Agent Wayne was sure Captain Carter and his trusty sidekick were part of the package, meaning Agent Green might have just walked into a snake's den. He glanced at the clock on the television: 3:48. He reached for his phone and found her number.

*****

There was freedom that came with driving around aimlessly. Agent Green took note of the rundown single-wides and the near washed-away structures that littered the scenery. This country was about as pretty as any land could get, but it was tainted by poverty, often followed by neglect. Still, she found herself fantasizing about living here, surrounded by the creaking wood of an old ranch home while outside her pair of Palominos (she had never even been on a horse) rushed by her flamboyantly large bay window. She struck the image down, forcing herself to focus on the job.

Lisa wanted to talk and most likely thought she had found a soul mate. Someone with whom she could share the grief and anger that had made her what she was. This didn't make Agent Green feel good; manipulating this poor girl to further a case was a step over the moral line. Yet, Agent Wayne said something was off about this place, and his gut was usually right.

It was then that her phone began to ring.

"Joyce Hicks, how can I help you?"

"Good one," said Agent Wayne.

"Did you find something?"

"Maybe," said Agent Wayne, filling her in about the HS Corporation and their odd interest in Lost City.

"Did you find anything out about its founder?" said Agent Green.

"Just that he started it back in nineteen-forty-nine."

"You might type in his name," said Agent Green. "You never know."

"What the hell," said Agent Wayne and she could hear the clacking of his keyboard.

"Holy shit."

"Did you find him?" she said.

"I didn't find him, but I found her, or at least a spitting image of her from about three hundred years ago."

"What are you talking about?"

"I'm sending it over to you," said Agent Wayne. "Check it out and call me back."

The line then went dead before she could respond. Within seconds, her phone beeped, and she gazed at the picture he had sent. It was a portrait of a man dressed in flowing robes. On his head was a crown, but his face was distorted with flattened cheeks and eyes that protruded well past normal. But it was the chin that caught her attention. The man was a mirror image of the woman that they were searching for. She widened the image, focusing on the words written near the bottom: King Lionus II of Spain. She had seen this image somewhere before but couldn't place it.

Agent Wayne picked up on the first ring.

"You don't seriously think they're related, do you?" she said and was answered by laughter.

"Was that funny?"

"Actually, yes," he said. "I just finished reading up on King Lionus. Guess what family line he comes from?"

"I have no idea," she said.

"The Henley's," he said.

"Like...THE Henley's? Like the Queen of Austria and the Romanovs Henley's?"

"The very same," said Agent Wayne. "And get this, they were quite fond of each other, which explains their odd looks. They even have a chin named after them."

Suddenly, it all came back. It was during her first year of college. She had been forced to take European History and had surprisingly enjoyed it. One reason was that she stumbled across the Henley name during her last semester. The family was eccentric because they were determined to keep their bloodline pure while unknowingly polluting their gene pool. It was the perfect example of irony. She remembered reading that hemophilia was common within the family, as well as the elongated chin that Agent Wayne had mentioned.

"Yes," she said. "The Henley Chin. But that is a sign of inbreeding and has nothing to do with that family. Anyone could have it."

"I know," said Agent Wayne. "I also know it's a reach, but it would explain a lot. For one thing, it would explain how Charlie became a millionaire almost overnight."

"But when would they have come here?" said Agent Green. "And why?"

"Maybe they were being persecuted," said Agent Wayne. "It's certainly possible, considering what I've read about them so far. Especially King Lionus' branch. They were very messed up. Apparently, he was the last Henley to rule Spain."

"Assuming for a second that you are right," said Agent Green. "Why would they associate themselves with Charlie?"

"That is the question," said Agent Wayne. "What could he possibly offer them in return?"

"Lisa is coming over tonight," she said as she rolled back into town. "Let me see what I can find out."

There was a long moment of silence.

"What is it?" she said, finally.

"First of all, good job gaining her trust," said Agent Wayne. "But that town scares me."

"Like Stephen King scared or Goosebumps scared?"

"Definitely The Shining," he said. "There's something going on there, and I think maybe the police are involved."

"You think they're on someone's payroll?"

"It wouldn't be the first time the law wasn't legal."

"Jesus, you sound like Billy Jack," said Agent Green, turning into the motel.

"Just be careful," said Agent Wayne. "And keep your phone close."

"I will, sir, ' she said, with a southern drawl, "I got my snub-nosed thirty-eight tucked into my right shit-kicker."

"You really are a strange one," said Agent Wayne. "I'll dig deeper into this wonderful family and see what I can find. Call me after she leaves, no matter how late. I'll be waiting."

"You can count on it," Agent Green said, killing the call.

Agent Green unlocked the motel door, aware of the creepy proprietor staring at her through the office window. She could only hope that it was because he was a pervert and not because she was being monitored. Agent Wayne was right. The town had a Jim Jones-like atmosphere. It wasn't something that you could put your finger on. It was more like a sinister silence, a thunderless storm that hovered, refusing to move.

Agent Green shut the door behind her, making sure that the lock was activated.

She sat on the bed, pulled out her Smith and Wesson, and placed it on the bedside table. She then grabbed her laptop out of her bag and turned it on. Agent Wayne's theory about the Henleys bordered on desperation. But there could be no denying that the old portrait of the sad king and the picture of the woman were similar. The results of inter-family breeding usually resulted in the same symptoms: the jaw, protruding brow, recessed cheekbones, and many others, but there were many features that the degenerative genes couldn't explain. The eyes being one. Both the painting and the woman's eyes held the same lurid cruelty. The dimensions of both faces were close to an exact match. They could be laid over each other, and no one would know.

There were still over three hours to kill before Lisa closed the Dollar Store. It would be enough time to do a little research of her own. Agent Green leaned back against the headboard, placed the computer on her lap, and typed in King Lionus II of Spain.

CHAPTER THIRTY-FIVE

A Chance at Freedom

By the time Charlie pulled into the driveway, thirty-three hours had passed. For Karen, these hours ticked away like a prison sentence. She sat there in the living room, barely moving, as the sun slowly worked its way from the east to the west. Her mind was lost in a marathon of fear and hopelessness. Her phone was clutched in her hand and had been for most of the time. It was the last thing that she owned that could provide a way. A way to what? Freedom? For that, she would have to have someone who cared, and there was no one. That thought brought her even more misery. It summed up her life and forced her to reflect on the decisions that she had made.

For so long, she had been tethered, linked to an abuser, while quietly enabling the abuse because she had nowhere else to go. But that wasn't quite true. She wasn't an invalid; she could have left Jimmy years ago. Why didn't she? The depressing truth revealed itself, causing her sinking ship to drop even lower: She had become complacent and lazy from the trade-off. Jimmy had given her a roof, food, and a car. All the essentials that one needed to survive, and all he had asked for in return was compliance, and she had agreed, not with words but with silent acceptance. She now understood why the beaten wife refused to leave, justifying the heavy hands as just another form of love, proof that he cared.

Thirty-three hours had provided her with plenty of time for reflection. So lost was she in this cognitive state that she only realized Charlie was back when the front door opened. She jumped off the couch as he walked in, her face heated as if he had caught her doing something wrong.

"Are you okay?" he said, closing the door behind him.

A flood of emotion consumed her, and she began to sob, her phone falling to the floor as her hands flew to her face,

"Hey, baby girl," said Charlie, coming to her and wrapping his arms around her waist.   "I'm sorry," he said. "That trip took a lot longer than I thought it would."

Karen sank out of his arms onto the couch. Charlie sat down beside her, placing his hand on her knee.

"I know this has been rough on you, stuck here alone."

"I just feel so lost," she managed to say.

Charlie squeezed her knee, gave her a beaming smile, and said, "I've got some bad news."

"Of course you do," she moaned.

"But I've got some really good news, too. Which do you want first?"

"Just tell me what's going on," she said.

Charlie sat back on the couch, folding his hands on his substantial gut.

"They poured sugar into your gas tank," he said.

"Of course they did," said Karen, her face dropping into her palms. "Why wouldn't they?"

"One of the reasons I'm so late is that I have a friend who owns a car dealership up in Stroud. He told me about a sweet Honda Civic that just came in. Cherry red with low miles."

Charlie pulled out his phone and showed her a picture.

"What do you think?" he said.

Karen looked at the car and felt her heart sink.

"That's great, but I have two hundred dollars," she said.

"Keep it," he said. "I already bought it."

"You what?"

"Yep," he said, leaning forward and resting his hand on her knee. "All we have to do is go up there in the morning and pick it up."

"I can't let you do that," she said.

"I already did it," he said. "Besides, it's the least I can do. Your car was ruined in my driveway. Hell, I might even be legally liable."

"No, Charlie," she said, "It's too much."

Charlie scooted himself closer to her side, placing his arm around her shoulders, and pulling her close. For a moment, Karen thought she caught a subtle whiff of alcohol hidden within the overpowering fragrance of his cologne.

"Listen," he said, his eyes locking on to hers. "I want this for you. I think you should take your bag and when we grab the car you should keep going. You need some time away."

"Where would I go?" she said.

"What about seeing your mom in Colorado?"

"I don't think that agent will let me."

"I don't think he can stop you," said Charlie. "You could ask him. I have his number if you want it."

"I have it," she said.

Charlie gave her a nod and stood up.

"I'm going to go take a shower," he said. "You should call him. Tell him you're going to visit your mom for a couple of weeks. The asshole has your number if he needs to get a hold of you."

He then made his way down the hall to the bedroom.

Karen watched him walk away, her mind racing. Charlie had bought her a car. A ticket out, which was surprising. She reached down and picked her phone up off the floor. Would the agent let her leave? Maybe if she told him her mother was sick and promised to return within a few weeks.

No. Better not to lie. She needed to go away, needed to leave this house, this town. This fucking state. He had told her that he wished she wouldn't, that it would look bad, but he also said he couldn't stop her if she wanted to go.

Karen scrolled to the agent's number just as the sound of running water reached her from down the hall. She paused momentarily, fighting the threatening tension, and placed the call.

*****

Charlie had turned on the water in the tub, removed his shoes, and then crept out of the bathroom, stopping near the bedroom doorway. He quickly looked past the frame just as Karen raised the cell phone to her ear.

The plan played out within his mind, fast forwarding from now until the moment he and Gloria were ascending on their flight. It took less than three seconds, long enough for a baleful grin to split his face. For a moment, he thought he might begin to giggle, so he raised his hand to his mouth. The booze from earlier was beginning to fade but still held a dying grip.

"Agent Wayne," said Karen, and Charlie listened.

*****

The King was unable to have children. His body had been so riddled with the various symptoms of inbreeding that he had barely been able to eat, much less reproduce. But he did have a sister, Margaret Theresa. Agent Wayne clicked on her name just as his phone began to ring. He glanced up at the clock on the television and saw that there was still over an hour left before Lisa Smith would arrive at Agent Green's room. The agent shuffled the papers on the bed until he finally found his cell. He glanced at the number and was pleasantly surprised.

"Hi Karen," he said. "Is everything okay?"

"Agent Wayne," she said. "I need to ask you something."

"Please," he said, pulling the scattered documents back together.

"Can I go see my mother?"

The agent paused for a second.

"Is she okay?" he said.

There was a long silence, and he could sense the struggle on the other line.

"Are you still there?" he pressed.

"I'm here," said Karen. "My mother's fine. It's just that I haven't seen her in a long time." Suddenly, her voice dropped. "I have to get out of here for a while."

"I understand," said Agent Wayne. "Karen, I'm not going to tell you not to go. You haven't been charged with anything, but I would like to be able to get in touch with you."

"You have my number," she said. "And I promise I'll answer if you call."

Agent Wayne let his gaze drop to where the image of the sickly king's sister stared back at him from his laptop screen. The resemblance was there, including the elongated chin, but a flare of intelligence within her eyes seemed to be missing from her brother.

"Do you have enough money?" said the agent.

"I'll be fine," said Karen.

Agent Wayne scrolled down to where Margaret Theresa's information began.

"And Charlie's okay with this?"

"It was actually his idea," said Karen. "He thinks I should get away for a while."

This grabbed the agent's full attention. He would have bet the farm that Charlie would do anything to keep Karen from leaving, including ratting her out.

I don't really know her that well, he had said.

His call to the agent had been shrouded with ulterior motives and designed to deceive. Why change now? What had happened?

"He suggested that I call you."

"Did he, now?" said the agent. "That *is* interesting."

"So, I can go?"

"As far as I'm concerned, you've done nothing wrong. When are you planning on leaving?"

"Tomorrow morning," she said.

"Do me a favor; promise you'll let me know as soon as you get there."

"I'll shoot you a text," said Karen.

The line went dead. He wondered if he were to call her back, would she answer? Probably not. He placed the cell phone on the night table and returned his attention to the laptop.

Like so many other women during those dark days, Margaret Theresa had been tossed into the background. She had married her cousin, Leon I of The Holy Roman Empire (also no surprise), and made her way to Milan, where they struggled to continue the Henley line. Out of six difficult pregnancies, four had managed to make it out of the womb, and of those four, only one survived into adulthood: a daughter named Maria Petra. The agent took notes of the five children who didn't survive. Their names and dates of their death had been documented.

He then saw that Margaret Theresa had died at the early age of twenty-one while attempting the birth of her seventh. Agent Wayne scrolled back up to the list of the deceased children. A sudden realization caused the agent's hand to freeze. All six pregnancies had been documented, the last one resulting in a stillborn a year before Margaret's death. And yet, Margaret Theresa's biography stated that she had died while giving birth. He typed in Margaret Theresa's lineage and then cross-referenced the results he had already found. It read the same: six names with only her daughter reaching adulthood. All these children had been given pre-ordained titles while Margaret was still early in her pregnancy, so why was there nothing about the seventh child, the one that had taken her life?

By the time Margaret Theresa had passed away, Spain was on the verge of financial collapse, being led by a child king whose deteriorating mind and abhorrent body did little to quell their fears. But as far as the agent could tell, Margaret Theresa had been mostly forgotten. Was that why her final child seemed to have gone unnoticed? Out of sight and out of mind? Perhaps, but the kid was still royalty, still a possible heir to the throne. Then another thought occurred to the agent: What if they didn't want the baby to be known? What if there was a reason that he remained expunged from the Royal Records?

Agent Wayne put the computer to the side and lay back on the bed, rubbing his eyes. He glanced at the clock and saw that Agent Green's visitor was due to arrive within the next fifteen minutes. He considered calling her and sharing what he had found. She, no doubt, was doing some reading on her own and might have a theory, but he decided against it. Better to let her focus on the task at hand.

He again looked over at his screen, where Margaret Theresa's eerie face covered the upper half of the monitor. How strange it must have been to be selected for breeding in a family that was generationally poisoning themselves. To go from calling someone a cousin to calling them a husband. Of course, she would have had no choice. None of them did. She had been pregnant seven times by the time she had died. Seven times, and yet only six were listed.

A child was missing. Not just any child, but a royal child. But what if this royal child was never supposed to be there in the first place? What if it had been chosen for something else? Or ordained, if you will? Agent Wayne grabbed the laptop and typed Spanish Territories in the seventeenth century. He stood from the bed, his hands rubbing together like a mad scientist, and walked over to the mini-fridge. He brought out a bottle of green tea that he had bought earlier while he and Agent Green were out purchasing that ghastly outfit and made his way back to the bed, gazing down at the screen. This theory went well beyond one of his customary long shots, yet it all seemed to fit. As if to confirm, the screen lit up with an image of early America, including popular shipping lanes.

The agent looked over the screen, his eyes locking on one in particular. It was a direct route from the shore town of Vigo, Spain, to the then-Spanish shores of Florida.

He popped the top off the bottle, took a small drink, and sat down. It had been a long time since he had taken an American history class, but if he wasn't mistaken, Spain was already losing ground by the time the seventeenth century reached its midway point. By then, the infamous Spanish Armada had met The Protestant Winds and was a thing of the past. Would they have just let the New World slip through their fingers without some kind of fight? Doubtful.

Perhaps what they needed was someone to rally around. Perhaps what they needed was a king.

CHAPTER THIRTY-SIX

Lisa Has a Beer

Agent Green was careful to pace herself. She sat on her bed telling a fabricated story, pausing here and there to wipe her eyes for dramatic effect, while Lisa Smith sat at the small round table by the motel door, popping the top of her third beer. The young woman could certainly drink and had shown little signs of even the slightest buzz. But the made-up story could only go on for so long.

Agent Green waited until Lisa finished the beer and was reaching for a fourth when she said, "That's enough about me. Tell me something about yourself."

Lisa glared at her for a moment.

"There's not much to tell," said Lisa, finally.

"Are you from here?" said the agent.

"Born and fucking raised," said Lisa, her words beginning to slur together.

After three beers, it seemed that the alcohol was finally starting to work.

"Do you like it here?"

"What's not to like?" she said sarcastically. "Every day is an adventure. I wake up, go to work, and then I go home just so I can get up and do it again."

"Do you have a boyfriend?"

"Hell no," said Lisa, with disgust. "And, after listening to you, I don't think I want one."

"They're not all bad," said the agent.

"Really? Then why did you end up here?"

Agent Green lowered her eyes.

"I'm sorry," said Lisa. "I didn't mean that."

She then chugged the rest of her fourth, reached for a fifth, and said, "I can be a bitch when I drink."

"It's okay," said the agent. "I'm just thankful for your help."

Lisa took a swig, let out a long belch, and said, "We girls have to stick together."

"Very true," said Agent Green, lifting her beer for a distant toast.

"You know, I had some problems with my old man."

Here it comes.

"That asshole waited until my mother died and then went for me like I was a fuck toy."

Agent Green was momentarily shocked by her statement. She knew all of this, of course, but the way Lisa assaulted her with the truth was like a brisk slap.

"The sonofabitch was in my room at least twice a week."

"Shit girl, I'm sorry," said the agent.

"Don't be," she said. "He eventually got his."

Lisa finished her beer and went for another.

"What happened to him?"

"He was killed about two miles away from here," Lisa said, her face radiating. "They found his body on one side of the highway and his head on the other."

"Holy Shit!"

"Yep. They never found out who had done it, but I don't think anyone really cared. I know I didn't."

"Did you see the body?"

"I was out of town when it happened," she said. "But I heard all about it. I didn't go to the funeral. Why would I? I was just glad that the bastard was dead."

Here, she paused with the beer halfway to her mouth and said,

"You can understand that, can't you?"

"Hell yeah, I can."

"I figured you could," said Lisa. "It's not like I was left with nothing out of the deal. I did get the family home, rundown as it is, and a sweet Thunderbird."

"You also have a pretty good job," said the agent. "You manage that place, right?"

"I do," said Lisa. "But it's not like they have a lot of manpower to choose from here."

"Still, the owners must really like you."

"Not sure if that's the right word. More like they trust me."

"Well, that's good, too," said the agent. "Are they around here?"

The sobering look that came over Lisa's face was immediate. She placed the can on the table and leaned forward, her brown eyes drilling into Agent Green.

"Why do you give a shit about who owns the Dollar Store?"

Agent Green was prepared for such a question.

"Listen, Lisa," she began, "I told you before that I don't have a lot of money. Shit, I don't even have a place to live. I'm looking for a new start. Somewhere where my husband won't think of looking for me. Does that make sense?"

"This town would certainly qualify," said Lisa, sitting back in her chair and grabbing the beer off the table. "So, what do you want, a job?"

"Are they hiring? I can meet with them."

"That probably wouldn't be the best idea," said Lisa. "Besides, I do the hiring. You know the job pays for shit, right? It's only minimum wage to start."

"I'm okay with that," said the agent. "Like you said, it's a start."

Lisa suddenly stood up and leaned on the table.

"Fuck, I'm drunk," she said.

She then shuffled over to the bathroom, unbuttoning her jeans as she passed through the doorway, not bothering to shut the door behind her. She dropped her pants and squatted on the toilet, releasing a thunderous stream.

"I might be able to get you on," she said, reaching over and grabbing a handful of toilet paper. "This place really is a shit place to live."

Agent Green averted her eyes just as Lisa was grabbing the handle. A swirling flush briefly echoed in the room.

"Are you sure you wouldn't be better off going on to Tahlequah or even Fayetteville?" Lisa said, stumbling her way out of the bathroom. "Hell, those're university towns. There's gotta be better jobs there."

Agent Green gazed up just as Lisa plopped down next to her on the bed. The girl's eyes held the disconnected look of someone reaching their limit. She sat there with her shoulders slumped, a slight sheen of sweat layering her forehead. The girl was attractive, though her face had the weathered look of someone who had seen too much. She had experienced too much. Compassion flooded over the agent. For a moment, she wanted to reach out and embrace this young woman, to pull her close and apologize for the horrors that this world had seen fit to bury her in. To tell her that all was not lost, but how could she? As of now, Agent Green was nothing more than a prop set up to pry into this woman's life.

"I'll tell you what," said Lisa. "You come by the store tomorrow morning, and we'll see if you still want to stay."

She then stood, tripping back a few steps, and said, "If you do, I'll give you a job."

"That's a deal," said the agent. "You're not going to drive home, are you?"

"I have to," said Lisa. "I've got to feed my baby."

"You have a kid?"

"Yep," said Lisa, with a smile. "I picked him up from the American Bulldog Rescue in Tahlequah a few years back. He was scheduled for the needle."

"Damn, Lisa. That was good of you."

"I understand what it's like to be tossed to the side," Lisa said, looking down at the agent with tears welling in her eyes. "I also know what it's like to be given a chance." She then lowered her head, and her shoulders slumped. "Can you imagine being killed because no one wants you? Just because of what you are?"

"Hey, Lisa," said the agent. "I think that's really cool."

"I only wish I had enough money to save them all."

Lisa reached up, wiped her eyes, and shook her head.

"This is why I rarely drink," she said with a laugh.

"Do you think you should drive?" said the agent. "I could take you."

"I'll be fine," said Lisa. "The cops here won't fuck with me; they know better."

She then leaned down to where her face was just inches away from Agent Green's and said, "Thank you, Joyce. This town is a lonely place. Maybe I'll see you tomorrow."

She opened the door, threw the agent a weak wave, and left. Agent Green sat there, listening as the Thunderbird's V-8 roared to life. A sudden squeal of rubber being laid to the road was soon followed by silence.

The cops here won't fuck with me. They know better, she said, and Agent Green believed her.

Agent Wayne had gotten the feeling that the police here had a little more on their minds than *to serve and protect.* Perhaps Lisa, like them, was nothing more than a well-backed front. But a front to what?

Agent Green grabbed her phone off the nightstand and saw that it was a few minutes after eleven. She pulled up Agent Wayne's number but hesitated. The evening with Lisa had been an emotional ride that had left her exhausted.

She mentally checked the pertinent points while preparing the report, but she would try to exclude Lisa from it if she could. The girl had been through enough.

Agent Green placed the call.

CHAPTER THIRTY-SEVEN

Jimmy Meets the Baby

Jimmy sat less than ten miles away, his legs drawn up to his chest and his arms braced together under his knees. He stared with numb amusement at the golden frilled collared shirt and Royal Blue coat hanging from the bars of his cell.

Would there be a wig?

This was his gift for being able to enter Marianna, his reward for inseminating the wicked queen's daughter, and by tomorrow night, he would be a full-fledged member of the family. Would it be legal? How could it be? There was no judge to document the act. There would be no papers filed. And yet, within the eyes of those who weren't afraid to murder, it was as good as a notarized judgment, and any attempt at annulment would result in immediate death.

Marianna had brought him his dinner just a few hours earlier, and she hadn't come alone; nestled within her right arm was the infant, his tiny hands clenching and unclenching as she slid the tray through the door. The child looked healthy and, despite the sharp point of its chin, seemed normal. Marianna had brought the baby close to the wall of bars, allowing Jimmy to reach his hand through the cage and touch the infant's soft skin.

"What's his name?"

"Ferdinand," she said.

Of course, it would be something like that.

"He's very cute," Jimmy said.

Yes, he was, and in a few years, he would be expected to mount his aunt and continue the line. Would he be cute, then?

She waited with the child as Jimmy ate the baked chicken and a side of walnuts. Her distorted face beamed with the possibility of having a child of her own. Jimmy smiled in between bites while watching Marianna, his own emotions zigzagging. He liked the young woman and, for now, needed her. But the thought of having a child with her was horrifying. And what would he do if the opportunity to escape did present itself? What if she was pregnant? Could he leave her then? In a New York minute.

Marianna had taken the empty tray and the child upstairs, only to return a few minutes later with the outrageous outfit. Jimmy could see her face flush with embarrassment as she hung the ensemble on the bars.

"Mother insists," she said sheepishly.

"I'm sure she does. Will we be married here in this cell?"

"Of course not," said Marianna. "I wouldn't allow it. We'll hold the ceremony in the ballroom."

"And then what?" said Jimmy. "Off to France for our honeymoon?"

This caused Marianna to laugh.

"Probably not," she said.

No, there will be no honeymoon for this transaction. The best he could hope for was a quick glance outside through a window, and then he would be led back to his cell, regaled in absurd clothes, and forced to climb aboard the princess in waiting.

"Try to get some sleep," she said, going to the stairs. "Tomorrow will be our day."

Jimmy had watched silently as she disappeared around the lava corner, sweat shining across his forehead. Of course, they would grab him early and march him over to the shower. They would watch as he tried to figure out how to put those clothes on properly. And then what? They would march him upstairs with the giant's hand wrapped securely around his neck. A sudden chill seized his body as an image of the queen, her eyes lasering into him, played out in his mind.

Without realizing it, he began to hum Annie's tune: *Tomorrow, tomorrow, I'll love you tomorrow...It's only a day away.* A wave of darkness swept over the chamber from the lights being switched off.

Jimmy lowered his head and began to cry.

CHAPTER THIRTY-EIGHT

A New Toy

Karen sat in the passenger seat of Charlie's Mercedes, gazing out the passenger window at a gray October sky. An uneasy feeling continued to churn within her stomach. She had made love to the man the night before, and not because of any desire, but because she felt she owed him. It was severance pay for services rendered. It mattered little. Her single bag lay in the back seat zipped. Charlie had insisted on giving her an additional five hundred dollars to go along with the two she already had.

That was more than most prostitutes make, she thought morosely to herself.

They had taken the Tulsa Turnpike off I-35 and traveled at a nervous ninety-five miles an hour. Charlie was listening tc Glen Beck, which did little to quell the uneasy feeling swirling within her gut.

Just one more hour, she thought to herself.

One more hour, and she would be in her new car. Of course, she would have to pretend that she would miss the man and promise to return to him after a couple of weeks. But she knew better. Karen could feel the beckoning freedom of the open road; it was like a doorway out of a burning house, and there would be no coming back.

I will no longer lie to myself: I'm fucking gone.

She would call the agent once she was at her mother's house, just like she had promised, but she had no intention of staying there.

"Oh shit," said Charlie.

Karen looked to the front just as Charlie was turning onto an offramp. The road T-d at a stop sign, and on the corner to the right was an old Stuckey's restaurant that looked like it had been closed during the last recession.

"What's wrong?" she said.

"Don't you see it?" he said.

The parking lot was a wide sea of cracked asphalt containing broken bollards and chipped curbs. Near its center was a late model RV. Posted underneath the left wiper was a For Sale sign.

"What about it?" said Karen.

"It's a classic," said Charlie. "That's a seventy-three Winnebago. That bastard's got a four-forty motor."

Karen looked at the RV. The side panels were faded, the grill had taken a shot or two, and it was cracked on both sides.

"Are you serious?" she said.

"Let's check it out," said Charlie, coming to a stop beside it.

He shut the car off and expelled himself from the Mercedes with surprising quickness for a man his size.

A moment of tension seized Karen. Her escape from the madness was again being delayed.

"You must really like RV's," she said sarcastically, opening her door and climbing out.

"I like this model," he said, his face beaming. "These are hard to find."

He then walked over to the entry door.

"It's probably locked," said Karen.

Charlie pulled the handle, and the door swung open.

"Why would they leave it unlocked?"

"They probably forgot," said Charlie, stepping up. "Holy shit! You've got to see this."

Karen made her way over to the metal stairs hanging off the sidewall. The lot was empty, the only sound coming from the wind rustling through a tree line that sat thirty yards away. The sun was gaining in its mid-morning climb, casting golden light on the RV's darkened side windows. She neared the steps but hesitated.

"Karen," said Charlie, "You have to check this out."

She went through the narrow doorway. To her right were the driver and passenger seats. Charlie was standing between them, each hand perched on a headrest. She turned back to where a small table, its paisley cover hanging near the floor, faced a mini fridge from across a narrow walkway. At its end, there was a closed door.

"Okay," she said. "Can we go now?"

"After I show you this," he said, brushing by her.

He squeezed his way down the aisle and opened the door. She watched with amusement as he then forced his paunch through the narrow opening.

"You have to come in here," he said.

Karen began to follow and then found herself being knocked off balance. Something had struck the RV, violently rocking it. A sound, like a rifle shot, rang in her ears as the entry door was slammed shut.

"Charlie," she cried out, rushing back to the door.

She pushed against it, but it wouldn't budge.

"Charlie," she cried out again. "I can't get the door open,"

She turned to where Charlie had disappeared just as an old woman in a wide-brimmed hat shuffled through the doorway.

"She is pretty," she said.

Karen took a step back, her heart thrumming in her chest.

"Who are you?" she managed to say.

It was then that her ankle was seized. She let out a scream and tried to pull away, but whatever had her was like a vice. A sudden sharp pain raced its way up from her calf. She looked down and saw a pair of corpse-colored hands jutting out from the low-hanging tablecloth. One held her ankle while the other removed a syringe. She again began to scream, but her voice tapered off. The interior of the RV began to spin, striking her with swirling colors. Karen had enough time to see Charlie gazing at her from over the old woman's shoulder, his face contorted into a madman's grin, before collapsing into the Winnebago's aisle.

*****

Charlie watched the RV disappear around a curve while shoving

Karen's cell phone and the five hundred dollars he had given her into his pants pocket. A bone-rattling roar of motors ignited from behind the vacant building. He turned just as three Harley Davidson's cleared the corner, coming towards him. They stopped a few feet from where he leaned against his Mercedes. It was Ben, his V.P., and that psycho Lester.

"You did good, Ringleader," Ben said over his rumbling motor. "When this is over, I want an office with a window."

Charlie ignored the bile in his throat and gave him a thumbs up. The three men then throttled towards the onramp. Charlie let out the breath that he had unknowingly been holding. His life was descending into darkness, and it was time to leave. Whether or not Ben could eliminate the family mattered little; either way, Charlie lost. He climbed into the car and reached for his phone. For a moment, he considered calling Gloria but decided against it. Her connection to Ben was too dangerous. Maybe someday, after this nightmare storm passed, he might. But not today. Today, he would book his flight, go home, pack, and hope that he was long gone by the time the bomb that was Ben went off.

CHAPTER THIRTY-NINE

A New Arrival

Marianna brought Jimmy his breakfast and paced from one side of the dungeon to the other. Every few steps, she would pause and look over at him. At first, he figured that it was her nerves. This was, after all, the big day. The day when they began the mission in earnest. How many times a day would he be expected to mount her? Two? Three? As many as it took. He slid the tray into the slot and watched Marianna make her way over.

"Where's little Ferdinand?" he said.

"I need to tell you something," she said, ignoring his question. "But I want you to know that I had nothing to do with it."

"You can tell me," he said.

"Mother has gone for a replacement for Nith."

This was no surprise. Jimmy had heard them discussing it on at least two occasions. But knowing that it would happen didn't alleviate the nightmare he would be forced to witness.

"Please tell me I won't have to watch your brother rape another woman."

Marianna's sapphire eyes locked onto his.

"This is my mother's fault," she said. "If she had just left Charlie's wife alone, the police would have nothing, and then we wouldn't need her, but since he has her, we have no choice."

"Who?" said Jimmy.

"The woman you used to love," said Marianna, her slanted eyes finding his.

At first, Jimmy didn't understand, but then her words began to bore into his skull like a slow-moving drill. He stumbled blindly to his cot, collapsing as Marianna continued to speak.

"Why do you care?" she said. "The woman left you for the very man who sold you out."

Jimmy placed his face into his hands, fighting back the horrific images flashing through his mind.

"She was my wife," he gasped.

"But not anymore," she said. "And as of tonight, I will be your wife."

"Are you fucking crazy?" he said. "You're going to bring my wife down here so I can watch your retarded brother rape her?"

Marianna's face darkened.

"Don't forget why you're still alive," she hissed, her hands strangling the bars. After a moment, she released her grip. "This is not what I wanted."

"And yet you won't stop it," said Jimmy, looking up at her. "Don't let them hurt her, Marianna. You have me already. I'll do anything you want, but you must let her go."

"I wish I could," she said. "But then I wish for a lot of things."

She then turned and made her way to the stairs.

*****

Agent Green sat beside Lisa at the Dollar Store's front counter, filling out the employment application. She was about to tell Lisa she would need a couple more days to think about taking the job when a Winnebago pulled into the parking lot. She gazed up just as the side door opened and felt her heart stop.

It was her.

The face had aged since the picture was taken, but there could be no mistaking that chin. Agent Green quickly looked back down as the woman entered the store.

"Mrs. Henley," said Lisa.

"Hello, Lisa," the woman said. "Is everything ready?"

"It's all here," said Lisa, reaching down and bringing up a plastic sack. This is the last of the formula, but I put in an order for more. We should get it by Thursday. Plus, we just received a shipment of Pampers, so you should be good for a while."

"Excellent," said the old woman, her gaze falling to where the agent was doing her best to look busy.

"Who is this?"

"This is Joyce Hicks," said Lisa. "She just got into town and is looking for a job. Joyce, this is Mrs. Grenalda Henley. She owns this place."

Agent Green produced the warmest smile that she could muster and reached out her hand.

"Hi, Mrs. Henley. It's very nice to meet you."

The old woman gave the agent's hand a quick shake and then dropped it.

"What brings you to Lost City?"

"Well, it's kind of a long story."

"Then save it," the old woman said. "I'm in a hurry."

She then gazed at Lisa and said, "Did you contact Carter for a background check?"

Lisa glanced at Agent Green nervously and said, "She just started the application. I'll send it over in a few minutes."

"Make sure that you do," said Grenalda. "I don't want any miscreants in my town."

She gave the agent a sour look, grabbed her bags, and exited the store.

"I'm sorry about that," said Lisa. "She can be quite colorful sometimes."

"Don't worry about it," said the agent, standing up with the application in hand. "Listen, I'm going to go back to the room for a while and get some rest. I'm still a little hungover. I'll finish this up later."

"I don't blame you," said Lisa. "Bring it back, and I'll get it sent over to the chief. You might even be able to start tomorrow."

"That works for me," said Agent Green, making her way to the sliding doors. "I'll be back in a couple of hours."

She left the Dollar Store, craning her head towards the direction that the Winnebago had gone. The faded rear of the RV was still visible, and the agent quickly opened the door to the Bronco and hopped in. She had just placed the key into the ignition when she was startled by an ear-rattling noise. The agent looked through the passenger window just as three Harleys thundered by. They blew past her, but not before she saw the skull-covered helmets emblazoned across the back of their vests and instantly knew who they were. But why would The Centurions be two hundred miles from their base?

Agent Green waited for them to pass. She then started up the Bronco, throwing it into Drive, and made her way to the road. The RV was still visible in front of the motorcycles, but just barely. Agent Green made the turn, careful to stay safely behind. She then grabbed her phone and placed a call to Agent Wayne, her heart hammering in her chest.

"Hey, Hicks."

"She's here," said Agent Green. "Holy shit, Wyatt. Her last name *is* Henley. I'm following them right now."

"What are they in?"

"An old Winnebago," said Agent Green. "I can't get the plate because I've got some bikers in between us. It's The Centurions."

"What the hell are they doing there?" said Agent Wayne.

"I was just wondering about that myself. They're a long way from home. What do you want to do?"

"We need to worry about that lady," said Agent Wayne. "Whatever the bikers are up to will have to wait."

"I'll keep following the Winnebago. Hopefully, I'll get an address."

"Okay," said Agent Wayne. "I'm packing up and heading that way. I'll call you when I hit town. Be careful, Joyce."

The line went dead. Agent Green continued to shadow the RV. Her knowledge of the Centurians was limited. She knew that they owned a few businesses throughout the Oklahoma City area, and most of those were purported fronts for their illegal activity. But she had never been given the task of investigating them. Her information came from news outlets and the Internet. The three bikers seemed to be keeping their distance from the RV, which the agent found strange.

The two-lane highway was a desolate run surrounded by oak trees and grassland, which was a perfect setting for these outlaws to open up. And yet they didn't. They seemed content with doing the speed limit. The brake lights from the motorcycles suddenly flashed, and the agent could see the Winnebago turning onto a side road. The bikers came to a momentary crawl and then sped off. Agent Green turned, following the RV. The road was a dirt-layered nightmare, barely wide enough for one vehicle. The Winnebago was now a hundred yards ahead of her, kicking up small clouds of washout. Agent Green looked down at her phone and saw she still had a weak signal. A flickering glint struck her eyes from the driver's side mirror. The bikers had returned.

These men were following either her or Mrs. Henley. Nothing else made sense. Agent Green forced in a deep breath and held it for three seconds, slowly releasing it. The R.V. was beginning to slow down, and the agent tapped her brakes. It then lumbered into a left turn. Agent Green looked in her rearview mirror at the motorcycles. They had closed the gap and were just fifty yards away from the rear of her car. For a moment, she considered following the RV but decided against it and drove past the turn. The bikers reached the intersection and turned.

Agent Green had her answer. She drove on, coming to a water-damaged driveway, and turned around. Both the RV and the bikers were out of sight by the time she made it back to the intersection. In the distance, she could see a small cloud of dirt rising over a faraway hill. She pressed down on the Bronco's gas while reaching into her boot and pulling out the .38.

The land was becoming thick with dead foliage. Each side of the road contained walls of ivy surrounding tall elms and cottonwoods. The Bronco continued, carrying her down into a valley. Again, she checked her phone and saw that she now had no signal. This would mean no GPS. As she was climbing out of the valley, the biker's headlights appeared in front of her. Agent Green was forced to slam the brakes and turn the wheel sharply to the right, barely missing the deep culvert made by last year's rain.

The bikers roared by, their faces plastered with grins. Agent

Green sat on the side of the road, her breath heaving as the Centurions vanished over the hill.

Agent Green allowed the shaking to subside and then pulled back onto the road. She had no doubt that the bikers had been following the RV, and they couldn't have gone much further. Agent Green continued. After another half mile, the open land on her right became bordered by strands of barbed wire. It ran along the road for another quarter of a mile, ending at a wall. This behemoth structure stood ten feet tall and was built out of cinderblock.

The agent followed it until she could see a break in the line. She slowed down the Bronco just as a metal spiked gate appeared flanked by two antique light posts. It took everything she had not to stop and get a better look. But what she saw through the gap as she went by was impressive enough. It was a mansion looking much like a government building in D.C., and the old Winnebago was sitting out in the front.

Agent Green had found the Henleys, and she was sure Agent Wayne was right. How they had ended up in this small town in Oklahoma was beyond her, but in her heart, she knew it was them. Agent Green drove on for another mile until she could find a spot wide enough to turn around. She passed by again, slowing for a look, unaware of the camera following her from within one of the light posts.

*****

It took less than five minutes for Agent Wayne to pack. He then reached for his laptop, pausing. The motorcycle club was bothering him. Why would they be in Lost City? Much like Agent Green, Wayne had never been assigned to investigate them, and his knowledge of the club was just as limited.

He pushed the bag over, grabbed the computer, and sat on the edge of the bed. He clicked on the OSBI icon and traced the cursor over to criminal records. The only thing he knew for sure about the MC was the name of their leader, and only because of how many times he had been in the news. Agent Wayne typed in Benjamin Lanchino and immediately saw a two-page rap sheet going as far back as 1988. It read like most career criminals, starting with petty larceny and moving into violent crime, but nothing seemed to stick. There was a four-year sentence that he had spent in McCallister for assault, but that was it. The rest had all been dropped.

He scrolled down until he saw the murder charge. which had been dismissed due to an eyewitness claiming to have been with him the night the crime had been committed. The agent expanded the report, reading the details, and then felt his breath catch in his throat. The witness' signed affidavit struck out like a viper. The agent closed the laptop and lay back on the bed. He pulled his phone out of his coat pocket and clicked on Agent Green's number. The call went straight to voicemail. Agent Wayne killed the call and let his thoughts wander.

All roads lead to Charlie, one way or another. An urge to cut through the bullshit struck him like a revelation. The time for games was over. He only hoped that he could make Charlie believe it.

CHAPTER FORTY

Karen Arrives

The metal door cried out, sending chills throughout Jimmy's body. The sound of heavy footfalls rumbled down the stairwell. Jimmy rose from the cot and made his way to the cell door. He wrapped his fingers around the cold bars, straining his neck, trying to look beyond the corner of the lava wall.

They have her! A voice screamed in his head. *They have her, and they're bringing her down to hell!*

It was pointless to try and argue with this voice, his voice. Marianna had said all that needed to be said, and soon, he would be forced to watch as the giant, the murderous beast, raped his wife. And he would be helpless, much like he had been with the woman before. Of course, he would die first. For them to think he would idly sit here in this cell while Karen fought against Nith was absurd. He would bash his head against the lava rocks before it came to that. Did they not know this?

The echoing footfalls receded, and he could see faint shadows spreading across the floor as they drew closer. The old woman was the first to appear. Her wrinkled face stank with exertion. She hobbled over to the other cell door as Nith stepped into view. Nothing could prepare Jimmy for what he saw, and he felt his knees unhinge. Karen lay over the giant's shoulder, her mouth open, a string of spit attached to the large man's stretched T-shirt.

"No," Jimmy moaned, his head now resting against the bars. "Please don't."

Nithard turned and presented Jimmy with a smile straight from the Devil himself.

The grind from the cell door being opened caused Jimmy to flinch. The old woman held it as Nith carried Karen's limp body in and dropped her on a cot at the back of the cell.

A sudden storm erupted in Jimmy's gut, and he was just able to make it back to the shit bucket before his stomach emptied.

After a moment, he lifted his head and saw the old woman standing near his cell.

"The wedding has been delayed," she said. "We have some company that must be dealt with first."

She then looked over at where the giant stood, looking through the bars at his new toy, and said, "He's not to touch her. At least for now."

With that, she turned and made her way back to the stairs, snapping her fingers. Nith responded like a dog' and was quickly at her heels. A blanket of silence followed the sound of the clanging door. Jimmy forced himself up and walked back over to the wall of bars, ignoring the acidy taste in his mouth.

"Karen," he said. "Karen, wake up."

He could see her lying motionless. No doubt Phillip had drugged her. Jimmy slunk down to the floor, his eyes never leaving her body and was grateful to see that at least she was breathing.

He's not to touch her. At least for now.

Comforting words, if they were to be believed. The Evil Queen probably meant for her twisted spawn to leave Karen alone, much like she had meant for him to leave the pregnant woman alone, and Jimmy saw firsthand how that had worked out. Whatever the old woman's reason, it wouldn't matter much to her son: The giant had an agenda of his own. But the wedding was off, at least temporarily.

We have some company that must be dealt with first.

A small glimmer of hope. Could it be the police? And how would the family deal with cops? Would they dare kill them? Of course, they would.

"Jimmy? Is that you?"

Jimmy felt his heart leap into his throat. Karen struggled to sit up, her hair hanging loose across her face.

"It's me," he said.

"Where are we?" she said, her voice slurred.

Jimmy considered the question and said, "We're in hell, Karen."

"What the fuck is going on?"

Jimmy told the tale, starting from when they had taken him from the murdered woman's house. He told her how Charlie had set them both up and found himself staring at her face as he did, curious to see her expression. He could see her complexion turn red even through the shadows of the bars.

"That sonofabitch," she said. "I was leaving him today. He had bought me a car."

"You don't really believe that, do you?" said Jimmy.

"What are we going to do?" she said, slowly standing and making her way to the bars.

"There's more," he said, lowering his head.

He didn't want to tell her about the previous occupant, but to hold back seemed like it would only make it worse. A rumbling whipped through his stomach as he prepared himself for full disclosure, for the full reveal of why she was there. The words came out with a stuttered rhythm, and he refused to look at her while he spoke. Finally, he ended with the birth of the child. Karen stood like a statue. Her face was etched with horrific disbelief. She slowly turned, returned to the cot, and sat, her elbows resting on her knees.

"They are using you to breed?" she said.

"Yes. And they are going to use you, as well."

"Fuck that," said Karen. "I won't do it."

"They cut her leg off, Karen because she tried to run. She was put in a coma while she was pregnant. They murdered her."

"So, what are you saying?" she said. "I should just let this monster fuck me?"

He thought, *"You let Charlie,"* but said, "I don't know what I'm saying. I only know what they will do if you don't."

A silence fell over them. Jimmy had left out the part of the giant raping the woman while she had been comatose, and maybe he should have told her. Perhaps then she would see just how hopeless her situation was.

"I'm going to be sick," said Karen, leaning her head over the five-gallon plastic bucket beside her bed.

A feeling of satisfaction inflicted Jimmy. How could she have fallen for Charlie? It then occurred to Jimmy that he had fallen for him too. Not sexually, of course, but had been drawn into his bullshit just the same. This woman across the way once loved Jimmy and had been there for him until she could take no more. And now she was here and was more than likely going to die.

"Karen," he said as she pulled her face out of the bucket. "I'm so sorry."

CHAPTER FORTY-ONE

Agent Wayne Talks to Charlie

Charlie was just pulling into Oklahoma City when his cell phone began to ring. He held the thing in his hand, gazing at the incoming number. It was the agent, probably wanting to get his side of the story as to why Karen had decided to leave. This, unlike the code, was a question he was prepared for. It was all a part of his plan. A plan that he intended to follow, at least until tomorrow's flight landed in Belize.

He drew a deep breath and consciously tried to erase the image of Karen collapsing in the RV. He replaced it with the imagined sorrow he had felt as he watched her drive away, knowing deep in his heart that he would probably never see her again.

"Agent Wayne," he said, his voice trembling with sorrow. "I'm glad you–"

"Enough shit, big man," the agent snapped, causing Charlie to tighten his grip on the steering wheel.

"What do you mean?"

"I just had an interesting conversation with your biker friend up here in Lost City."

A pain, like a needle being thrust into his gut, made Charlie wince.

"I don't know what you're talking about," he managed to say, but his voice sounded weak.

"Save it, Charlie," said the agent. "Mr. Lanchino was quite forthcoming."

Flashes of light began circling in front of Charlie's vision, and the air suddenly became warm. He found himself having to pull over onto the shoulder.

"Look, I don't know what he told you, but I haven't done anything."

If Ben talked, tomorrow's flight wouldn't be soon enough. Charlie began to shake, his brow now magically coated with cold sweat.

"The one thing I can't figure out," continued the agent, "is why the Henleys would want anything to do with a loser like you."

It was as if a noose had been tightened around Charlie's throat. All he could manage was a choked grunt, and then his nerves exploded like compressed gas. Charlie threw the phone out of the window and punched the gas. A horn blared from behind, and he heard the screech of tires being locked up. He gazed back in his rearview mirror just as a kid driving an old Ford Taurus regained control. Charlie could care less. What he did care about was getting out of this state, and not just this state, but the country.

Could he make it to the airport before the cops found him? He would have to. Fuck Belize. He would jump on whatever flight was available and go from there.

*****

"Charlie? Are you still with me?"

The phone was dead. Agent Wayne had played his hand and had come away a winner.

But it still didn't answer the question of why. Agent Wayne dialed Agent Green and filled her in on what had happened.

"Holy shit," she said. "This could be bad."

"I think it will be," he said, packing up his laptop and grabbing his bag. "Have you seen The Centurions?"

"I just got back to the motel, and there's no sign of them."

"They're around somewhere," he said, going to the cruiser.

"Do you think we should call this in?"

"What would we tell them?" said the agent, throwing his things into the backseat. "We don't have any proof. And don't forget, I lied to Charlie about talking to Lanchino."

"Yeah, that could be a problem. So, how do you want to handle this?"

"Keep your eyes open and listen for that glorious sound of roaring hogs," he said, pulling out of the hotel's parking lot. "And call me if you see them."

CHAPTER FORTY-TWO

Agent Green Gets Taken

Agent Green placed the phone on the nightstand and lay back on the bed. It might have been a mistake forcing Charlie's hand. If something was happening and Charlie was involved, it was a sure bet that the man wouldn't hang around until the dust settled. His connection to the bikers could lead to anything: drugs, theft, murder. Just how far in with them could he be? And then there was his connection to the family. What would they want with a guy like Charlie Wheaton?

A knock on the door caused the agent to jump. There was no way it was Agent Wayne; he was leaving Tahlequah. She reached into her boot and brought out the .38.

"Who is it?"

"It's Lisa."

Agent Green had forgotten about the application she was supposed to have returned to the store for Lisa to process. This would be as good a time as any to tell the girl that she had changed her mind.

"Hang on," she said, placing the pistol under the pillow.

She then walked over to the door, unlocked the chain, and began to turn the handle. The door crashed in, knocking the agent over the small table, her face scraping across the weathered carpet. She tried to crawl over to the bed, to where her gun lay hidden but was driven down by a knee to her back.

"That'll be enough of that," said a gruff voice.

Agent Green twisted as well as she could and saw a middle-aged man wearing a police uniform now kneeling on her. His gun was pointed at her head. Behind him stood Lisa, her face a portrait of rage.

"Find her I.D.," the cop said.

Lisa made her way to the agent's purse, which was sitting next to her laptop, and dumped it on the bed.

"Don't bother. My name is Joyce Green, and I'm an agent with the Oklahoma Bureau of Investigation."

"Yeah, right," said the cop, digging his knee deeper.

"Holy shit," said Lisa, holding up the agent's wallet. "She's telling the truth."

The cop reached for the ID and held the picture close to Agent Green's face.

"Why don't you get off of me, and we'll just chalk this up to a mistake."

"Yeah," said the cop. "I don't think so. Why don't you tell me why you're here?"

Agent Green tried to pivot to her side and was just able to see the double bars on the man's collar.

"I'm on official business," she said. "We're conducting an investigation."

"Without notifying my office?" said the cop.

"I believe you were contacted by an agent the other day. Aren't you Captain Carter?"

"I am," said Carter. "And I remember that freak. He was looking for a woman but wouldn't tell me why."

"It's a need-to-know thing," said the agent. "I'm sure you understand."

"What I understand is that you are harassing people in my town without a warrant."

"I told you we are investigating. We're not here to arrest anyone."

"So why lead me along," said Lisa. "Why the fuck would you invite me over."

"I was just doing my job," said the agent.

"Well, your job sucks," said Lisa. "And I hope they kill you."

"Shut up, Lisa," said Carter. "Give them a call, tell them who she is, and see what they want us to do with her."

Lisa took her phone out of her back pocket and walked out the door, shutting it behind her.

"Why are you doing this?" said the agent.

"I'm like you, just doing my job."

"But you're an officer," said the agent. "We're on the same side."

"You have no idea what you're talking about. There are no sides in a country that's falling on its ass. All you have to do is look around. But shit flies straight in this town. We've made sure of that."

Lisa came back in, her face flushed.

"They want us to take care of it," she said.

"Sucks to be you, little lady," said the cop, reaching into his utility belt and bringing out a set of cuffs.

Agent Green was lifted with her hands secured behind her back. Lisa walked over to where the grip of the .38 was peeking out from under the pillow.

"What about all of her shit?" she said, grabbing the gun.

"I'll have Reynolds clean up the mess," said Carter, pushing the agent out the door and towards the back of his late model Chevy.

The sky was rapidly darkening as the sun began to settle behind the western mountain range. Captain Carter opened the back door and forced Agent Green in. He slammed the door shut and told Lisa to watch her. Carter went back into the motel room, no doubt giving it one last look over before taking Agent Green out to wherever she was going to die.

"Lisa," she said. The window was cracked, so the girl had no trouble hearing her. "You don't have to do this."

"Shut up," said Lisa. "You were leading me on."

"Only partially," said the agent. "I really do want to help you."

"It looks to me like you're the one who needs help."

"There are more of us here," said the agent. "And there's more of us coming. Don't be a part of this. As of now, you've done nothing wrong. But if you kill me, you'll lose everything. Think about your baby. Do you want him to go back to the pound? Does he deserve that?"

Lisa's face darkened as the agent spoke, her hand gripping the agent's gun.

"Tell me something," she said, turning towards Agent Green. "Did your father even touch you?"

Agent Green could have lied and could have continued with the psychological fib that had brought Lisa to her in the first place, but she decided against it. The time for that was over. It was best to let sincerity have its say and hope that it would be reciprocated.

"Only to hug me," she said. "I know what happened to you, Lisa. I read your file. The only thing I don't understand is why you didn't kill that bastard yourself."

"Don't you think I wanted to?" she said, tears flowing. "Sometimes, he would finish and then just roll off of me and pass out. I could have killed him then. I wanted to."

"You're a braver woman than I am," said the agent.

Lisa looked at her doubtfully.

"No, I mean it. I can't imagine going through what you were forced to go through. I would have killed myself."

Lisa looked up at the sky. Her tears had ceased, but the drying tracks still glistened in the fading orange light.

"It's still an option," she said, sticking the gun into the waistband of her jeans.

Carter walked out of the motel room, closing the door behind him. He tossed Lisa the key to Agent Green's Bronco and said, "Follow me."

He then walked over to the driver's side of the Chevy and climbed in.

"Where are we going?" said Lisa.

"Payton's Bridge," said Carter, starting up the car. "Or what's left of it."

He pulled out onto the road without giving Lisa another glance.

The agent felt her heart pounding and forced herself to take deep breaths. The shadows began swallowing the world, and she could smell the dying foliage in the fall air. Captain Carter drove on as if she wasn't there, gazing from side to side with a slight smile decorating his face. The bastard was enjoying this. Just one less uppity city bitch that the world would have to deal with.

"So, you work for the Henleys," said the agent, and it wasn't a question. "They must pay you very well for you to risk everything by killing an OSBI agent."

"You're damn right, they do," said Carter.

A sudden chime sounded in the cab. Carter reached into his breast pocket and pulled out Agent Green's cell phone.

"Solly," he said, using a horrible Asian accent. "She no home."

He then lowered his window and tossed the phone out. Agent Green looked back and saw that Lisa had come to a stop. Was she grabbing the phone? The agent quickly turned back before Carter could become suspicious.

"Did you murder the old woman in El Reno?"

"I had nothing to do with that," said Carter.

"What about the salesman?"

Again, Carter laughed and said, "Better him than me."

"What do you mean?"

Carter gazed back at her in the rearview mirror, his eyes narrowed.

"You really don't know what you're involved in, do you?"

"Why don't you fill me in," said the agent.

Agent Green was sure that he wanted to. The man was wrapped in his own ego, chomping at the opportunity to prove his superiority. Besides, it wasn't like she was going to be able to tell anyone.

"They're all fucked out," said Carter.

"And I should know what that means?"

"It means that they can't have kids because they've ruined their bloodline."

The truth struck the agent with enough force to cause her to flinch.

"They're kidnapping people to breed with," she said in an almost whisper.

"Now you've got it, sweet cheeks," said Carter. "And let me tell you, I'd hate to be the girl picked for Nithard the Retard."

Carter banked the car to the right, the headlights revealing a narrow dirt road. Within seconds, they came to a wooden blockade with Bridge Out painted across its face.

Carter came to a stop and threw the car into Park.

"I'll be right back," he said, opening the driver's door. "Don't go anywhere."

He then walked over and moved the warning sign out of the way. He drove on for another fifty yards and then stopped.

Agent Green could see the jagged edge of the washed-out bridge shimmering within the headlights. A perpetual roar was coming from the darkness.

"Lucky us," said Carter. "The current is up."

His gun was out, and he pointed at the agent. Lisa pulled beside them as he dragged Agent Green out of the car.

"Park it where the bridge begins," said Carter.

Lisa drove the Bronco ahead, stopping in between the entrance guard rails. She left it running and got out, walking back next to Carter.

"What now?" she said.

"Now, our pretty agent from the city is going to have a seat in her truck."

"And then you're going to shoot me," said Agent Green.

"You *are* good," said Carter.

"It won't look like an accident if I have a bullet in my head."

"By the time you wash up, you'll be in Muskogee," said Carter.

"My office knows I'm here," said the agent.

"Good for them," said Carter. "All they'll have is a bloated body and a rusted Bronco."

"And a bullet," said the agent. "Unless you think that nine-millimeter will go all the way through. That's a hell of a gamble."

"Oh, no!" said Carter, with feigned fear. "Then, if they find the gun in the river, they can trace it back to me. Enough bullshit, get in your truck."

Agent Green began to make her way to the Bronco, daring a look at Lisa, who was standing there with her eyes saucer wide, her hand clutching the agent's gun.

"It's a lot to risk," said the agent. "Losing your baby."

"How did you know about the baby?" said Carter, momentarily pausing.

"She doesn't," said Lisa in a shaky voice. "Let's get this over with."

Carter reached out and opened the Bronco's driver door.

"Get in," he said.

The agent paused. A tree line stood ten yards away, its fall-stripped branches scraping together in the breeze, calling out to her. But she would never make it. For the first time since joining the OSBI, she was sure that she was going to die. An image of her bronzed name being placed next to all the others who had fallen in the line of duty flashed in her mind. All she could do now was hope Agent Wayne would figure out what had happened and stop them.

Agent Green slid into the driver's seat, hoping her face didn't reveal the terror now consuming her.

If I'm going to die, I'll do it with dignity.

Carter waited until her legs were in and then shut the door, pointing the gun at her head.

"Try not to move around too much after you're hit," he said, his low-lit smile like penetrating evil. "I still have to uncuff you, and I'd rather not get blood all over my shirt."

"I can't make that promise," said the agent, and she was surprised at how steady her voice sounded.

She closed her eyes and made a silent prayer. The gentle whisper of the wind blended with the river, and she focused on those sounds.

A gunshot shattered the tranquility, and Agent Green did move.

CHAPTER FORTY-THREE

Wayne Returns, and Lisa Makes a Choice

The winding two-lane highway held Agent Wayne's speed in check. At best, he could do fifty miles per hour on the straight-aways but would then have to tap the brakes as the road veered to the left and right. His Crown Victoria's high beams pierced through the darkness in a losing effort. On each side of the road, the slim shoulder would suddenly vanish, leaving treacherous drops into hidden, silent pools of water.

He had passed the Centurions. They had gathered at a dive- bar in Hulbert, a blip of a town fifteen miles outside of Lost City. Had it not been for the bizarre voice at the other end of Agent Green's phone when he had called her, he would have pulled to the side and waited. But something was wrong.

Empty streets greeted the agent as he pulled into Lost City. The motel looked forsaken, with its dark windows and abandoned parking lot. Agent Wayne brought the cruiser to a stop in front of door number two. He exited the car with his hand placed securely on the butt of his pistol. The door was locked. He gave it a quick rap with his knuckles and then stepped to the side, his ear placed on the panel. There was no sound. Further to his right was the office with a NO VACANCY sign flickering above the door. He gazed down the street to where the Dollar Store's sign stood like a frozen silhouette.

Had she checked out? That wasn't a part of the plan. She was supposed to meet him here. Someone had gotten to her. Could it have been the biker? That would explain the van. If it were them, he might have made the biggest mistake of his life by not stopping when he had the chance. Of course, they might still be at that bar. And yet, it felt wrong.   Why would The Centurions kidnap an OSBI agent? No, somebody would have to have a lot to lose to pull a stunt like that. What had Agent Green stumbled on?

Agent Wayne's eyes drifted back to the motel office as a sudden blast of light washed over him. He turned and saw the unmistakable grill of an old Chevy Impala and a row of blue and red lights perched upon its roof. Following the car was Agent Green's Ford Bronco. He squinted through the beams and felt his heart plummet. The girl driving the Bronco was not Agent Green.

*****

Agent Green heard the shot and fell to her side. She lay there listening but could only hear the rushing tide of the river fighting for dominance against her panicked breath. The driver-side door flung open.

"Get out," said Lisa, the agent's gun clutched firmly in her hand.

Agent Green struggled to sit up and slide out of the Bronco. She forced her knees to lock and willed them to stop shaking. Laying three feet from where she stood was the body of Captain Carter, a bullet hole above his right ear.

"Thank you, Lisa," said the agent.

"Don't thank me yet. I could still make this look like you did it."

"Why would you want to?" said the agent.

"You really don't know what you're into, do you?" said Lisa.

She was right, of course.

"I know about the Henleys," said the agent. "I know that they are kidnapping people."

"Did you know that they are killing people?" said Lisa.

"Like the old lady in El Reno?" said the agent.

"She's just one of many. They killed my dad."

"Is that why you stay here?" said the agent, ignoring the tingling in her confined wrists. "Do you feel like you owe them?"

"I *do* owe them," said Lisa. "Look at all they have done for me."

Yes, it was true, and it was pointless to argue against it.

"Granted," said the agent. "Your father had it coming, and I wasn't kidding when I said I admired you. But what about the old woman in El Reno? She didn't do anything to anyone. Did she deserve to be murdered?"

"I don't know," said Lisa, the gun lowering. "Maybe she did, and maybe she didn't. For all we know, she might have beaten her kids."

"That's a dangerous way to think, Lisa."

"So, what would you have me do? Rat out the only people who ever cared for me?"

"Do you really believe that they care?" said the agent.

Lisa lowered her head. Her face was lost within the shadows of Carter's Impala headlights.

Finally, the girl's face lifted.

"If I help you, what will happen to me?"

"Like I said before, you've done nothing wrong."

But it suddenly occurred to Agent Green that she didn't know if that was true.

"What do you want me to do?" said Lisa.

"The first thing is to get me out of these damn cuffs. I can't feel my hands."

Lisa made her way over to the dead man, crouching down beside him. After a moment, she returned with a set of keys in her hand and walked around to the back of the agent. Agent Green hid the anxiousness coursing through her as best as she could. The girl could still change her mind. A sigh of relief escaped from the thump of the handcuffs hitting the dirt. The agent brought her hands to the front, rubbing her wrists.

"Here," said Lisa, handing the agent the gun. "If you're going to arrest me, just get it over with,"

"I can't do that," said the agent, taking the .38. "You've got to drive my Bronco."

"What? Why?"

"I'm taking Carter's car and we're going back to the motel. But first, help me move his body."

Together, they dragged Carter into the thick brush lining the side of the dirt road.

"Isn't this illegal?" said Lisa. "It being a crime scene and all?"

"Correct me if I'm wrong, but if he is on Henley's take, then so are the other officers."

"That's true," said Lisa, "and Reynolds knew we were coming to see you."

"So, if he comes out here, he won't find anything."

"I understand," said Lisa.

Agent Green took a moment and searched through the pockets of the dead man.

"Ah ha!" she said, coming away with his cell phone.

The agent stood, and Lisa followed her back to the vehicles. She grabbed Carter's keys from Lisa and went to the Impala.

"Follow me to the motel," she said. "And don't stop for anything."

CHAPTER FORTY-FOUR

An Imminent Threat

The agent had been dealt with. At least Grenalda Henley hoped that she had. There was still no word from Carter, and he wasn't answering his phone. Grenalda gazed down at the diamond-clustered watch on her thin wrist. It read 8:46 pm. It had been over an hour and a half since Lisa called her about the agent's identity. She stood over Phillip's shoulder, who was perched at a desk, gazing at a computer monitor with information about the Centurions filling the screen. Lining the wall above them was a row of small video screens, each one showing a different exterior angle of their mansion. To Grenalda's left by the doorway was Nithard, his massive shoulders wider than the door frame. To his right was Marianna, with little Ferdinand sleeping in her arms. Her family, a family that was finally beginning to grow, was now in jeopardy.

Anger flooded the old woman's veins. How could that fatherless bitch be so stupid? Lisa had almost brought the wolves to the door. But that wasn't quite true, was it? No. Genalda had been paving the way for a long time, beginning with taking Charlie under her wing. A trembling sigh escaped from her misshapen mouth, causing Phillip to look up at her with concern.

"What is it, mother?" he said.

"I'm scared, Phillip," she said. "I've made a horrible mistake. I should have never allowed myself to get involved with Charlie."

"It was a plan forced out of desperation," said Phillip. "How could you have known that the man was a bastard?"

"I should have known," she said. "And now look at what's going on. We have the OSBI on one side, and these outlaws are coming at us from the other. And they can all be traced back to that fat man."

"Carter will take care of the agent," said Nithard, his voice sounding like distant thunder. "As for these guys, I'll deal with them."

"What do you think they want?" she said, ignoring the giant.

"Considering what I've read and how that motorcycle gang and Charlie are so close, I have to assume that those bikers have been told about us."

"But why?" said Grenalda.

"Perhaps Charlie is using them to get to us. Or maybe they are afraid of being implicated in something. Surely, Charlie has utilized them before. Perhaps they were unknowingly a part of a scheme related to us."

Grenalda looked down at Phillip, her eyes wide.

"Yes, of course," she said. "That woman he brought us. That idiot could never have pulled that off alone."

"It's very possible that these gentlemen were the ones who actually carried out the dirty work."

"So now what?" said Grenalda. "They want us to pay them to keep their mouths shut?"

"I seriously doubt that," said Phillip. "I don't think money is the issue."

"What do you mean?" said Nithard.

"I think they're going to make sure that we keep our mouths shut, and it won't be with a promise."

"They wouldn't dare," said Marianne.

"I think they very much would, and most likely soon, considering how far away from home they are."

"Would they come here?" said Marianne.

"Indeed, they have already been here," said Phillip, pointing at the center screen on the wall. "And these people are not to be taken lightly. They are killers."

Grenalda found herself thinking about her husband. He would

have known what to do. Of course, if he were still alive, she doubted very much if they would have been in this situation to begin with. He would never have brought in an outsider like Charlie for a long-term plan. He would have known better. This thought only intensified the guilt, drawing out another sigh.

"Are we really going to let these beasts attack our home?" said Marianna, her voice riddled with anxiety. "What about the baby? What if something happens to him?"

That thought had been like a stone weighing on Grenalda's chest. The risk of losing the child, the first of what was supposed to be many, left the old woman feeling breathless. This could very well be the end of them all. Nithard was a true monster. He could probably handle two or three of them by himself. But these men, these creatures, wouldn't be armed with sticks and knives. They would be carrying the latest in automatic weapons and quite possibly more.

Grenalda managed to keep her gaze steady as she looked over at Marianne.

"When they arrive, I want you to take the child and wait for us in the basement."

"But what if something happens to you?" said Marianna. "How will I know?"

"We'll come get you when it's over," said the old woman.

She again looked down at her watch and saw that it was now after nine, and still no word.

"I'm going to try Carter again," she said.

She grabbed the phone off the desk. It was answered on the third ring.

CHAPTER FORTY-FIVE

Unwelcome Company

The embrace was a surprise, but Agent Wayne couldn't help himself. The image of Lisa driving Agent Green's Bronco sent a current of dread, and for one horrific second, he was sure that the agent was dead. But then she climbed out of Captain Carter's patrol car. That was when he rushed to her, his arms outstretched. Agent Green patted him on the back like a soothing mother would.

"Why, Agent Wayne, this seems less than professional."

"I thought you were dead," he said.

"Actually, so did I," she said.

Lisa stood in the background, her head lowered, kicking at loose rocks in the parking lot.

"What the hell happened?" said Agent Wayne, releasing her.

Agent Green told him how she had been abducted from her room and how Lisa had saved her in the end. She also filled him in on what Carter had said.

"So, they're kidnapping people to continue their bloodline," said Agent Wayne. "That would explain a lot of unanswered questions." He then looked over at Lisa and said, "What can you add to this?"

"I didn't know anything about that," she said. "I knew that they recently had a baby. I had to take them formula and diapers, but I never asked any questions."

"What about the bikers?" said Agent Wayne. "Do you know anything about them?"

"What bikers?" said Lisa. "We don't have any bikers here. Mrs. Henley would never allow it."

It was then a phone rang. Agent Green reached into the back pocket of her jeans and pulled out Captain Carter's cell phone. She held the screen up to Lisa and said, "Do you recognize this number?"

"It's them," said Lisa.

After a couple of seconds, the line went dead.

"They're going to think something's wrong," said Lisa.

"And they'll be right," said Agent Green.

"Lisa," said Agent Wayne. "There's no reason for you to be involved any further. You've helped us enough, and we can't put you in further danger."

"He's right, Lisa," said Agent Green. "Thank you for saving me. But you should go home. Take care of that dog of yours."

"You're going to arrest them," said Lisa. "And then what am I going to do? I'll be out of a job."

"They are killing people, Lisa," said Agent Green. "What's to say they won't kill–"

A roar from the east cut her off. Slicing through the darkness was a pair of growing beams.

"Get behind a car and duck down," said Agent Wayne, already making his way to the Impala.

Agent Green grabbed Lisa, and together, they dropped to the side of the Ford Bronco. The rumbling motor grew closer, echoing off the empty buildings like an oncoming storm in a canyon. Within moments, a dark van zipped by, its taillights faintly glowing red.

"It's the Centurions," said Agent Wayne.

"What are they doing?" said Agent Green.

Carter's phone rang again.

"Let Lisa answer it," said Agent Wayne.

"And what do I say?" said Lisa, her voice shaking.

"Tell them that bikers just passed through town, and then tell them I want to speak to them."

Lisa looked at the agent for a moment, unsure of what to do.

Finally, she reached out her hand and took the phone from Agent Green.

*****

There was no casual greeting upon hearing Lisa's voice.

"Where's Carter?"

"He's no longer with us," said Lisa.

"What does that mean? Where is --"

"Listen to me," said Lisa, cutting her off. "A van full of bikers just passed through town heading your way."

The knuckles of the old woman's hand threatened to burst through paper-thin skin. They were coming. Lisa had seen them. But how could she know they were bikers if they were in a van? Could Lisa be a part of it? Could Carter? That wasn't possible.

"There's more," said Lisa, her voice trembling.

"What is it?" hissed Grenalda, but she wasn't sure that she wanted to know.

"Someone here wants to speak with you."

There was a muffled sound of the phone being handed off.

"Mrs. Henley, this is Agent Wayne of The Oklahoma Bureau of Investigation. The Centurions are coming for you. I know this is Charlie's doing, and I also know that you have the salesman."

"I don't know what you're talking about," she said.

"That's fine," said the agent. "I must have made a mistake. But just in case, I want you to know that these guys don't care about age or gender; they'll kill everyone."

Grenalda turned her gaze to where Ferdinand was being held in Marianna's arms. She could see that her daughter had overheard the agent.

Agent Wayne was telling the truth, as Phillip had already confirmed. The motorcycle demons might be able to be defeated, but even if they were, the agent knew about the liar. The family would be going down one way or the other. But maybe not all of them. Perhaps there might be a way to save Marianna and Phillip. Grenalda clutched the phone closer to her ear. She then looked to where Nith stood like a hell-spawned soldier awaiting his orders. She turned back just as a

245

shadowy shape flitted across one of the screens. Phillip reached for the keyboard, and Grenalda watched as he maneuvered the security camera, panning the picture to the right.

"They're here," said Phillip.

The old woman placed her free hand on his shoulder, trying to steady the wave of terror threatening to consume her.

"Can you track them?"

Phillip pivoted the camera to the right, stopping on another shadowy form. He began zooming in on the figure when the screen went blank. Within moments, the other screens started to flicker and then die. Nithard turned and left the room without a sound. Grenalda watched him leave in silence and couldn't help but wonder if she would ever see him alive again. A part of her hoped that she wouldn't. It would make things much easier.

"Mrs. Henley, is everything alright?"

Grenalda had forgotten that the agent was still on the phone.

"If you want to save the salesman, you had better hurry," she said, killing the call.

She then turned to where Marianna stood frozen, her tilted eyes a caricature of fear.

"Go to the basement," the old woman said, but the girl didn't move. "Marianna, do as I say!"

Marianna blinked as if coming out of a dream. She spared a horrified look at her mother and then shuffled out of the room. Phillip clicked away at the keyboard, but the security screens remained dark.

"They cut the lines," he said.

"All of them?" said Grenalda.

"It appears so," said Phillip.

He then slithered off the desk and crawled to a small shoe closet near the corner of the room. He opened the panels, and hanging from one was a compact crossbow and five steel-tipped bolts attached to its stock. From the opened cubby came a cold, damp breeze. An odor, like saturated earth, filled the room. Phillip reached in his hand and fumbled around for a moment. Within seconds, a row of lights flashed, weakly illuminating a narrow tunnel.

"Perhaps you should also go to the basement," he said.

"Nonsense," snapped the old woman. "I'm not leaving you boys alone."

Phillip seemed to want to say more but then decided against it. He lifted himself into the tunnel.

"Phillip," said Grenalda. "Be careful."

The bald man gave her a razor-thin smile and closed the panels behind him.

Grenalda stood silently watching the place where Phillip had disappeared. The boy was anything but helpless, and he had his hidden arsenal placed within the tunnels he had created. But his physical disabilities inhibited him, and if they were to catch him, there would be no mercy. These bikers were used to people fearing them; they made their living by promoting terror. Perhaps it was time for them to meet someone who wasn't so afraid. Someone who had crossed the lines of murder on more than one occasion. What's the worst they could do, kill her? She was already dead. A sudden shattering of glass was soon followed by a wall-rattling explosion. The beasts had breached the gates and would soon raze the remains. Grenalda knew how it worked.

The fear that had been lingering within her veins dissolved. She considered finding a weapon, but what good would it do? These men were armed to the teeth. No. Her best weapon right now was time, and she needed to buy as much of it as possible. Grenalda made her way out of the room.

CHAPTER FORTY-SIX

Freedom

"What was that?"

Karen was standing at the wall of bars. Jimmy leaped off his cot just as the metal door grind from above echoed throughout the dungeon. It was followed by a muffled boom.

"Was that an explosion?" said Karen.

"I don't know, but someone is coming," said Jimmy.

Marianna came around the lava rock corner, her thin hair clinging to her face. The baby was clutched in her arms and was beginning to cry. Marianna rushed to the center of the room and collapsed to her knees.

"What's going on?" said Jimmy.

Marianna spun around, and Jimmy could clearly see the terror decorating her face. She had the look of the cornered animal he had destroyed a thousand years ago.

"We're being attacked?"

"By who?" said Jimmy. "Is it the police?"

"No," she managed to stammer. "It's bikers, friends of Charlie."

Jimmy gazed over at Karen, who was staring down at Marianna with a hate that he could almost smell.

"What bikers?" he said.

"I don't know," said Marianna. "But they're here, and they want to kill us."

"Good," said Karen. "Let them."

Marianna's head whipped towards Karen, causing her to step back.

"They're not here just to kill us," she said. "They'll kill everyone. The agent said so."

"The cops know we're here?" said Jimmy.

"They do now," said Marianne, her lower lip quivering. "Thanks to that bitch, Lisa."

That name mattered little to Jimmy. What did matter was that the police were close. All they had to do was survive until they arrived.

Do you really think they'll let you be taken alive? A voice whispered in his mind, its tone very familiar.

Jimmy shook his head, clearing out the unwanted words. But that voice was right. There was no way this family would let them go. They would kill them both first. Jimmy gazed up at the keys hanging on a hook across the room.

"How many bikers are there?" he asked.

"I don't know," she said.

"Marianna," said Jimmy. "Come over here."

The woman looked at him for a moment, her eyes glowing with distrust.

"You don't have to come in, but I need to talk to you."

Marianna slowly rose to her feet, the baby held close to her breast. She stumbled towards the cell, her eyes never leaving his, stopping just inches from the door.

"Marianna, we are supposed to be married," he said in the softest voice he could muster. "You are going to be my wife."

She looked up at him, her offset eyes welling with tears.

"You don't love me," she said. "If you could leave, you would."

"At first, yes. And can you blame me?" he said. "I had just been kidnapped. But then I got to know you. You are the only reason I didn't kill myself. Did you know that?"

The tears were now rolling down her cheeks.

"The time we made love meant more to me than you'll ever

know," he continued. "And you were right; the world is full of monsters, so what do I really have to lose? Don't you understand what I'm trying to say?"

Marianna held his eyes, and he could see that she yearned to believe. To be loved was all that she had ever wanted. The chaos from above had made her terrified, had broken the promised chain of events that were hers by birthright, and she was now losing everything—but perhaps not everything if what Jimmy was saying was true.

"What about her?" she said, cocking her head back to where Karen now stood, watching them through her cage.

"Oh honey, he's all yours," said Karen. "We're divorced."

Another explosion sent particles of dust raining down upon their heads. Marianna stepped back, the fear again painting her face.

"Listen to me," said Jimmy, pulling her gaze back. "I want to help you. I want to help Ferdinand. We can beat them."

Marianne was frozen. Jimmy could see the conflict playing out within her disfigured face. This went against her mother, possibly against her better judgment, and yet, she needed to believe. Finally, she stepped closer to the cell, her shoulders slumped, her arms shaking.

"Do you love me, Jimmy?" she asked.

He almost leaped forward with an answer that would have locked him away forever. Instead, he drew a long breath and slowly let it out, his eyes locked onto hers.

"I don't know, Marianna. I only know that I miss you when you're not with me."

Marianna gazed at him, her ice-blue eyes unwavering. She then turned and made her way over to the keys, grabbing them off the wall.

"I'll let you out," she said, returning to his cell door. "But she stays."

"Fuck her," said Jimmy. "We don't owe her shit."

Jimmy forced his body to remain still as the key entered the lock. He stepped out of the cell before the door opened entirely, like a dog left alone for too long.

"Are you seriously going to leave me here?" said Karen. Jimmy could see that she sincerely believed that he would.

After all he had put her through, who could blame her? He ignored her question and focused on the infant clutched in Marianna's shaking arms.

"Marianna," he said. "You're trembling. Let me carry him."

Without hesitating, Marianna handed the baby over.

"What do we do now?" she said.

"We need to arm ourselves," said Jimmy. "Do you have any guns?"

"Not down here," she said.

Just narcotics and knives, thought Jimmy to himself.

"What is that on the table?" he said.

Marianna followed his gaze. There was never a moment of doubt. Jimmy didn't have time. He curled his right hand into a fist and aimed for the woman's elongated chin. A sharp, nauseating crack filled his ears. Marianna turned back towards him, her eyes, at first wide with shock, rolled back into her skull. She collapsed to the floor, her arms splayed out as if being nailed to a cross.

"Holy shit," said Karen. "Did you just kill her?"

"I hope not," said Jimmy, reaching for the keys.

He walked over to Karen's cell and opened the door.

"Here. Take the baby."

Karen stepped out of the cell, grabbing the wide-awake Ferdinand.

Jimmy made his way back to Marianna, knelt, and placed his finger on her throat. She had a pulse. He then took her by the wrists and dragged the unconscious woman into his vacated cell, putting her on his cot. Jimmy gazed down at her for a moment. Blood was streaming out of the corner of her mouth.

"I'm sorry," he whispered and then exited the cell, locking the door behind him.

Karen came over with Ferdinand now nestled against her shoulder. From above, they could hear the cracks of gunfire and the sound of breaking glass. They gazed up the metal stairway to where the door stood waiting.

"What are we going to do?" said Karen.

It was a question that was impossible to answer. There was a war upstairs, and they wanted only one thing: a way out, like a family of refugees. But there would be no liberation. According to Marianna, the attackers were just as bad, if not worse, than the ones who had held them hostage. They could stay here and wait for the police to arrive, but what if they came too late? Jimmy's eyes drifted to the infant. He lay cradled within Karen's arm. The baby had yet to make a sound. Perhaps they had been sedating him, as well.

"Jimmy," said Karen, her voice sounding distant. "Are you okay?"

And unlike the other question, this one was easy to answer.

"No," he said. "Come on, we have to get out of here."

Jimmy took her free hand, and together, they began to climb the stairs.

CHAPTER FORTY-SEVEN

An Injury at The Fence

Lisa sat in the passenger seat of the Bronco while Agent Green clutched the steering wheel, her eyes locked onto the road. At first, Agent Wayne opposed bringing Lisa along because of the safety issue and because he wasn't completely sure that Lisa was on their side. She was right, after all. Her life was about to change forever. However, Agent Green insisted that without her directing them, she would never have been able to find the house at night. He sat in the back seat with his hand resting on his .38. The road was like driving in a cave, and it seemed that even the Bronco's high beams struggled to penetrate the shroud.

"Go left here," said Lisa.

A narrow dirt road appeared like a magician's trick and Agent Green tapped her way into the turn.

"This is the road those assholes ran me off," she said. "The house is just a mile or so up on the right."

Agent Wayne leaned forward between the women, struggling to keep himself steady as the Ford's suspension was tested by the gullies of the battered lane. A distant silver light appeared on their right and began to grow. Within moments, they could see it was the reflection of a back bumper. It was the van, parked next to the tall cinder block wall.

Agent Green stopped a few feet from the back of the van. Agent Wayne pulled his .38 and exited the Bronco. He stood behind the open door momentarily, watching for any sign of movement. The van appeared to be empty.

"Wait here," said Agent Green, opening the driver's door.

Lisa reached out her hand, gripping the agent's knee.

"Be careful," she said.

"I intend to," said the agent, and made her way out of the Bronco.

A sudden blast from beyond the wall filled the night, causing her to pause. Agent Wayne rushed to the van's rear, grabbed the access ladder attached to the back door, and went to the roof. Another explosion rippled through the darkness.

"That was a gun," he said. "We've got to get in there."

Agent Green climbed up to where Agent Wayne stood calculating the odds of jumping over.

"We're going to have to go for it," he said.

He then placed his hands on the top of the wall and hoisted himself. He straddled the edge for a moment trying to gauge the distance down.

"I can't see shit," he said.

"It can't be more than ten feet," said Agent Green. "That's nothing for a spry lad such as yourself."

"Very encouraging," said Agent Wayne.

He then lowered himself over the other side, his hands gripping the top like a cliff.   "Here goes nothing," he grunted and let go.

A sound of scraping metal was soon followed by a heavy thud like a bag of flour hitting the ground.

"Wyatt?" said agent Green, her voice a forced whisper. "Wyatt, are you okay?"

"Don't come down yet," he said in a strained voice. "There's a ladder."

Agent Green could hear something being dragged across the brush.

"Okay," he said. "You're clear for landing."

Agent Green pivoted her way over the wall and landed a few feet away from where Agent Wayne sat, his back resting against the cinderblock. His right leg was bent, and he was holding his ankle.

"I think it's broken," he said.

Agent Green knelt beside him, placing her hand on his shoulder. They had called for backup before leaving the motel but could not give the exact location. Even Lisa didn't know the physical address to this place, so the agency was going to send their two closest agents from Tulsa to Lost City and await further instructions. That was forty minutes ago, and the drive from Tulsa was over an hour. That would mean, at best, the agents were still thirty minutes out.

"Does your phone have a signal?" she said.

Agent Wayne reached into his front pocket, pulling out the Android.

"Barely," he said.

"We should call an ambulance," she said.

"Not until this is over. Let's get our back up here first and then I'll go."

"Drop a pin and let them know where we're at," she said, rising to her feet.

"I don't think you should go in there alone," said Agent Wayne, and as if to prove it, another sound of gunfire blasted through the night. A thud startled them both as Lisa landed to their right.

"What happened?" she said.

"You were supposed to stay in the car," said Agent Green.

"Yeah. Fuck that," said Lisa. "I'm not staying alone."

"Good," said Agent Green. "You can wait here with him until the cavalry shows up."

"What are you going to do?" said Lisa.

"My job," said Agent Green, pulling out her .38.

They watched her disappear into the shadows just as a flicker of orange lit in the distance.

"She's going in there by herself?" said Lisa.

"No," said Agent Wayne.

He took a deep breath, pulled his gun and lifted himself off the ground, using the wall as a brace. He tentatively stepped out onto his bad ankle. Pain erupted, dropping him to the ground, his gun skipping out of his hand and clanking off the ladder. The impact of hitting the dirt sent a wave of torture up his spine. He sat there for a moment allowing the pain to run its course. Finally, he was able to open his eyes and turned towards Lisa.

Both she and the gun were gone.

CHAPTER FORTY-EIGHT

Battle In the Mansion

Grenalda made her way down the hallway. Portraits of those long gone stared accusingly through the thickening smoke rising from the floor level. They would soon be reduced to ash, and she could do nothing to stop it. She cleared the archway and paused on the landing. The crystal chandelier swung from left to right, its long chain groaning from the strain. Her sixteenth century table was directly under the crystal, and it was beginning to smolder. Small flames sparked throughout the room, caused by whatever had been thrown through the large picture window to the right of the door. Motion pulled her vision away from the disaster.

A man was approaching the foot of the stairs. He was wearing a ski mask, his torso covered in a leather jacket that hung down to a pair of faded jeans. In his gloved hands was an AR-15.

"You bastard," she said.

That caused the man to pause. It was then that another masked man appeared at the broken window. He leaped through the frame, and she saw that he was much larger than the one standing at the foot of the stairs. The man flanked the other, his sawed-off shotgun raised.

"Holy shit," the big one said. "You *are* ugly."

"You're the ones wearing a mask," said Grenalda.

"Go get her ass," said the man.

The one closest to the stairs began to make his way up to her, his automatic rifle leveled at her chest. She considered falling back towards the hall for a moment, but it would do no good. There was nowhere to run. Plus, they were focused on her, which at least gave the others time. The man stepped onto the landing and took her by the elbow.

"Come on, you old prune," he said, pushing her towards the stairs.

She glared at Ben as she descended.

"Just two of you?" she said. "That's not very smart."

"Don't you worry about that," he said. "What you should be worried about is where the other members of your fucked up family are, because it's about to get ugly."

He then pointed the sawed-off at the chandelier and let loose a round. The crystal shattered, sending razor-thin pieces of shrapnel down on Grenalda's head. The repercussion still hung in the air as he pumped out the empty shell, loading another.

"The next one takes the old bitches left hand, and then her right!" he said. "I could go on, but I think you get the idea."

The house remained silent, except for the popping of the spreading flames.

"Bring her here," said Ben, walking over to the stairwell. "Put her hand on the rail."

The man dragged her by the left arm and forced it onto the banister.

"If he tries to leave," began Ben. "I have a guy outside with an AK-47 waiting."

"I don't know what you're talking about," she said.

"Fuck it," said Ben, lifting the shotgun. "Let's start with the hand and see what happens."

A cry from behind startled the big man. He spun around, allowing Grenalda to see past him. The calmness that she had forced herself to embrace fled like water down an open drain. Her knees unhinged and she fell to the floor.

"No," she whispered. It was the only thing she could manage to say.

*****

The metal door was much heavier than Jimmy expected. He waited with Karen behind him until it stopped against the hallway wall. An instant whiff of burning wood mixed with sulfur filled his nose, making his eyes water. He spared a quick look back at Karen and the baby. Ferdinand's eyes were wide open, but the child had yet to make a sound. Karen choked back a cough and turned her head away from the doorway. Jimmy hunkered down and motioned for her to do the same. Together they began to creep up the picture-laden hall.

He could hear voices. What they were saying wasn't what concerned Jimmy; it was from where they were saying it. It sounded as if they were directly in front of them. He brought Karen to a halt, trying to remember the layout of the house. How many days ago had it been? A week? A month? Jimmy couldn't remember.

He recognized the hall they were in, but his mind was blank as far as how to get out.

"We can't just stay here," said Karen, her mouth inches from his ear.

Jimmy began to move. The tall archway grew with each step that they took. Within moments they found themselves standing at the threshold. The wide-open foyer now lay before them. Jimmy stopped mid-stride, causing Karen to run into him. But it couldn't be helped, for what he saw was like a level of hell. Scattered flames burned throughout the room. Broken glass lay sprayed across the floor with prismatic orange light. The gold base of a chandelier hung twisted off a long chain. Underneath it stood three people, two were wearing ski-masks and with them was the evil queen, herself.

"Fuck it," said one of the men, and Jimmy noticed that the guy was huge. Not quite as big as Nith, but close. "Let's start with the hand and then see what happens."

It was then that little Ferdinand had finally decided he had had enough. He began squirming in Karen's arm with a strength that surprised her.

"Oh shit," she hissed, placing her other arm under him.

The infant took a deep breath, held it for a second, and then released a sound like an enraged banshee. The big man turned, and Jimmy felt his spine freeze. The man was holding a twelve-gauge shotgun shaved to the stock. Jimmy barely noticed the old woman falling to the floor. His eyes were locked on the gun.

They'll kill us all, Marianna had said, and Jimmy had no reason to doubt her.

"Hey," he said, stepping out into the large room. "Thank you for saving us."

"Who the fuck are you?" said the big man.

"My name is Jim Varnett," he said, motioning for Karen to follow. "These people kidnapped us."

The man stepped towards them, his gun pointing at Jimmy's head.

"They seem to do that, a lot," he said.

He motioned him to the side and stopped a few feet from where Karen struggled with Ferdinand.

"Did they kidnap the kid too?"

"That baby's mother was murdered," said Jimmy. "I saw them do it."

"I see," said the man.

Suddenly the old lady spoke, her voice laced with venom.

"That's Ben Lanchino, liar. He's with the Centurions. He's friends with Charlie. All you're doing is digging your own grave."

The large man began to laugh. He spun towards the old lady and said, "You're right, you old hag."

He then reached up and pulled off his mask. The other man did the same.

"What's the point of wearing these things if you already know who we are?"

Ben turned back to Jimmy, his bearded face glowing from the flames.

"So, you know Charlie Wheaton?" he said.

"I used to work for him," said Jimmy.

"Ah, so he sold you off, just like he did his girlfriend over there."

"Listen, man," said Jimmy. "I have no doubt that you have a beef with these wackos. If you just let us go, we won't say a word."

"You see that's the problem," said Ben. "There's already been too much talking going on."

"But not from us," said Jimmy. "We don't know shit."

"We'll see about that."

Ben walked over to where the old woman was perched on her knees, her heavy chinned face stone still, eyes blazing into his. He placed the barrel on the top of Grenalda's head.

"This is your last chance, kids. Come out or I pull the trigger."

Jimmy felt his heart switch from jackhammer to live wire. This man was going to do it. Where was the giant? And where was Phillip? Had they abandoned the wicked queen?

The flames continued to grasp at whatever they could find. One fire was consuming an old table near a set of antique curtains. Once those ignited, things would move along a lot quicker. Jimmy noticed a pile of ash being pushed away from a wall vent near a baseboard. The iron vent cover was slowly being slid open. From out of the gap appeared a miniature crossbow and he could see the steel tip of a bolt reflecting in the fire. A twang rang out. The bolt flew, its slanted upward journey ending in Ben's right thigh.

It was then that the wicked queen chose to act. She lunged up, grasping the shotgun, just as Ben cried out in furious pain. The other man leapt towards him, spinning his AR-15 around in blind confusion. A blast thundered through the room with a flash that left phantoms dancing in front of Jimmy's eyes.

A voice burst over the residual ringing in Jimmy's ear.

"MOTHER!"

An adjoining panel to their left splintered, throwing chunks of wood like an exploding grenade. Jimmy looked over to where Grenalda lay on her side, most of her head missing. A sound, like falling boulders, rocked the floor as a shape filled the shadowed void of the shattered doorway and Jimmy knew that the giant had at last come, and he was pissed.

CHAPTER FORTY-NINE

Green Gets Help and Ben Meets the Giant

Agent Green crouched behind the Winnebago. The fire in the house was intensifying. There was violence happening within those walls, and more than likely people were about to die, if not already dead. Perhaps she should have listened to Agent Wayne and waited; she was hopelessly outnumbered. But there were innocent people inside. The salesman being one, and probably others. By the time the backup arrived it would most likely be too late.

Suddenly, a voice spoke from behind.

"Well, hello there."

The agent spun around and found herself staring into the barrel of an assault rifle. The man had crept up behind her without making a sound. How had he done that? She cursed under her breath. She had been too lost in her thoughts and had forgotten rule number one: Always pay attention to your surroundings.

"Easy now," the man said. "Toss that gun over here and have a seat."

Agent Green briefly wondered if she could get a shot off before being ripped apart and decided she most likely couldn't. She tossed her .38 at the man's boots and dropped to the ground.

"So," said the man. "Who might you be?"

"Agent Joyce Green with the OSBI. You must be with the Centurions."

"What gave it away?" the man said.

From the house the orange light continued to grow,

"Aren't your friends in there?" she said. "Shouldn't you be helping them?"

"They're doing just fine," he said. "Let's talk about you. What are you doing here?"

Agent Green gazed back at the house and thought she could hear screaming. The man in the mask seemed unconcerned. This was no surprise; these men were used to terror.

"We're here for the same reason," she said. "To stop this crazy family. That's why you're here, isn't it?"

"Maybe," he said. "Maybe not."

Another explosion came from the mansion followed by a roar, causing the man to flinch.

"It doesn't look like you're here to sell cookies," said Agent Green.

A painful cry carried over the flames.

"Lester!"

"You must be Lester," said the agent. "Give me my gun and I'll help you."

The man gazed over at the flames dancing through the broken window. The agent could see indecisive fear reflecting in his eyes.

"We have to hurry, Lester," she said. "They're going to be killed."

"I have a better idea," he said, turning his gaze and his gun towards her.

For the second time that day, Agent Green was sure that she was going to die.

"There's more of us here," she tossed out, but he believed it about as much as Captain Carter had earlier.

"Can't wait to meet them," he said, leveling the rifle at her chest.

A sudden shot rang out. Agent Green fell back as the front of the man's head broke open, spraying the agent with blood and bone. He dropped to his knees and collapsed onto his side. Behind him was Lisa, a smoking barrel of a .38 extended in her hand. The girl's arm dropped to her side, the pistol falling to the ground. Within seconds her knees unhinged, and she followed.

Agent Green fought back a wave of emotion and crawled over to where Lisa now sat with her legs drawn up, her head resting on her knees. The agent came to a stop beside the grief-stricken girl and threw her arm around her. Twice in one day she had almost died and both times had been saved by a girl whose only concern in this world was for a dog. But Lisa was no killer. Agent Green could see that now. So, the agents' salvation would come with a price, which included sleepless nights and horrifying nightmares. Agent Green could not let her face that alone. She would do whatever it took to see that Lisa came out of this as best as she could. But first she would have to survive.

She looked over at the Winnebago. It would have to do.

"Come on," she said, rising to her feet.

Lisa looked up at her with a vacant stare. Agent Green took her by the arms and gently helped her to her feet.

"Where are we going?" said Lisa.

"I want you to wait inside of the RV until I get back."

Lisa's eyes widened, and her hands reached out to the agent.

"You can't leave me alone," she said.

"Lisa, you've done enough," said Agent Green, taking her hands. "Keep the gun and use it, but only if you have to. I'll be back."

Lisa followed the agent to the RV's door. Agent Green silently prayed that it was unlocked and felt a wave of relief when the panel opened. The girl walked up the steps and then turned back.

"I feel horrible," she said.

"I know you do, honey," said the agent.

But she didn't know. How could she? She had never killed a person, much less two in one night.

"Just stay here and I'll be back. I promise."

She watched Lisa stumble into the darkness of the RV's aisle and then shut the door. The silhouette of the man's body lay six feet away. Walking over, Agent Green holstered her .38 and picked up the assault rifle. The agent could still hear the crashing sounds of a struggle, which was good. At least they were all still occupied. She began to make her way towards the large front door, checking the rifle and ensuring it was locked and loaded.

*****

The giant thundered forward. The man with the AR-15 managed to get one shot off, catching Nith on his right shoulder. The impact of the bullet caused his arm to kick back but didn't break his stride. The man attempted to squeeze off another round but was struck by a massive fist. He was sent sprawling across the floor, the gun flying from his hands. Ben was able to chamber a shell into the sawed-off and was taking aim just as a second steel-tipped bolt caught him in the lower back. He screamed out in pain and his shot went wide, blasting a hole in the wall to the giant's right. Nith was on him before Jimmy could blink.

Jimmy watched in awe as Nith grabbed the man by his shoulders, scooting the biker back. Ben lashed out with his hands, slamming them against the giant's arms, trying to free himself, but it was like striking an iron rail. The biker planted his booted feet, and yet they continued to slide like a car being pushed by a semi-truck. Disbelief and fear painted Ben's face. Within seconds the biker's back struck a wall. The giant released the man's shoulders and took him by the throat.

"Lester!" Ben managed to scream.

An image of Nith coming into his cell flashed in Jimmy's mind, and he shuddered. He had been pissed about the murdered woman when he had challenged the beast, but now all he could do was cringe. He watched as Ben's feet rose from the floor. A heated blast came from the front window. The fire finally caught the ancient drapes. The flames raced up, licking the ceiling. All around them the fire continued to grow, and soon there would be no way out. And still Jimmy couldn't take his eyes off Nith. Ben was kicking out with his boots, clipping the giant's thighs and even landing a couple of shots on the man's crotch. But the giant hardly seemed to notice, and Jimmy watched in horrific fascination as the biker's eyes bulged from his skull and his legs went still.

A furious scream erupted. The man that Nith had knocked to the floor was up and charging at the giant's back.

"Watch out!" said Jimmy, and even years later he could never really say why he had warned the killer, although he was glad that he did.

Nith released Ben, who fell lifelessly to the floor, and turned just as the man was leaping, a bowie blade cocked in his right hand. The giant caught the man's wrist and then shot his other hand out, gripping the man's throat. A sound, like a branch being broken, split through the crackling flames. The giant let go of the man, who then crumpled to the floor, the enraged look on his face now replaced by one of shock. His legs twitched for a moment and then stopped.

Nith walked back over to where the man who had murdered his mother lay. Ben tried to sit up but couldn't get his arms to comply. The giant stood over him for a moment, his massive chest heaving. He then lifted his foot and put it down on Ben's head. The biker let out a final scream.

"We have to get out of here," said Karen.

She was correct; their time for escaping was running out. A sudden crash caused Karen to cry out as the chandelier smashed to the floor, its chain winding across the headless queen. The front door and both flanking windows of the foyer were engulfed in flame.

"I don't think we can go that way," said Jimmy.

A mountain suddenly eclipsed the orange glare, and Jimmy felt his heart freeze. Nith was blocking the way. Blood was streaming down his gorilla-like arm, sweat boiling out of his protruding forehead. His bulbous eyes glared down at Jimmy like laser-sights. Would he kill them both? Or would he spare Karen until later?

"Where is Marianna?" he said.

He had forgotten about Marianna. The girl was most certainly going to die. Did he dare tell the giant the truth? It probably wouldn't matter either way. If Nith wanted to kill them, there would be little they could do about it.

"I left her in the basement," said Jimmy.

"Is she alive?" said Nith.

"Yes," said Jimmy. "She's in my cell. The keys are on the floor."

The giant looked past them down the hall. Smoke was filling the area, but the flames had yet to make their mark. He then looked down at Karen and the baby held in her arms.

"Is he okay?" he said.

"He is for now," said Karen. "But he won't be if we don't get out of here."

The giant gazed at the infant for a moment and Jimmy thought that he could see tears forming in the corner of the creature's eyes.

"Follow me," said Nith.

He turned and headed for the front door, knocking away burning debris. Karen gave Jimmy a questioning look to which he could only answer with a shrug and together they followed Nith. The giant stopped a couple of feet away from the inflamed panel. The heat was overwhelming, and Jimmy could feel his lungs beginning to roast within him.

"Stand back," said Nith.

He then let fly a kick that shattered the door into a dozen flaming pieces, A rush of cold October air raced into the room, sending welcoming chills throughout Jimmy's body.

"Go," said the giant.

Jimmy nudged Karen in front of him and then began to follow when the giant gripped him by the arm, stopping him in his tracks.

"Take care of him," the giant said. He then released Jimmy's arm, turned, and made his way back into the flames.

*****

Jimmy and Karen slowly stumbled their way down the front porch stairs just as a woman holding an assault rifle appeared out of the darkness.

"Stop right there?" she said.

"We have a baby," said Karen.

The woman lowered the gun and then looked over to where Jimmy now stood shivering.

"Are you James Varnett?"

"I am," he said, collapsing to the ground.

The woman rushed over, slinging the AK-47 over her shoulder. Jimmy lay there gasping for air. The nightmare appeared to be over, but his mind refused to believe.

"Come on," said the woman, pulling Jimmy to his feet. "Help is on the way."

The mansion lit up the sky, the roaring flames drowning out the distant pounding of the oilrigs.

"Is there anyone else inside?" the woman asked.

"Yes," said Jimmy.

The woman stood there for a moment gazing at the inferno.

"They're on their own," she said, finally.

She motioned for them to follow her, and they stumbled toward the Winnebago. She brought them to a stop just outside of the RV's front door.

"Wait here," she said, opening the door and climbing the short stairs.

Jimmy and Karen sat on the cold ground, watching the flames continue to feed. By the time the fire department arrived, nothing would be left of the mansion, and that was fine with Jimmy. It was strange, these feelings that pulsed through him. Did he want the family to die? He should, after all that they had done to him—and not just to him but to the woman whose child Karen now held. But he found himself hoping that they had found a way to survive.

The door to the RV opened, and the agent descended. Her eyes glistened in the fire's light, and a pistol was in her hand.

"What were you looking for?" said Karen.

"It's gone," said the agent.

Jimmy and Karen stood up, readjusting Ferdinand just as he let out a small burp. Together, they followed the agent into the darkness.

CHAPTER FIFTY

Belize

It had not been easy. Charlie found that it was possible to drop the weight if he only drank bourbon mixed with water and stayed entirely off beer. He also cut his food intake to just half of what he had been consuming while in the States. The results were a staggering loss of one hundred and ten pounds. Add to this his now bearded face and deep tan, and he was just another middle-aged beach bum walking the surf of Belize.

The first flight he managed to catch landed him in London. He was forced to stay there for three days until he was finally able to transfer his funds into the secluded FFG Financial in Switzerland. From there, it was just a matter of calling a guy in Belize. By the time he arrived in the rented Cessna, the meager beach house was furnished and waiting.

After a couple of months, he dared venture into Belmopan and purchased a Wi-Fi router and laptop. The signal was weak, but it was good enough if he stayed on the front porch. The news article, dated October 23rd of the previous year, was titled *A Mysterious Ruin*.

A mansion had been burned to the ground with five bodies found inside. It went on to name Ben Lanchinno as one of the five. The article also described three victims as the owners of the home. One (Grenelda Henley) and the other two (who had been found crisped in a basement) as her children.

The article read like a robbery gone wrong. Could it be that they had nothing on him? It was hard to believe that if Karen had survived. Maybe she hadn't. Maybe the family had killed her before Ben had arrived. The important thing was that both the Centurions and the family were gone. He shut the laptop and grabbed his burner phone. He walked into the front room, closing the door behind him to quiet the crashing waves and placed a call. Gloria answered after the third ring and to his delight she was happy to hear from him. Two days later she was on a plane.

Three years had gone by since that article, enough time for him to feel the weight of his past beginning to lift. There was still the occasional news check, because it never hurt to be sure, but it was as if the entire event had been forgotten.

Thank God for a crazy world. The media had their hands full, and the death of a few criminals wasn't exactly earth shattering.

Because of this, Charlie decided to live a little. He had already purchased a boat, nothing fancy, just an inboard that sat nestled in the newly built dock that he had contracted out to the natives. He also hired a local caterer to provide them with authentic Belizean meals. Gloria was quite fond of Bamboo Chicken, complemented with roasted walnuts. It was not his favorite, but if she was happy, so was he.

On their last day together, they sat on the porch, drinks in hand, gazing out at the blue rolling water. The sun descended, and soon, it cast palm tree shadows over the sand. He took the woman's hand as the catering van pulled into the stone-paved driveway.

"Thank you," said Gloria.

Charlie squeezed her hand, and together, they watched as the men unloaded a rolling tray draped with a long paisley cover. They then began placing metal-covered plates onto it. This was his life now. Gone was the fabricated Truth. He had played the part of the servant long enough for both the family and Ben. Their deaths only proved that in this dog-eat-dog world, it paid to have balls the size of a cannon and luck to match.

These pretentious fantasies continued to march through his mind as the men rolled the tray up the slanted walkway onto the porch.

There was never any guilt about what had happened, and as far as Karen and Jimmy, they were just the unfortunate victims of a war: A triumvirate gone bad, if you will. We all have an inescapable *Truth* at our core. Some people refuse to listen, and those people lose in the end. Karen and Jimmy had found this out. But Charlie knew. Had always known. The fact that Gloria was sitting next to him proved it. Perhaps, at some point, he might be tired of her; if that happened, he would have no reservations about sending her on her way. But she did know a lot, like where he was, for starters. That might have posed a problem for the old Charlie, but not now. He would find a way for her to disappear if the time came.

The caterers loaded back into the van and departed.

"Let's eat," said Gloria. "And then go for a swim."

Charlie smiled at her and reached for the lid to one of the trays. At first, he thought she was choking on her drink. Gloria's face had gone ashen, her eyes widening. A spray of crimson-laced foam burst from her mouth, splattering Charlie's face. She tried to speak but could only manage a constricted hiss.

"What's wrong?" he said, leaping to his feet.

Something bit his ankle, causing him to jerk back.

Gloria began to shake, rattling in her chair. Charlie attempted to move towards her, but it was as if his legs had become severed. A numbness crept up, passing his knee and he felt his bowels release. The smell filled his nostrils, causing him to gag. Gloria had become still, her fear-stricken eyes frozen and motionless. The cold continued its march up Charlie's body, passing through his abdomen. Again, he tried to move but only managed to catch himself on the rolling tray. He teetered there momentarily and then collapsed to the planked deck, his breath coming in short gasps.

The tray's paisley covering was pushed to the side, revealing a dark opening. Within the shadows, two points shimmered in the fading sunlight.

"Hello, Charlie," said a voice.

Charlie could see a scar running across a pale skull as it slithered towards him.

"No," Charlie whispered.

Phillip dropped the syringe he had been holding and replaced it with a long, serrated blade.

"You've lost weight," Phillip said, crawling onto the paralyzed man. "Perhaps it's time to lose some more."

CHAPTER FIFTY-ONE

Picking Up the Pieces

Agent Green parked her Bronco near the back of the lot. Next to her sat Agent Wayne, who was wearing a T-shirt with an image of Yoda on the front. She shut the Bronco off, and together they watched as Jimmy and Karen held hands on a bench, their attention held by a boy playing on a swing. Considering all they had been through, it was good that they had decided to give it another go at their marriage. The second wedding had been small, with only the two standing before a judge and the agents as witnesses. Perhaps it would work this time. Agent Green could only hope. A bark came from the backseat and Agent Green turned, reaching out to give her adopted American Bulldog a scratch behind the ear.

"Do you have his leash?" Agent Wayne said.

"It's under your seat," said Agent Green.

Agent Wayne pulled out the retractable line and hooked it to the dog's collar. They climbed out of the Bronco and crossed a narrow rock bridge. It was then that Jimmy looked their way. He rose from the bench, his smile beaming.

"Hey guys," he said.

The agents gave him a wave.

"So, you three are packed and on the road?" said Agent Green.

"Yep," said Karen. "We were headed to Dallas when you called."

"That sounds like a good plan," said Agent Wayne.

"My mother insists that we move closer," Jimmy said. "And I guess we all agreed."

"We did," said Karen. "Besides, we're going to need help raising this guy."

"Still no luck finding Charlie?" said Jimmy.

"Well, actually, that's one of the reasons we called you," said Agent Wayne. "Charlie was found dead."

"No shit," said Jimmy. "I guess the wheels of justice caught up to him, after all."

"It appears so," said Agent Green. "You didn't happen to travel to Belize last week, did you?"

"I don't even know where Belize is," said Jimmy.

They all smiled at that. And they all knew the truth. Only three of the four family members were found at the mansion, and all of them had normal legs. It also explained the strange phone call that Jimmy had received just two weeks after the adoption papers for the infant had been finalized. A bank account had been set up in Jimmy's name containing two hundred thousand dollars, promising more if he continued to treat the child right.

He is a prince, after all, the man had said.

Of course, there could be no drinking and surprise UAs were a part of the deal. But that was okay. To Jimmy, those days had become like Grenalda Henley; it was a thing of the past. Jimmy had decided against sharing this information with the agents. What good would it do? All the guilty parties were accounted for. Except for Phillip, but he was sure that the deformed man was as gone as the mansion.

*****

Agent Green broke away from the group and walked out to where a dark-haired child was now running from one swing to the other, giving them a joyful push. The boy was large for his age, and the agent could see the faint tip of his family trait at the end of his chin. But besides that, he seemed normal.

The boy looked at her, his ice-blue eyes narrowing. For a

moment she thought that perhaps the boy didn't recognize her. It had been over two years since she had appeared at Jimmy and Karen's adoption hearing.

"I know you," he said.

"Yes, you do honey,"

"You helped my mommy and daddy."

"I did."

"You helped me."

"I was happy to do it," said Agent Green, extending her arms. "Now come here and give me a hug."

The boy let out a sudden barking laugh and raced into her arms, throwing them around her neck. The agent gave a muffled giggle of her own as he squeezed her close.

The boy was strong, very strong.

The End